TWICE
TO DIE

R.J. JAGGER

THRILLER PUBLISHING GROUP, INC.

Twice To Die

Thriller Publishing Group, Inc.

Copyright©RJJagger

Library of Congress Control Number: Available

ISBN 978-1-937888-39-8

Printed in the United States of America

"Verdict: The pacing is relentless in this debut, a hard-boiled novel with a shocking ending. The supershort chapters will please those who enjoy a James Patterson–style page-turner"
LIBRARY JOURNAL

A "clever and engrossing mystery tale involving gorgeous women, lustful men and scintillating suspense."
FOREWORD MAGAZINE

"Part of what makes this thriller thrilling is that you sense there to be connections among all the various subplots; the anticipation of their coming together keeps the pages turning."
BOOKLIST

"This is one of the best thrillers I've read yet."
NEW MYSTERY READER MAGAZINE

"A superb thriller and an exceptional read."
MIDWEST BOOK REVIEW

"Verdict: This fast-paced book offers fans of commercial thrillers a twisty, action-packed thrill ride."
LIBRARY JOURNAL

"Another masterpiece of action and suspense."
NEW MYSTERY READER MAGAZINE

For Eileen

ACKNOWLEDGEMENTS

Many thanks to Esperanza Marcias for her talents and skills in seeking out and destroying the many typos and errors that lived in the initial manuscript of this book.

DAY ONE

July 8
Tuesday

1

Nick Teffinger, the 34-year-old head of Denver's homicide unit, parked the Tundra in front of a hooker bar on south Broadway and crossed the street to Tokyo Jack's. Inside, pre-lunch, the place was dark and the customers were few. A waitress pouring coffee at a booth spotted him, came over and put him in a full-length squeeze with the pot still in hand.

Her touch was as he remembered.

She led him to a red vinyl booth in a dim corner back near the restrooms and said, "It went down right here."

"Okay, walk me through it."

"It's pretty simple. A guy came in, sat back here and ordered a cup of coffee," she said. "This was last night about seven. There were hardly any customers at the time. It was about like it is now."

"You were his waitress?"

"Right."

"Describe the guy."

"He was black, somewhere in his mid-thirties and dressed really nice, in a suit," she said. "His hair was short but it was dyed blond. He had sort of a jet-set look to him, if you know what I mean. He had a tan leather briefcase that he kept on the table right in front of him."

"Okay."

"Nick, I haven't taken any drugs in over a year."

"I know."

"I'd be dead if it wasn't for you."

"That's not true. Tell me what happened next."

She ran a finger down his chest.

"I never showed my gratitude. I get off at eight tonight. We could get a room or something."

He squeezed her hand.

"Be careful or I'm going to call your bluff one of these days. What happened next?"

She focused and then said, "He was here for about ten minutes and then a blond woman came in and joined him. She was like a goddess, Nick, honest to God. You've seen all those models on the covers of those magazines? She blows them away."

"So she was nice, huh?"

"Let me put it this way," she said. "Don't look her in the eyes, Nick. You'll be ruined if you do."

"Ruined? That's a pretty strong word."

"Yeah but that's what you'll be. She had a tattoo on her neck. It was some kind of Kanji thing. I have no idea what it meant. Anyway, she ordered coffee, which I got, and then I was over there in that area where I had two other tables going, sort of keeping an eye on them in the mirrors."

"Show me."

She took him across the room and showed him how a mirror by the bar angled into another one over by the restroom and reflected into the booth.

"I use the mirrors sometimes to keep track of things," she said. "Anyway, the man opened the briefcase. It was pointed away from the main room but into the mirror behind him. It was filled with money and I mean a ton of the stuff. On top of it all was a picture of a woman."

"Did you get a look at her?"

"No. I could tell it was a woman but that was it," she said. "Anyway, to me it looked exactly like the kind of thing that someone would give to a hitman. My curiosity went through the roof. What I ended up doing was going through the kitchen and around to the restrooms the back way. I hugged the wall right around the corner. Let me show you where."

She took him over.

Her position was five or six feet behind the table, out of line of sight.

"They talked about the woman taking the mark by Friday night at the latest. Mostly they used the term the mark but at one point the man said her name, which was Susan Smith."

"Susan Smith."

"Right."

"She was the mark?"

"Right, Susan Smith. Anyway, ten minutes later the little goddess left with the briefcase. The man stayed for another five minutes, finished his coffee and left."

Teffinger nodded.

"Did he leave you a tip?"

"Yes, five dollars. You want to put it towards that room?"

2

Outside the July sun beat down with every ounce of scorch it had, intent on wringing the last living drop of juice out of every person and plant and dog and bug in the city.

It felt good for the first thirty steps.

By the time Teffinger got to the Tundra he'd had enough. He cranked over the engine, turned the AC on high and dialed Sydney Netherwood, the newbie. As it rang he pulled up an image of the woman's taut African American body and her smooth mocha skin.

"That call this morning is legit," he said. "The mark is someone named Susan Smith. Find everyone in the city who has that name and get me what you can on them."

A beat.

"What's in it for me?"

"Same as me. A paycheck at the end of the month."

"I get that without dropping everything," she said. "You want me to drop everything, right?"

"Right."

"So, what's my motivation?"

"How about saving someone's life?"

"Susan Smith's?"

"Exactly."

"I don't know the woman," she said. "What else you got?"

He exhaled.

"Okay, lunch."

"That's better. See, you can get to the right answer if someone gives you enough time."

He pulled into Broadway traffic, cut over to Santa Fe and swung north back into the guts of the city, punching the buttons in hopes of getting a Beatles or Beach Boys song only to find that Sydney had set all the presets to hip-hop.

50-Cent's In Da Club came through.

He let it play.

The bass twisted into his brain.

The hitwoman—the goddess—was from out of town. Denver didn't have the depth to support a hit person, not to mention that a woman that riveting would have come across Teffinger's line of vision sooner or later. The caveman genes in the back of his skull would have made him focus at her. He would have memorized her every detail. He would have seen the tattoo.

No, she wasn't from here.

She was from out of town staying at a hotel.

That's where he'd find her, in one of the better ones.

Goddesses don't live low.

He found her on the fourth try, registered at the 1,000-room Sheraton strategically located in the heart of the matter, mere steps from both the 16th Street Mall and the financial district. According to the guy working the reception desk—a college-looking kid with a Bob Baxter name tag—the woman's name was Portia Montrachet. She was staying in 1215, booked through Saturday morning.

Teffinger pulled a fifty out of his wallet and pushed it across the counter.

"It's important that she doesn't know anyone was asking about her."

Bob shoved the bill in his pocket.

Teffinger was halfway across the lobby when he had an idea and turned back.

"I wanted to ask you one more thing," he said. "Is she with anyone?"

"No."

"How about a black guy with blond hair?"

"No."

"You haven't seen a guy like that around?"

"No."

"Okay, thanks."

He headed across the lobby and out the revolving doors. Then he went back in.

"Bob, stop making me leave before I ask all my

questions. Did she rent a car?"

"Let me check." The man punched buttons on a computer screen and nodded. "She rented a black Mustang. You want to the plate number?"

"Sure, why not?"

He wrote it down.

Then he walked away.

"Hey," Bob said.

Teffinger turned.

"Aren't you going to ask me the next question?"

"Don't have one."

"You will."

"You're probably right," Teffinger said. "Don't ever get as old as me. The mind stops working in a straight line." He drummed his fingers, trying to remember what it was that he was supposed to remember. Then it came to him. "Is the room next to Ms. Montrachet's available?"

"I told you you'd have another question. Let's see; 1214 no, 1216 yes."

Teffinger rented 1216 through Saturday morning under the name North Reynolds, not really having a plan for it yet but reasoning it couldn't hurt.

Then he left.

Back at homicide Teffinger headed for the coffee and from there over to Sydney who had eight or ten fresh stacks of papers on her desk.

"So far I have eleven Susan Smiths," she said.

"Eleven?"

She nodded.

Teffinger picked up the nearest pile.

On top was a printout of a driver's license for one Susan Smith, a 32-year-old who lived west of Colorado Boulevard. Below that was her rap sheet, fairly clean except for a few minor alcohol-related infractions. Below that was her Facebook page, dated today, with a photo that matched the driver's license.

The other piles were similar.

"Our hitwoman is someone named Portia Montrachet," Teffinger said. "She's staying at the downtown Sheraton, room 1215. Do me a favor and run that name to ground. I'm sure it's a fake but I don't want to find out later that it isn't."

Sydney gave him a look.

"When do I get that lunch?"

"Next week."

"That's what you always say."

Teffinger shrugged.

"It's not my fault that when next week comes, it's now this week instead of next week."

"So under your reasoning, next week never comes."

He nodded.

"Precisely."

"That's pretty tricky reasoning."

"It doesn't come easy. I have to work at it."

As Sydney worked the computer for Portia Montrachet, Teffinger told her about the black man with the bleached hair. "We'll run him down," he said, "but my guess is that he's not the one who wants the mark hit.

He's an intermediary."

"What makes you say that?"

"The system is built in layers," he said. "No one who wants someone dead can just look in the phone book under hitmen. They have to leak their desire to someone, who knows someone else, who knows someone else. It's all smoke and mirrors. The black man is a link in that chain but isn't the start of that chain. Even if we find out who he is, working upwards from there will be difficult. He'll be smart enough to cover his tracks."

Sydney frowned.

"So far no one named Portia Montrachet exists," she said. "She's not in any of our databases and Google never heard of her. She must have used a credit card to register. Maybe we could get a lead from that."

Teffinger didn't answer.

One of the Susan Smith piles on the desk had his attention.

He picked it up and couldn't believe what he saw.

3

What he saw on the top of a Susan Smith pile was a face he recognized, intimately recognized to be precise. Looking into those eyes again for the first time in over two years, a memory flashed in his brain with such vividness that he might as well have been right there.

He was in Razzle.

It was Saturday night.

The bodies were sardine tight and every inch of the club dripped with smoke and perfume and sex and wild abandon and pounding bass. He was leaning against the bar with three Buds in his gut and a fourth in his hand, watching a pretty little thing gyrate on the dance floor and imagining what it would be like to slip his hand up between her thighs.

It was then that something happened.

A woman appeared from out of nowhere, her face suddenly in front of his, close, dangerously close, so close that he could feel the warmth of her breath. She rubbed her stomach on his and gyrated to the beat, letting her long raven-black hair swing from side to side.

She said nothing.

Her eyes said it all.

Her hips said it all.

Ten seconds, that's how long it took before Teffinger was addicted. Her face was dark and mysterious and filled with lust.

Her eyes came close.

Her tongue licked his lips.

"Nick, are you okay?"

The words came from Sydney.

The memory flashed off.

He tapped the pile and said, "I know this woman. Her name's Del Ray Rain. She's a flight attendant."

Sydney's face washed in confusion.

"Her driver's license says Susan Smith. Her website says she's a lawyer. What's going on?"

Teffinger shuffled through the pile.

In it was a printout of the front page of a website for Susan A. Smith, Attorney-At-Law. The photo of the attorney unquestionably belonged to Del Rey Rain, the flight attendant. He rolled the papers up, tapped them on the desk and said, "I'll be back."

"Where you going?"

"To talk to the mark."

"You think she's the one?"

"I'm positive of it."

"How?"

"I don't know. I just do."

The woman's office turned out to be an old but still-standing brick structure on the less-trendy edge of Wazee, three or four blocks from Coors Field in LoDo. It probably started life as a store or small manufacturing facility of some sorts before decades of abuse dragged it to near-death. Now, like more buildings than not, it was patched, upgraded, converted and reinvented. Burnt-orange designer awnings framed a weathered oak door. What the address lacked in prestige was balanced out with sunlight, parking and reasonably priced eateries.

Someday the area might be trendy.

That day wasn't quite here yet.

Fire shot through Teffinger's veins as he walked to the front door.

The woman's eyes were dangerous.

They could shift his world.

They could make him be stupid.

They could make him do things.

They could make him feel things.

Screwed into the front door was a tasteful brass plaque:

Law Office of

Susan A. Smith, Esq.

The brass was darkened with age. It had been there for years, including the period two years ago when the woman was busy telling Teffinger she was a flight attendant.

He turned the knob and stepped inside.

What he expected was cramped dark wood, half-dead ferns and saggy bookshelves. What he got was a vaulted foyer, sunlight streaming from a skylight and rich Delano oil paintings on textured vanilla walls.

A contemporary receptionist desk was unoccupied.

Fresh tulips poked out of a crystal vase.

"Anyone home?"

No one answered.

He eventually found her in the upper attic storage area, sitting on the carpet with her back against the wall and her legs stretched out. A large storage box was at her side, pulled off a shelf of more of the same. The top was opened and several files were out. A band of sunlight sprayed through an open window, striking her thighs. She had her skirt hiked up to catch the rays.

She was shuffling through papers in a manila folder.

"So, you're a lawyer," Teffinger said.

The woman looked up.

Her eyes locked on his, first hard, then like a watercolor.

"Nick."

"Not that it matters much anymore," he said, "but why'd you keep it from me? The fact that you're a lawyer?"

She set the file down.

"I'm sorry about the way things ended," she said.

"Don't worry about it."

Her eyes darted.

"Do you hate me?"

He thought about it.

The answer surprised him.

"Sometimes," he said. "But only in the middle of the night."

"I almost called you a hundred different times," she said.

"Why didn't you?"

"Do you want the truth?"

He smiled.

"The truth in a lawyer's office? Is that physically possible?"

She stood up, hesitated, and took a step to him. She put her arms around his waist and buried her face in his neck. She smelled like an oasis and the pressure of her thighs against his shot fire through his veins.

"Not calling you was the hardest thing I've ever

done."

"Then why didn't you?"

"Because you scared me, Nick."

"Bullshit."

"I don't mean in a mean way," she said. "I'm talking about the opposite."

4

Teffinger sat down on the floor, leaned back against the wall and said, "Technically I'm here on business. We have credible reason to believe that a hitman—a hitwoman, actually—is in town to kill a target by the name of Susan Smith. We know of eleven women in town by that name and there are probably more. What I want to know from you is whether you're the one she's here for and, if so, why."

The woman smiled, waiting for the punch line, then got somber.

"Are you serious?"

Yes.

He was.

"No," she said.

"You're not the one?"

She shook her head.

"If someone wants you dead, that's the kind of thing you can feel."

Teffinger shrugged.

"Maybe yes, maybe no," he said. "Maybe it's a brother or a girlfriend of someone you didn't get off."

"You mean revenge?"

"Sure, why not?"

She chewed on it.

"It doesn't fit," she said. "Revenge would come with warnings. It would be like headlights coming up a dark road."

Teffinger raked his thick brown hair back with his fingers.

It immediately flopped back down.

"You're a lawyer," he said. "People tell you things they don't tell anyone else. Maybe someone's reconsidering whether they want someone running around who knows something about them."

The woman shook her head.

"Theoretically it's possible but I can't think of any real life fits."

"Maybe it's not related to your practice. Maybe you saw something you shouldn't have."

"No."

"Did you take something?"

"No."

"Are you into drugs?"

"Nothing you don't already know about."

"Do you owe anyone money?"

"Yeah, Visa."

"Are you pressuring anyone about anything?"

"No."

"Did you break anyone's heart?"

She paused and sighed.

"I'm not the target, Teff," she said. "I'll keep my eyes open but you'll be better off concentrating on the other Susan Smiths." A beat then, "Tell me about the hitwoman."

He told her.

She was going by the name Portia Montrachet.

She was attractive, blond, and had a Kanji tattoo on her neck.

He didn't have a photograph yet but would by the end of the day.

"Where's she staying?"

Teffinger frowned.

"I don't want you trying to make contact with her."

"I won't."

"Good."

"What's your plan to stop her?"

"That's still a work in progress."

"Let me help."

"No."

"Come on—"

"It's a police matter."

"It's also a matter for Susan Smith," she said.

"You already said you're not the one."

"True, but we both know I can make mistakes. Just being on the list gives me some entitlement, don't you think? Besides, it will give us a chance to get reacquainted."

Back at homicide, Sydney had collected even more information on the Susan Smiths. With coffee in his left hand, Teffinger went through the files one by one, looking for a situation or personality trait or occupation that could possibly trigger a hit.

A few red flags rose.

The 28-year-old Susan Smith who lived on Clarkson was one. She had some minor scratches in her record, including a few that had landed her free room and board at the public's expense for a short period of time. Currently employed as a Merry Maid, it was possible that she snooped around when she should have been cleaning and ended up taking something. Or maybe she found a more interesting kind of dirt, the kind that could be used for blackmail. It would be interesting to know whose houses she'd been in recently and whether any large sums of money had mysteriously appeared in her bank accounts.

He handed the file to Sydney.

"Take the lead on this one," he said. "See if she got herself in over her head on something. Get her to say something that would support a warrant to get into her bank records."

Sydney took the file.

"You're weird today," she said.

He raised an eyebrow.

"Meaning what?"

"Meaning your old flame."

He shrugged.

"She said I scared her."

Sydney wasn't impressed.

"You're a lot of things, Teffinger, but scary isn't one of them."

Two more files caught his eye.

One was a lawyer who had been disbarred for three years for putting retainer funds into an operating account and then drawing on them as a loan, allegedly with intent to repay it next month. She was in year two of her disbarment period and, apparently, was talented enough to land an interim job as a legal assistant at one of Denver's largest law firm, Tracer & Banks. In that position she'd have access to a lot of confidential information.

The other file of interest was for a model. Teffinger recognized her from some of the clubs around town. The word was that she had a cocaine habit and a penchant for screwing powerful people.

He handed the files to Sydney.

"Two more."

She made a face.

"What are you going to be doing while I do all the work? Repeat, all the work."

He stood up and headed for the coffee.

"I'll be doing something I shouldn't."

5

Working the net, Teffinger found a real-life New York limited partnership by the name of 47Drop that was in the business of developing upscale residential high-rises in the heart of prominent cities across the country. He also located and printed out information regarding ownership of land and properties in Denver that would potentially be suitable for leveling and development of the types of structures that 47Drop maintained in its portfolio.

Then he headed home, showered, and put on his crispest white shirt, a lagoon-green silk tie and his most expensive summer-weight suit.

He put the files in a tan leather briefcase and drove out to Denver International Airport where he rented a white Range Rover.

From there he drove to the downtown Sheraton, snaked back and forth through the parking garage to see if Portia Montrachet's rental was there—which it was—and then parked as close to it as he could.

He headed up to his room, 1216.

His ear went to the wall.

There was movement in the adjacent room.

The woman was there.

He opened his door three or four inches to be able to hear her when she left. Then he waited, with the jacket on and the briefcase sitting by the door where he could grab it on the way out.

Half an hour came and went.

The woman didn't emerge.

Ear to the wall, Teffinger detected water running. She was showering.

Twenty minutes later she emerged.

Teffinger grabbed the briefcase, stepped into the

hall and closed the door, jiggling the handle to make sure it was locked. Then he looked over, ostensibly surprised to see someone there.

He smiled but said nothing.

Instead he turned right towards the elevator bank.

The woman followed five steps behind.

Teffinger pressed the down button and faced forward.

He looked good.

He looked important.

He looked like money.

He looked like he was hung like a T-Rex on a Saturday night.

Come on, bite.

Seconds passed then the woman said, "In town on business?"

He looked over.

She was more than he expected.

He tried to appear unaffected by her goddess eyes and her goddess face and her ample goddess chest tucked under a sleeveless pink blouse.

"Yeah. You?"

"Same. Your eyes are two different colors. One's blue and one's green. I've never seen that before."

He cocked his head.

"I think it's from the New York water."

"Is that where you're from?"

He nodded.

"Right. How about you?"

"Same; New York. I have a flat over on 84th."

"Well, small world."

"So they say."

The elevator came, replete with half a dozen sardines already packed in and facing the front. They stepped in and did the same. At the lobby the woman said, "My name's Portia. Why don't you take me out to dinner tonight?"

Teffinger frowned.

"I have a business engagement."

"Oh."

He paused in contemplation and said, "I should be back around nine. We could get a drink if you'd like."

"Sounds good."

"My treat," he added.

She smiled.

"What's your name?"

"North," he said. "North Reynolds."

She straightened his tie.

"There, all better."

Two heartbeats later she was out the revolving doors and down the street on foot. Teffinger suppressed his urge to follow and instead headed for the Range Rover.

At the office he called his old high school buddy, Matt Vernon, in New York, and said, "Matt, it's me, Teffinger. I need to be from New York tonight. Tell me some stuff that only the locals know."

"Okay but on one condition."

"Here we go …"

"Take Jena out and get her drunk," he said. "She

still talks about you."

Jena.

Jena Vernon.

She was Matt's younger sister, three years younger than them, in 9th grade when they were in 12th. Now she was a reporter for the Channel 8 news and, for the last three years, a mutual booty call, although no calling by either side had been done for the last six months.

"Sure, why not?" Teffinger said.

6

With Sydney busy giving warning to all the Susan Smiths on the list, Teffinger paced next to the windows with a cup of coffee in his left hand and a phone in his right, calling hotels in hopes of finding the black man with the blond hair. Outside, across Cherokee Street, old houses had been converted into bail bond junkets and painted cartoon colors. Neon signs burned in the windows. A kid on a skateboard shuffled past.

Then something happened.

The receptionist at the Westin had some interesting news. A black man with bleached hair, nicely dressed, had checked into the hotel late Sunday and back out early this morning.

His name was Oscar Benderfield.

"Do you know where he was going?"

"The airport. He took the hotel shuttle. Where he was flying to from there, I have no idea."

Teffinger got the man's credit card number and from there traced him to be a private investigator out of Washington, D.C. That confirmed his earlier suspicion that the man hadn't been the one who wanted Susan Smith dead but instead was a link in the chain; part of the smoke and mirrors.

So who was he working for?

He called the homicide department in D.C., explained who he was and got connected to a man named Randy Johnson, who answered in a deep growly voice with a thick drawl that sounded like it got honed on Bourbon Street down in the guts of the Big Easy.

"Oscar Benderfield is a high-priced low-life," Johnson said. "Most of his clients are law firms. He gets things done for them, and I'm not just talking about investigations and information gathering."

"Meaning what?"

"Meaning whatever needs doing," Johnson said. "He's given us occasion to sniff around more than a few times but we never come up with anything other than a bad smell. He's a guy who knows how to cover his tracks. My guess is that you could break into his office right now and go through every file in there without finding a shred of evidence as to who he's working for or why."

Teffinger cocked his head.

"Look," he said. "He's flying back even as we speak. Whoever hired him might be waiting for a report on how the handoff went. That might be done in a meeting rather than by phone. Is there any chance you could put a tail on him for a day or two?"

A pause.

"Manpower's tight," Johnson said.

"I appreciate that."

The man exhaled.

"I'll make you a trade. I'll tail our P.I. friend if you come out to D.C. at some point in the next six months and do a training session with our detectives."

Teffinger grunted.

"That might set them back."

"Not from my angle. I saw you talk out in San Francisco last year."

"Then you should understand what I mean."

Johnson chuckled.

"Do we have a deal or not?"

Yeah.

They did.

7

Tuesday night after dark Jori-Lee Kent paused at the sidewalk next to the ornate brick security wall encompassing the mansion and reflected on the seriousness of what she was about to do.

The city wasn't as dark as she'd like.

There were too many streetlights and wandering

cars. There were too many urban lights bouncing off a low blanket of clouds. In typical D.C. style, the air was humid and muggy. A mosquito drilled fangs into her arm and she slapped it dead.

She wore black jeans and a black T with gray Nikes down below. Her long brown hair was tucked under a baseball cap.

No one was in close proximity.

She exhaled one last time, quieted the lightning in her veins as much as she could and maneuvered her 26-year-old body over the wall, landing on landscaping rock between two bushes.

Her heart pounded.

This was crazy.

She should back out now while she still had the chance.

Lights were on inside the structure.

No one was home though. She knew where the owner was. He wouldn't be back for over an hour.

She headed across the grass.

The motion of her body ignited a floodlight and brought a blinding glare into her eyes. She sped up, concerned but not overly. No one from the street could see her through the wall. The nearest neighbor was fifty yards away with plenty of trees in between.

Several of the rear windows were cranked open.

She slipped on latex gloves, worked the screen out of a window and entered.

The air was coffin quiet.

She headed up a winding staircase to the upper level.

The master bedroom was at the far end of a walkway that opened on one side to the level below. She had a feeling that if she was going to find what she was looking for, it would either be buried somewhere in the master closet or inside a safe.

The bedroom was dark.

She closed the window coverings, turned on the lights and dimmed them to half. The room was something out of an interior designer magazine, fitted pitch-perfect with contemporary textures and colors. The dresser drawers contained nothing of interest.

The master closet was larger than most bedrooms.

Twenty tailor-made suits hung on sculpted wooden hangers. A hundred or more silk ties were neatly folded on top of a built-in dresser made out of the same blond wood as the shelves.

In the far corner, hardly visible, were two black briefcases.

She picked one up.

Something was inside.

The latches were locked. She turned the tumblers to zero on the chance that the pre-sets had never been changed. They hadn't. The latches sprang open.

There was a small MacBook Air laptop inside.

She set it on top of the ties and opened it up.

There was no password protection.

The screen sprang to life.

She opened Documents and found a large number of files, too many to look through. She headed downstairs with a racing heart, found the home office in a separate room off the dining room, and rummaged through the drawers until she found a box of blank thumb drives.

She took one upstairs, copied the contents of the Mac, stuck the drive in the pocket and put everything back exactly like she'd found it.

Then she got the hell out of there.

8

Portia had the look. Teffinger had only seen it briefly in the elevator and then down in the lobby when she straightened his tie, but that had been enough. She was the kind of woman he could wrap around every night and think about every minute.

That was the problem.

At exactly nine he knocked on her door, shifting his feet and reminding himself one last time not to fall in love with her.

She was a killer.

Susan Smith—maybe even his Susan Smith, Del Ray—was depending on him. The next two hours were business, potentially pleasurable business, but business all the same.

The door opened.

The woman wore a bra and panties but no clothes. Her body was tanned and taut and belonged to a California surfer girl, straight out of a Beach Boys song. Her hair was thick, straight and freshly washed.

Her eyes were green.

He hadn't noticed that before.

She smelled like Paris.

She pulled him inside and said, "I'll be ready before you blink. Do you feel like getting a little crazy tonight?"

"Sure."

"Good. I've found a place for us to go."

"Where?"

She smiled and headed for the bathroom.

"I'll tell you when we get there."

"Mystery woman."

"Always."

While she was in the bathroom, Teffinger cast his eyes around for the briefcase. It wasn't in sight or under the bed. He had his eye on the closet, wondering if he had enough time to open the door and take a quick peek inside. He thought better of it. Even if it was in there it would be closed. He'd have to undo the latches and pull the top up to get to the photo inside. Legally, that would be a search without a warrant. As nice as it would be to know which of the eleven Susan Smith's was the mark, it wasn't worth jeopardizing the legality of the investigation.

He stood at the window.

Denver was thick with twilight.

Streetlights were on.

Headlights were on.

The air was full of mischief.

The bathroom door opened.

Portia was now in a short red dress that framed

her body to perfection, tighter up top at the cleavage but flaring dangerously loose over her hips, barely covering her posterior. She wore no nylons.

Her lips were the same red color.

So were the high-heels.

"Acceptable?"

Teffinger swallowed.

"I suddenly feel understated." In jeans and a white cotton shirt with no tie, the words were more than true.

Portia linked her arm through his.

"You're fine," she said. "Tonight's my treat so just sit back and enjoy." She pulled a flask out of the top dresser drawer, shoved it in her purse and said, "Let's go."

"Let's."

Downstairs in the lobby Portia hesitated for a moment as she looked around and then headed over to a stunning little blond in a white skirt sitting in a white leather chair by the fireplace.

"Are you here to meet Portia?"

Yes, she was.

"That's me," Portia said. "You're prettier than I expected. What's your name?"

"Seven."

"As in the number?"

"Right, six plus one."

"This hunky guy here is North." To Teffinger, "She's from Escorts en Secret. She'll be partying with us this evening, unless you have an objection."

Teffinger didn't and extended his hand to prove it.

The woman's skin was pure sex.

Her eyes were voodoo blue.

They jammed into the back of a cab with Teffinger in the middle. Portia pulled out the flask, took a hit, passed it to Teffinger and told the driver, "B.T.s."

"The strip club?"

"Right, the strip club. Not the church."

They ended up in a dark roped-off couch area of the club, an oasis in a world of high-energy, pounding music and twisting sin. There were several stages and most had two dancers getting down and dirty and wrapping their thighs around the faces of as many female takers as males. In the middle of the club was a gyrating dance floor. The women were amateurs. Most had their tops off.

There had to have been five hundred people in there.

Over in the far corner was a stage of male entertainers, muscular men with swagger and attitude, awash in a sea of hollering women laying down green and getting their faces close in. The lucky ones got their drunken bodies pulled onto the stage and placed into a compromising position.

Portia got very touchy very fast.

Drinks landed on their table.

Dancers came over to party.

Hands went to Teffinger's thighs.

Lips landed on his.

Sexy little thighs straddled his lap and the heavenly weight of beautiful young things grinded down for attention.

An hour into it, Portia's hand slipped into Teffinger's pants.

He needed to pull it out but the fire in his veins wouldn't let him.

The plan changed, just like that.

The whole world changed. It shrunk and turned into Portia. There was nothing else, only her; her and her short little dress and her sweet little mouth and the smoothness of her golden skin.

"You're an evil little thing," he said.

"Me? I'm an angel."

DAY TWO

July 9
Wednesday

9

Jori-Lee woke Wednesday morning with a scary realization of just how serious a secret she was sitting on. The files she extracted from the Mac-Book last night weren't just explosive, they were almost beyond comprehension.

She needed to figure out what to do.

She needed to do that this morning.

At five-one, she wasn't big.

Her apartment wasn't much bigger. She had to suck her stomach in to turn around. The thing that made it tolerable was the fact that it was temporary. Her Harvard law degree, now two months old, would make sure of that—assuming she passed the bar in October, which she would as long as she got time to study.

She showered, dressed for work and took a look at herself in the mirror. A mildly but not wildly attractive face stared back. Above her left eye was a jagged three-inch scar, not highly-contrasting or thick or deep, but perceptible and capable of causing confusion when the person looking at her for the first time tried to figure out what was wrong.

There was no great story to it.

She fell off her bike when she was ten.

No foreign spies or acts of courage were involved.

Her stomach churned.

The thing she wanted more than anything in the world was to not go to work this morning.

She had to though.

She had to make sure that everything was normal and no one knew about what she did last night. She needed to know that her face hadn't been captured on a security camera or that someone had seen her and made a phone call. She needed to know that the FBI didn't have her in its crosshairs.

She made two extra copies of the flash drive.

One went into the bottom of her purse.

Another went into a box of frozen Lean Pockets in the freezer.

The third went into an envelope, stamped and addressed to herself.

She dropped it in a mailbox.

Then she got on an eastbound bus.

Thirty-five minutes later, at One First Street, she stepped off.

10

Teffinger woke late Wednesday morning with Portia on one side and Seven on the other. Both women were passed out. Portia was face up. Seven was face down. Both were on top of the covers. Both were naked. Teffinger's head still spun to the trance of the liquor and the smoke and the pounding speakers and the gyrating bodies and the raw shameless sex of last night.

He twisted onto his back and stretched.

His watch said 10:32, five hours past what it should.

He shouldn't have done what he did last night but he did it and that was all there was to it, and now he needed to deal with it. To be fair, there had been too much beer and body contact and dark lighting for too many hours for the night to not have ended in some kind of grand culmination.

Having officially and irrevocably slept with Portia, his credibility as a witness against her was forever tainted.

If she ever came to trial and he had to testify against her, the defense would say he'd been jilted or rejected after the fact.

Now he was out for revenge.

Now he was lying.

Just look at him.

Still, the case wasn't necessarily in the gutter. What he needed to do was be sure it got built on physical evidence.

He slipped out of bed without waking either woman, grabbed his clothes and made his way next door to his own room—the room of North Reynolds—for a shower and a change. Forty-five minutes later he walked into homicide, deflected a stern look from Sydney and headed for the coffee. He stayed there and drank half the cup slow enough that he didn't burn his tongue, then topped off and headed for his desk.

Sydney plopped down in a chair, looked at her watch and then at him.

No one was overly close.

They had privacy if they kept their voices low.

He leaned forward and said, "I ended up spending some time with Portia last night."

"I'll bet you did. Did you sleep with her?"

Teffinger exhaled.

"Technically, yes."

"Technically?"

"Right, technically."

"As in, you didn't enjoy it?"

"I wouldn't say that."

"So you did enjoy it?"

"Well, yes, technically speaking," he said. "In my defense, though, someone else slept with her too."

"Who?"

"Seven."

"Seven men?"

"No, one person, a woman. Her name is Seven."

Sydney rolled her eyes. "Who's Seven?"

Teffinger shrugged.

"She's an escort with something called Ladies en Secret. That's probably not her real name."

"Is she an accomplice?"

"I'm not sure there's anyone to be an accomplice to," Teffinger said. "If Portia's a killer, she's keeping it well hidden. She doesn't fit the profile. She's not detached or cold or calculating. I didn't pick up any personality flaws or deep hidden issues. All night long, she didn't say a single thing that was incriminating."

"So what is she then, a link in the chain to someone else? A courier or something?"

"I don't know. I need more time with her."

"I'll bet you do. Who paid for Seven?"

"Portia did."

"Lucky you. Did you ask her what the tattoo on her neck says?"

"No."

"Why not?"

"Because every guy in the world who's had the chance has asked her that," he said.

"So you're not every guy?"

"There you go."

An hour later his phone rang and the voice of his D.C. counterpart, Randy Johnson, came through. "Have you ever heard of a law firm called Overton & Frey?"

"No."

"Well, let me tell you about them," Johnson said. "They're relatively well-connected as D.C. firms go. Their office here has 150 or so lawyers and they have branches all over the world—London, Paris, Hong Kong, you name it. They're the go-to firm for the big and relevant. One of their top partners out here in D.C. is a man named Leland Everitt. Have you ever heard of him?"

"No."

"Well, our P.I. friend Oscar Benderfield has," Johnson said.

"Meaning what?"

"Meaning they had a little meeting just a while ago. I'm not talking about a lunch meeting. I'm talking about a quick little meeting on a street corner, four blocks off the grid. We don't know what they talked about but the interesting thing is that Everitt gave Benderfield a briefcase."

"Money?"

"Given what you told me about what happened in Denver, my guess would be yes," Johnson said. "Benderfield took it back to his office and that's where he's been for the last hour. When he leaves, we'll be with him. It'll be interesting to see if he passes it on to someone else."

Teffinger raked his hair back with his fingers.

It immediately flopped back down.

"If it's for Portia, she's still out here in Denver," he said.

"Has she made a move yet?"

"No."

"Have you found out anything on her?"

"Just one thing," Teffinger said. "Her skin is very, very smooth. I'm guessing she uses lots of lotions."

11

Teffinger walked into the law building of Susan A. Smith and found her in the back office on the main level pacing next to the windows and talking animatedly into a phone. The startle on her face from seeing him wore off quickly and she motioned him to have a seat. He looked around, saw no coffee and left in search of the kitchen.

He had a cup out of the cupboard and half filled when the woman walked in.

"The black man with the bleached hair is someone by the name of Oscar Benderfield," he said. "He's a private investigator from D.C. Do you know him?"

She hopped on the counter.

Her skirt rode up.

She dangled her legs.

"No."

"One of his clients is a lawyer by the name of Leland Everitt. He's a senior partner in Overton & Frey, which is a mega firm with a main office in D.C. and branches all over the world."

She wrinkled her brow.

"I've heard of them but not that particular lawyer."

"Were you ever involved in a case with that firm, where they were on the other side or something like that?"

"No."

"How do you know about them?"

"I don't remember," she said. "Maybe on the news. Maybe one of their lawyers spoke at a seminar I attended. Maybe I read something in the paper—something like that. I don't recall. Whatever it was, though, it wasn't anything direct. I don't have any tangible connection to them."

"Is there any reason anyone in that firm would want you dead?"

She ran a finger down his chest.

"Nobody wants me dead. I already told you that. I'll tell you what. If it will make you feel better, I'll have a look at this supposed killer. What'd you say her name was? Portia Montrachet?"

Teffinger winced.

"Stay away from her."

"Why?"

"It's dangerous."

"More dangerous than her killing me?"

"You might not be the target," he said.

"We both know that you think I am," she said. "Deny it if it's not true."

He went to speak. No words came out.

"Just stay out of it."

She smiled.

"You said she's pretty," she said. "Maybe I'll like

her. Maybe she'll like me. People don't kill people they like."

"Yes they do," he said. "They do it every day."

"I'll give you a choice. Either I'm going to head over to her hotel and see if I can buy her a drink or you can guard me tonight and we'll see if she shows up."

Teffinger swallowed.

"Don't play this game."

"A or B," she said. "Your choice."

He played out both scenarios.

"Give me a couple of hours to think about it."

She looked at her watch.

"Take until five."

12

Del Rey lived in Mesa View Estates, an up-scale custom enclave riding up the side of Green Mountain. Her particular house was a stucco ranch with a walkout basement nestled in a cul-de-sac and adjacent to open space, with commanding views of the eastern plains that swept all the way from Rocky Flats to Denver to Douglas County. As twilight set over Colorado and the flatland lights began to twinkle, Teffinger parked the Tundra two blocks away, hoofed the balance and knocked on the woman's door

Bad thoughts chewed at his brain.

In his last communication with Portia this afternoon, she told him she couldn't do anything with him tonight because she had business. That business, if Teffinger's instinct was right, was the murder of Susan Smith.

Tonight was the night.

All the Susan Smiths in the city had been warned to stay away from their homes and to keep an extra careful watch no matter where they were. Most of them planned to hole up at a hotel or with relatives or friends. A few said there was no reason for anyone to kill them and that they weren't going to get paranoid over something that was someone else's business. For those Susans, patrol cars would be making regular sweeps.

Del Rey, however, was the target.

Teffinger could feel it.

He could smell it.

He could taste it.

He could feel it pulsing in his veins.

When he closed his eyes, he could see Portia sneaking through the open space with a dark heart hammering to a voodoo beat.

There was a good chance Teffinger would be forced to kill her.

He told himself that he could.

He also told himself that the thing he just told himself might not be as true as he wanted it to be. She was under his skin in a way he hadn't anticipated.

Teffinger wasn't a stranger to Del Rey's house. Most

of the sex they had during their brief but explosive collision with each other took place there. When the woman opened the door, Teffinger wasn't prepared for what he saw.

She wore a short, loose sundress; the kind of flimsy thing he could rip off her body with one good yank.

Her hair was soft.

Her eyes were trouble.

Her lips were moist.

Her skin was golden.

Down below she was barefoot.

Addicted, that's what Teffinger could get if he didn't guard against it; addicted again, to be more precise. She was the cure, or at least could appear that way. The lightning in his chest was already sparking.

"Come on in," she said.

"Any sign of her yet?"

"No."

"She's coming tonight," he said. "Tonight's the night."

"How do you know?"

"I'm paid to know." A song was coming from the other room, one Teffinger had never heard but already liked. "What's that song?"

"You don't know?"

No.

He didn't.

"It's called Touch Me I'm Going to Scream."

"Who sings it?"

"My Morning Jacket."

"Never heard of them."

"If you want, I can put it on repeat. We can go down in the dungeon and have some fun."

Teffinger pulled up a memory.

Del Rey was on her back on a green leather table, dressed in white panties and a little schoolgirl outfit. Her knees were bent 90 degrees, her legs were separated and her ankles were tied to the feet of the table. Her arms were pulled up tightly over her head. Her elbows were bent at the end of the table and her wrists were pulled down towards the floor and inescapably tied.

Her body was stretched tight.

Her eyes were blindfolded.

Her blouse had ridden up to showcase a taut stomach and a pierced navel.

A petite vixen in similar attire was running her fingertips lightly over Del Rey's exposed flesh, in the initial throes of teasing her captive into an orgasmic frenzy.

Teffinger was sitting in the corner chair with a Bud in hand, watching for now, free to join in whenever he wanted.

"Teff, I said do you want to go down in the dungeon and have some fun?"

The words snapped him back.

The answer inside his head was, Yes.

The answer that came out of his mouth was, "What we need to do is check the perimeter and then lock up. Then I want you to follow your normal routine."

She ran a finger down his chest and said, "You can't resist me forever."

That was true.

He knew it.

She knew it.

"For the moment let's just concentrate on keeping you alive."

"That'll take care of itself. I'm not the target. I already told you that."

"We'll find out soon enough."

She turned, bent slightly at the waist and rubbed her posterior into his lap. "I'll make you a deal," she said. "If I'm right, you have to be my slave for a hour. If you're right, I'll be yours."

He raked his hair back with his finger.

It hung for a heartbeat and flopped back down.

"Deal," he said, "but for dinner, not slave. Loser pays."

"Okay."

Before bed Del Rey took a shower, then turned off the lights and slipped her naked body under a thin sheet. Teffinger sat on the bedroom floor with his legs stretched out and his back against the wall, resisting the urge to yank the cover off and take her to a place she'd never forget.

"Pleasant dreams," he said.

"Wake me if you hear anything."

"I will."

"I'm glad you're here."

"Yeah, no problem."

Within minutes the woman was asleep. Her breathing was deep and steady and familiar. He'd heard it plenty before and never gotten tired of it. Thinking back, he wasn't sure how he let her slip out of his life. He did know one thing though; he wouldn't make the same mistake twice.

Time passed.

Not a sound came out of the world that shouldn't be there.

His thoughts wandered.

His eyes got heavy.

Don't sleep.

Don't sleep.

Don't sleep.

He splashed cold water on his face and took a walk through the upper level of the house, finding nothing out of whack. Then he headed down the open staircase to the walkout level, a large space with ten-foot ceilings.

Everything was normal.

All the sliding glass doors were locked.

The wall-to-wall windows were locked.

No glass was broken or cut.

The dungeon was built into the back corner. It was a large windowless room with a carpeted floor and textured walls. Teffinger stepped inside, closed the door, brought the recessed lights on and then dimmed them to shadows.

Everything was as he remembered it.

He turned on the sound system.

A sultry voice dropped out of ceiling speakers. The words were French and the melody was haunting. The woman singing it understood lust. She understood passion. She understood the meaning of life.

Suddenly the door opened and Del Rey walked in.

She was naked.

She attached padded cuffs to her wrists and ankles and then stood in the middle of the room. She raised her arms and spread her legs. Immediately above her wrists, chains hung down from the ceiling.

"Don't deny me," she said.

DAY THREE

July 10
Thursday

13

Thursday morning Teffinger woke up next to a soundly sleeping but otherwise very much not-dead Del Rey. He slipped out of bed without waking her and took a quick walk around the perimeter, which showed no evidence of tampering or attempted break-ins. His phone had no messages or missed calls, which wouldn't be the case if one of the other Susan Smiths had been murdered. His gut feeling about last night had been wrong.

So, what did the Portia do last night?

Had she been doing final surveillance?

Had she parked her little killer body out in the open space and studied her prey through binoculars?

Did she spot Teffinger?

Was his cover blown?

Del Rey appeared in his peripheral vision, walking his way in a vision of white panties and an upper-body jiggle, scorching the image into Teffinger's brain where it would live forever.

"Is everything okay?" she said.

"Yes."

"Soap me up."

"Soap you up?"

"Yeah, in the shower." She grabbed his hand and pulled. "Come on. I won the bet by the way."

"I noticed."

"You're not going to re-neg, are you?"

"Do I have a choice?"

"No."

"Good."

It was mid-morning in homicide, at the start of the sixth or eighth or tenth cup of coffee, when Sydney walked over to Teffinger's desk with a serious face and said, "Come on. Someone just found a body."

"Where?"

"A stone's throw from Susan Smith's place."

"Which Susan Smith?"

"The model."

She was the one he'd seen at the clubs, the one who ended up spreading out in the beds of the powerful and the relevant; the kind of men who could fill a briefcase with hundreds and hand it to the right person if need be.

He drained what was left in his cup and grabbed his jacket.

"Get down to the body," he said.

"Where are you going?"

"To see Portia Montrachet."

"You think she's still in town?"

"If she is it's not by much," he said. "Go confirm

the body belongs Susan Smith and call me. As soon as I get your call I'm going to arrest her."

Portia wasn't at the hotel but hadn't checked out. Teffinger paced in the lobby with coffee in hand, picturing himself getting fired, and justifiably so, once it came out that he did the incredibly stupid act of sleeping with a person who was under suspicion of being an assassin.

His phone rang.

Sydney's voice came through.

"The body doesn't belong to Susan Smith," she said.

Teffinger halted mid-step.

"It doesn't?"

"No."

"Are you sure?"

"I'm positive," she said. "Get down here though. You need to see this."

14

The dead body sent a cold chill up Teffinger's spine and into his brain. The victim's face, now battered and listless, belonged to Portia; the hair, now messy and tangled, belonged to Portia; the body, now quiet and without dance, belonged to Portia. Teffinger knelt close. The familiar scent of the woman's perfume pulsed through the air and made him flash back to the night before last, drunker than drunk, with his face between her thighs and the moans of her lust in his ears.

She hadn't gone easily.

There had been a struggle, a violent one. Her face was beaten. Her clothes were ripped and dirty, indicative of a fight that ended up on the ground. Her panties were ripped off and twenty feet from the body, which itself was in an alley.

A knife was in her gut, still there, buried up to the handle.

Portia.

Portia.

Portia.

Whoever killed her would pay. Teffinger would spend the rest of his days tracking the guy down. No matter how long it took it wouldn't be too long.

"Teffinger are you okay?"

The words came from Sydney, standing close by with a concerned look on her face.

"Yeah," he said.

"You don't look okay."

"I'm fine."

He raked his hair back.

It immediately flopped down.

"She deserved something, but not this," he said.

Over the next two hours Teffinger's theory of the crime became clearer. Portia's purse wasn't far from her body. It was undisturbed, including her wallet, which contained over $5,000 cash. Also inside the purse was a .357 Tarus with a detached silencer. She had definitely come to the area with the intent of murdering Susan Smith. The target, though, hadn't been home, forcing Portia to wait. That was the fatal element. During that wait she encountered a stranger; a stranger who saw a beautiful woman alone and lingering in the shadows, a stranger who quickly got bad thoughts into his nasty little head.

He started off friendly.

She wasn't interested.

She had business at hand.

The man looked around and found no one in close proximity.

Things escalated.

The whole sick thing probably didn't last more than two minutes.

Susan Smith, the target, wasn't anywhere to be found until mid-afternoon when she showed up in high heels and a sinful night-before dress. Teffinger intercepted her from behind with a hand to her elbow in the lobby of her building, The Terrace, and said, "We need to talk."

She turned, studied his face and said, "I've seen you on TV. You're that detective."

Teffinger nodded.

The woman smelled like smoke.

"Nick Teffinger," he said. "I've seen you around at the clubs. I came over once to buy you a drink."

She wrinkled her forehead.

"Are you sure? I think I would have remembered—"

He shifted his feet.

"Another guy got there first, he beat me out by a half second."

She smiled.

"Next time be faster."

"Next time I will."

Her space, on the second of ten floors, was a lot more opulent than Teffinger anticipated, replete with high ceilings, floods of sunlight, rolling open spaces and rich contemporary textures. The pallete was muted with strategically placed color splashes.

"Business must be good," he said.

"Good enough."

"How do you afford something like this?"

She smiled.

"People give me money."

"Why?"

"Because they like me." She headed for the wetbar. "Do you want a drink?"

No.

That was the correct answer, No.

He went to say it but the words that came out were, "Sure, why not?"

"Diet coke and Absolute?"

"Fine."

He explained the situation, namely that the killer—a woman who went by the name of Portia Montrachet— came to take her mark last night. Luckily for

Susan, the woman ended up in an encounter that left her dead. "The important thing is that whoever hired her will have another go at it. You're not off the hook." He took a hard swallow and added, "You need to be honest with me tell me what's going on. If I don't have the information to stop this at the source, it won't stop. So tell me, what's the source?"

The woman pulled a pack of cigarettes out of her purse, tapped two loose and extended the pack towards Teffinger.

He declined.

She lit up.

"There is no source."

Teffinger frowned.

"Don't play this game. It's dangerous."

She blew smoke.

"I'm a big girl, Mr. Teffinger. I can take care of myself, if there was even something to take care of, which there isn't." She tapped ashes into a tray, read the expression on his face and leaned back. "I'll make you a deal. You can take me out tonight and ply me with drinks. You can pick my brain while my defenses are down."

He considered it.

It was wrong.

It was stupid.

It wasn't the way investigations worked.

It wasn't the way to maintain professional boundaries.

He stood up and headed for the door. Halfway through he turned and said, "I'll pick up you up nine."

"Perfect."

15

The afternoon was a flurry of motion, but whether that motion was forward, sideways or backwards, only time would tell. A search warrant for Portia's hotel room turned up the suitcase and the money. Unfortunately, though, the photo of the mark--Susan Smith--wasn't inside or anywhere to be found, either in the room or in the woman's rental vehicle.

As for her murder, none of the private security cameras in the area shined on the location in question. The cameras in the fringe areas where Portia may have walked en route contained no footage of her. No witnesses came forward. The alley contained a lot of junk ranging from empty cans to spent cigarette packs to who knows what. The fresher pieces were meticulously collected and bagged on the chance one belonged to the killer. Still, it wouldn't lead to the person's identity; it would only tie him to the scene after they knew who he was. Two stray pieces of trash, however, rose above the others; not in the alley but just outside on the sidewalk. The first was a spent book of matches, burnt amber in color with a black abstract dragon on the front, somewhat in the nature of a tribal tattoo. The second was a discarded cigarette, thrown down after only a few puffs and then burnt to the filter.

Neither contained prints.

"Find out where the matches came from," Teffinger told Sydney.

"You're not serious."

He was; very, in fact.

"The guy could have lit the butt in the first few moments when he was talking to Portia, then threw it down when things escalated. That's why it was hardly smoked." He raked his hair back, focused on the matchbook and said, "It could be from a tattoo shop. Maybe our guy's an ink nut. Go back over the tapes and mark anyone and everyone with tattoos, male and female, or even tattoo-looking, even if you can't see anything visible."

"Tattoo-looking?"

"You know what I mean."

"Not really."

"That's a long shot."

"I'll take a short shot if you have one."

She screwed a serious expression on her face and said, "I've been thinking about what you said before, about how Susan Smith told you she was a big girl and could take care of herself."

"Well, she is, but she can't," Teffinger said. "She doesn't really appreciate the depth of the problem."

"That's not what I'm getting at," Sydney said. "What I'm getting at is that maybe she already took care of the problem. That's why she's so relaxed, at least short-term."

Teffinger raked his hair back.

"Meaning what?"

"Meaning that maybe she was laying in wait."

The words landed with the force of a two-by-four, not because they were farfetched, which they were, but because Teffinger should have come to the theory himself. "Are you saying Susan Smith killed Portia?"

Sydney shrugged.

"Obviously I don't know," she said. "It's possible though, you have to admit. I mean, I've been in contact with her. She knew she was a target. She knew to be on the lookout for Portia—an attractive female with a tattoo on her neck—who I described to her. She discounted the whole situation to my face like I was out of my mind, but maybe all the while she knew she was the target. Rather than let that fact on to us—because we'd press her to tell us all the hows and whys, which is something she'd no doubt rather keep secret—she laid in wait."

Teffinger leaned forward.

"Or had someone lay in wait on her behalf," he said.

"Right, she could have hired someone, or had a friend, or maybe even some type of accomplice involved. Then she, or they, made it look like some kind of a sex thing gone wrong."

Teffinger chewed on it.

It made sense, logically speaking.

Down in his gut, though, it didn't resonate.

It was thin.

It was watery.

"Store it away as a theory," he said. "We'll drag it out later if we need to."

Sydney shook her head.

"It's a mistake to take her out tonight," she said. "If she killed Portia, you'll be tainting the investigation."

"Yeah, well, that's my new MO."

"Plus there's the danger to you."

He smiled.

"That's cute. I'm going to get some more coffee. You want some?"

Time passed. Clouds rolled in late afternoon. Instead of vaporizing and blowing to Kansas, they grew mean black bellies and put on a bad attitude. At twilight they cleared up without dropping a drop.

Teffinger and Sydney were the only ones left in homicide.

A pizza box with three pieces sat on the corner of Teffinger's desk.

His stomach was a grease pit.

Just as he was about to leave, Sydney pulled him over to the security tape and pointed. "What do you think about this guy?"

Teffinger studied the screen.

The guy in question looked like a boxer, with a square chin, a furrowed brow and a cat-like movement. Teffinger's first thought was that he didn't know if he could take the guy in a fair fight. His second thought was a lot darker and a lot more relevant.

"If he can't kill someone, no one can."

Sydney studied his face.

"There's no tattoos showing," she said.

"Find out who he is."

Two minutes later he was in the Tundra, heading west on the 6th Avenue freeway, en route to get ready for the big adventure with Susan Smith.

Del Rey called just as Teffinger exited at Union.

"What are you doing tonight?"

"Investigating."

"Till when?"

"I don't know," he said. "It'll probably be long. Past midnight—"

"Come over when you're done."

He chewed on it.

The chew tasted good.

"Okay."

Del Rey.

Del Rey.

Del Rey.

She had a hold on him again.

He didn't care.

Even if she dumped him again, he didn't care. It would be worth it.

"See you then," she said. "The key will be under the front mat."

16

Humidity choked the air and sucked the energy out of every pore of Jori-Lee's body as she jogged through the twilight streets of D.C. She hoped the run and the setting sun would get the legal briefs and deadlines and daily mess of One First Street out of her head long enough to let her think.

So far it wasn't.

So far all she could concentrate on was to not get hit by a car or trip on an uneven sidewalk or rip her face on a low hanging branch.

Still, she was alive.

She wasn't in a cell.

She wasn't disbarred.

She wasn't under a swinging light bulb in a dark concrete room being battered by the FBI as to what the hell she was doing the other night and who was she working for.

A mile passed, then another.

Heavy breathing came from behind.

She turned to find a woman approaching, a woman on a jog on a hot summer night, just like her except at a faster clip.

The woman came alongside and fell into step.

She was fit, curvy and had a body built for sex.

"Nice night," she said.

"Yeah."

"I've seen you around. You work at One First Street."

"Maybe."

The woman pulled a piece of paper out of her bra and passed it over. A glance showed that it contained a phone number; nothing else, just a number; typed, not handwritten. The area code wasn't local.

"Tell Mr. Robertson to call that number tomorrow at exactly seven p.m."

"Who are you?"

"Just tell him to do it."

The woman veered off and was gone.

17

When the time came, Susan wasn't in the mood for crowds, particularly drunken ones. She had two bottles of white wine and said, "Let's just go somewhere quiet and chill."

"Where?"

"I don't care. Surprise me."

Teffinger's first thought was Red Rocks, parked up high where the lights of Denver twinkled all the way to the Kansas line. His second thought was a lot better. They ended up at Chatfield Reservoir, anchored at the west end of the lake in a 29-foot Beneteau; a friend's from the marina, not his. The air was still and the water was glass. Five miles to the west, the foothills were a dark jagged band under a fading orange sky that would dissolve into total darkness within the next ten minutes. The oppressive heat of the day was losing its fight with the thin Rocky Mountain air, now down to 80 and sinking.

A hundred yards off, near the shore, two fishermen in an aluminum boat were working the lines.

"I used to do a lot of fishing when I was a kid," Teffinger said. "Back then I was just an amateur baiter. But, like everything in life, I got better. Now I'm what you'd call a master baiter."

Susan punched his arm.

"You're terrible."

He smiled.

"Thank you."

The talk was small, the moon was up and the wine was a song in Teffinger's head. Susan slipped out of her pants to cool off and stretched out on the cushions. A flash of white cotton appeared between her thighs whenever she shifted her legs, which seemed to be a lot.

Teffinger swallowed.

Don't screw her.

Don't jeopardize whatever it is that you have going on with Del Rey.

Don't get stupid.

"Stupider."

"Yeah, whatever."

"I'm serious, stupider."

"I heard you the first time."

He took a long swallow of wine, looked at the Susan-silhouette and said, "It's going to be a shame if all this disappears."

"If all what disappears?"

"All things Susan," he said. "Tell me who's out to kill you. Tell me why."

She exhaled.

"I'm not sure I'm drunk enough yet."

"Then keep drinking."

She drained what was left in her glass, slowly unbuttoned her blouse and set it to the side, then removed her bra and laid it on top of the blouse. She stretched out on the cushions face down, wearing only the panties, which were now nothing more than a hypnotic accent defining her curves.

"Give me a massage," she said.

"You need to talk."

"I'll talk during the massage. I like it rough. Dig deep."

Teffinger laid his hands on her back.

Her skin was soft.

Her muscles were taut.

"Talk," he said.

"Relax me first."

He obliged.

The touch of her flesh lit a fire under his skin.

"There's a law firm down in the financial district called Colder & Boggs," she said. "They're fairly big, about a hundred lawyers. They mostly do high-stakes litigation and specialize in class actions. The Colder part of the namesake comes from Jack Colder. Have you ever heard of him?"

"No."

"Well, lucky you," she said. "There was a time four or five years ago when him and me were pretty close. He figured out quickly that money made me happy and one of the things he wanted to do more than anything was make me happy. A lot of money flowed my way. I didn't know it at the time but he thought he was buying my soul one installment at a time. The time came when he considered me paid in full."

She sighed.

"So what happened?"

"His attitude changed," she said. "The money kept coming but a dark side of him came out that I never knew about. Well, that's not exactly true. I'd seen it before but it had never been directed at me. Now it was coming my way."

She rolled onto her back.

"Do my front," she said.

Teffinger obliged.

"It took a while for things to fully end," she said. "It was sort of like a slow painful dance. During that period, I met a man by the name of Seth Lightfield."

Teffinger knew the name but couldn't place it.

"He was a dancer," Susan said. "He's backed up lots of big names, including Madonna and Brittany Spears. He lives in Denver when he's not on the road."

It came to him.

"Was he a tall muscular guy with long hair?"

"Yes."

"I remember him," Teffinger said. "Someone put a bullet in the back of his head."

"Right," she said. "Now you know who."

"Colder."

"Right, Colder."

"Did he ever admit it to you?"

"No, we stopped talking months before that." She exhaled. "I don't have any proof if that's what you're getting at. Now he's after me."

"Why? Why now?"

"Because deep wounds never heal," she said. "Haven't you ever loved anyone that deep?"

He had.

It never turned crazy afterwards but, way down, the makings were there.

"So why didn't you tell me this before?"

"Because I didn't think he was serious," she said. "I thought he was just messing with me. I didn't want to give him the satisfaction of a reaction."

DAY FOUR

July 11
Friday

18

Friday morning with a jolt of caffeine in hand, Teffinger pulled the Seth Lightfield file out of storage and searched it for anything that hinted at Jack Colder being the killer. Nothing of that sort was there. Moreover, there was no DNA or fingerprints or witnesses to match to the man. Teffinger had motive but not a scintilla more.

Well, that wasn't exactly true.

He had a bullet to the back of the man's head.

Maybe Colder hired Portia Montrachet to do the deed; and now, a year later, he hired her again to take out the more hateful part of the equation, Susan. A bullet to the head would be Portia's style against a man like Lightfield. Maybe she even used the same weapon against him that she left behind in her purse. Ballistics could tell.

Sydney showed up at 7:30 wearing a white blouse that played well against her mocha skin. She filled a coffee cup, plopped down in the chair in front of Teffinger's desk and studied him over the rim as she took a sip.

"I hate you," she said.

He smiled.

"Why?"

"Because you had sex this morning."

He went to deny it but knew she'd know he was lying.

"And?"

"And I didn't," she said.

"Well, don't worry about it," he said. "It's actually underrated."

"Do you mean overrated?"

He raked his hair back.

"No, under."

He brought her up to speed on what Susan Smith told him last night about Seth Lightfield and Jack Colder, the lawyer; together with his theory that Colder either killed Lightfield or hired Portia, or someone like her, to do it. Now he was after Susan.

"I know Colder," Sydney said.

The words were a rock to the face.

"You do?"

She nodded.

"He dated a friend of mine back in the day," she said.

"A black woman?"

She smacked his arm. "Yes, a black woman, you should try it some time Teffinger. You might be surprised."

"I already have."

"And?"

"And I got no complaints."

"No complaints?"

"Right."

"Well, all I can say is you didn't do it right," she said. "If you'd done it right the answer wouldn't be, And I got no complaints. The answer would be, And I never went back to white."

He smiled.

"Next time I'll try to do it right." He sipped at the caffeine. "Maybe you'll give me some pointers."

She soured her face.

"In your dreams."

He smiled.

"Work up a warrant to get Colder's phone records for the three or four month period preceding Light-field's murder. I want to see if he was in contact with Portia Montrachet or that bleached haired investigator out in D.C. What was his name?"

"Oscar Benderfield."

"Right. Another field, that's weird."

"Weird just follows you around Teffinger."

He cocked his head.

"There's actually some truth to that. What'd your friend who was dating Colder say about him?"

"She said he gave her money."

"What else?"

"I don't remember."

"Call her up and get everything you can on the guy."

"That won't be possible."

"Why not?"

"She's dead."

The words hit hard.

"How'd she die?"

"Do you mean was she murdered?"

"Right."

"Not that I know of," she said. "I didn't hear much about it. It was a year or two afterwards when I found out."

"What was her name?"

"Female," Sydney said. "Female Natja."

The word rhymed with Tamale but when Teffinger ran the letters it made his forehead wrinkle.

"Is that spelled F E M A L E?"

"Yes."

"So the parents named their daughter Female?"

"It's pronounced Fa-Maul-E."

"Right, I understand." He headed for the door and said over his shoulder, "Get the details of her death."

Then he was gone.

19

Colder & Boggs, P.C., turned out to be a boutique firm of about thirty lawyers operating out of a high level in the epicenter of the financial district. Teffinger paid more than his monthly mortgage to park the Tundra and then worked his way into and through an opulent deco lobby and up an enclosed metal stairwell floor by floor until his quads burned and his chest heaved.

Five minutes later he was past the receptionist and easing into a leather chair at an expensive wooden table in the corner of Jack Colder's office.

Outside the glass was a commanding view of the mountains.

In the corner was a pinball machine with a King Kong theme.

Colder had a swagger.

He had the face to charm, the body to command and the penetrating eyes of a predator. In a different time and place, he'd be the king.

Teffinger pulled up a picture of Portia Montrachet on his phone, held it for Colder to see and said, "Do you know this woman? Her name's Portia Montrachet."

The man showed no reaction or hesitation.

"No."

"She got murdered last night," he said.

"And that involves me, how?"

"I don't know that it does," Teffinger said. "In her purse was a piece of paper with a handwritten phone number on it. The number is the one for this law firm."

As the words left his mouth, Teffinger had one thought and one thought only. Don't look like you're lying.

Don't look like you're lying.

Don't look like you're lying.

"And?"

"And I thought the firm might be doing some work for her," Teffinger said.

"If it was it wasn't through me," Colder said.

"I know that," Teffinger said. "Because if that was the case my life would be too easy and that's not how my life works. What I was hoping is that you could check around and see if she was a client. If she was, then the lawyer she was dealing with may be able to shed light on why she was killed."

Colder frowned.

"Who our clients are or are not is a matter of privilege," he said. "We can't disclose information like that without authority from the client or a court order."

"Well, given her state, I doubt she's going to object." Teffinger leaned forward. "Between you and me, I'm going to find the person who killed her and use my every breath to make sure he rots in hell. You can save me some time. If she was a client, I'll get a search warrant at that point. I just don't want to waste my time getting a warrant if there's no basis for it."

Colder shook his head.

"I understand you're pressed for time but that doesn't change my obligations as a lawyer," he said. "I'm sorry."

Teffinger nodded.

"It never hurts to ask," he said.

"No, it doesn't."

Back at homicide Sydney said, "I don't get it. I don't

see what you accomplished, not to mention that what you've been telling me every time I turn around is to always talk to the suspect last, after you have all the facts rounded up."

"I wanted him to feel the heat of a detective sitting in his office," Teffinger said, "I didn't want to do it in a way that would implicate Susan Smith though, so I made up a little excuse. Hopefully he'll be jarred enough to back off, at least temporarily."

"Tricky."

"If it works." He took a sip of coffee. "The fact that I lied to him isn't a license for you to do the same. Do as I say, not as I do."

"As if I ever do either."

He smiled.

"Good point."

She got serious.

"So what did you think about him? Is he our man?"

20

Jack Colder's cell phone records showed no communications to or from Portia Montrachet or the D.C. investigator, Oscar Benderfield; not four years ago in the months leading up to Seth Lightfield's murder; not recently; not ever. The records did show a long-lived relationship with Susan Smith, just like she said, abruptly ending three months before

Lightfield was murdered.

The negative didn't mean much, not to Teffinger.

Colder could have used landlines.

He could have used someone other than Portia to kill Lightfield.

Sydney's face appeared in front of his.

She was excited.

She was stressed.

"Come look at this," she said.

This was the surveillance tape that showed the boxer, stopped on still frame.

"What do you see?"

Teffinger studied it, not seeing anything he hadn't seen before.

"I don't know; the boxer."

"What else?"

"Nothing."

"Look in the background."

He did.

Several people were walking.

One was a woman.

She looked vaguely familiar.

Sydney tapped on the woman's face and said, "Do you recognize her?"

No.

He didn't.

"She's Susan Smith, the Molly Maid."

He looked closer.

"No she isn't," he said.

"Yes she is."

They compared the photo of the woman from

her file against the one on the screen.

"There's a resemblance but it's not her," Teffinger said.

"Then you're blind."

He could argue but she'd win. Also, deep down, he had to admit she had a ten percent chance of being right. "Okay, run her down and find out."

"What do I get, if I'm right?"

He could already feel the pain in his wallet.

"Lunch," he said.

"Your treat."

"That was implied."

"I've been tricked by implied before," she said. "Say it."

He swallowed.

"Fine; lunch, my treat. Happy?"

She tweaked his nose.

"See, that wasn't so hard."

Lunch was with Del Rey at Wong's on Court Street. Her step had the spring of a teenager. Teffinger thought it was because the other Susan Smith was now confirmed as the target, but there was a different reason.

"I won my motion hearing this morning," she said.

"Didn't know you had one."

"Federal court," she said. "Smell my neck."

He obliged.

It was a designer perfume, not a Saturday-night sex trap. It was something more understated, more professional.

"That's the smell of justice," she said.

"Justice?"

"That's right."

"There's no such thing."

She leaned back and studied him. "You should spend the night tonight."

An image flashed up, an image of him, Del Rey and an exotic raven-haired woman with a jungle vine tattoo wrapped around her right thigh, down in the dungeon one steamy drunken night. "Hey, do you remember that woman who joined us once, the one with the tattoo?"

She did.

She did indeed.

"What was her name again?"

"Trouble."

Teffinger smiled.

"Do you still see her?"

"Why? Do you want another one?"

"No, I was just curious."

"I haven't seen her in a long time," Del Rey said. "She moved."

"Where to?"

She wrinkled her brow, focused on the distance and then came back. "I can't remember. I'm thinking La La Land but I'm not sure; somewhere on the west coast. I have another one like here in town if that's what you're getting at. I don't mind."

Teffinger raked his hair back.

It immediately flopped back down.

"No."

She had a hesitant look on her face as if she wanted to say something but wasn't sure she should.

"There's something you don't know about that night," she said. "I recorded it."

"You mean on videotape?"

"DVD actually."

"Do you ever watch it?"

"I'm embarrassed to admit it, but yes." A beat then, "I can make a copy for you if you want."

He considered it.

Then he said, "No. I'll just stick with what I have in my mind. Paul Simon taught me that."

21

Colder had covered his tracks well but a man of his power and stature had enemies. Teffinger needed to find the one who had the dirt.

Sydney showed up mid-afternoon looking like she could use a drink. "I tracked down Susan Smith the Molly Maid and showed her the security tape," she said. "She says that's not her."

Teffinger tilted his head.

"That gets me out of lunch."

"Not totally."

"You said it wasn't her."

"No, what I said is that she said it wasn't her. I think she's lying."

"Why?"

"Just the way she acted. I'm thinking that whatever it is that's going on, she can't let us know about it. Either she did something illegal or she's expecting a big payoff, or something like that. Whatever it is it's worth the risk of getting killed over."

Teffinger wasn't impressed.

"If this is about lunch, I'm still going to take you. I probably owe it to you a hundred times over anyway. I want you to get on Jack Colder's tail. Follow him around. See what he does."

"You're not serious."

"I am," he said. "Also find out who his enemies are."

"How?"

"I don't know but do it quietly."

She wrinkled her brow.

"No offense Teffinger but the more I think about Colder the more I don't see him involved."

"Why not?"

"You mean besides the lack of any evidence?"

"Right."

"Well, basically, he's a guy," she said. "Guys don't hold grudges for four years. Most guys I know can barely remember what they had for breakfast."

The corner of Teffinger's mouth turned up.

Then he got serious.

"He's strong enough."

"To do what?"

"To hold a grudge. Most guys wouldn't have the strength. He does. Until someone better comes along, he's our prime suspect. Remember, he owned her at one point. You don't just let something like that go." He stood up. "I got to run."

"Where you going?"

"To find the boxer."

It took some time working the net, but Teffinger eventually traced the matchbook found at Portia's crime scene, the one with the tribal dragon, to a tattoo place on Broadway called Ink Insanity, which sat between a gay bondage paraphernalia shop and a Chinese massage parlor.

The place was empty except for a tatted-up pretty in her early twenties, at war with the world judging by the piercings and the paint. She was in a vinyl chair with her legs propped up and an iPad in her lap.

On the counter were complimentary matchbooks.

The covers had tribal dragons on burnt orange backgrounds.

Teffinger picked one up and tapped it on the counter.

"It's hot out," he said.

A fan blew at the woman's legs. They were pale but had a nice shape, riding up into a part of daisy dukes.

"Yeah."

"Is that bike parked out front yours?"

"Yeah."

"I've seen you around," he said.

"Yeah? Where?"

"The Grizzly Rose down in Golden."

"I don't go there."

"Then maybe it was The Little Bear. Do you go there?"

"Sometimes."

"That must be it."

He took out his phone and pulled up a picture of the boxer. "My name's Nick Teffinger. I'm a detective here in Denver and I'm trying to find this man," he said. "Do you know who he is?"

He studied her eyes as she studied the photo.

She knew him, he could tell.

"No," she said. "What do you want him for?"

He pulled up another photo, one of Portia, and said, "This woman was killed Wednesday night. The boxer was in the vicinity. I'd like to talk to him."

The woman didn't take her eyes off the photo.

Then she looked up.

"She's pretty."

Teffinger tapped the book of matches on the counter and said, "Matches like these were found at the scene. Help me out."

She hesitated.

"What's in it for me?"

"I don't know. What do you want to be in it for you?"

She shrugged.

"Let's just say that I have rent coming up."

Teffinger pulled five twenties out of his wallet and laid them on the counter. The woman scooped them up and stuffed them in her bra.

"Danny Rainer."

"You sure?"

She nodded.

"He lives somewhere off Colfax. You didn't hear it from me."

"What's your name?"

"Christina."

He headed for the door.

"You have yourself a nice day, Christina."

"You too. Come back some time. I'll give you a free one."

"A tattoo?"

"No. Something better."

Outside the sun was busy beating every living thing into a dry lifeless pulp. Teffinger got the Tundra's AC blasting and ran a background check on Danny Rainer.

The man was clean.

A quick web search led to something else he didn't expect. The man owned a majority interest in Rainer, Ltd., a holding company operating under several trade names and engaged in the business of constructing custom high-rise condos and lofts with units in the $500,000 to $2,000,000 range. Rainer Place One was currently being framed in LoDo and already 60% pre-sold, according to the website. Rainer Place Two was slated to begin in two years in the adjacent lot.

The man had money.

If you threw a suitcase full of green into his sea,

all you'd get would be a little splash. The surface wouldn't rise. The world wouldn't change.

Did he kill Portia?

Did he stop finding ways where money could make him happy?

Did he develop a dark side to get the kicks that worldly possessions could no longer give him?

Was he addicted to danger?

Had he turned himself into a hunter?

Teffinger merged into the sticky Broadway traffic and pointed the front end of the Tundra towards LoDo. Maybe Rainer would be down at the site watching his newest masterpiece go up.

The size of a man is related to the size of what he does. If nothing else, the project would give Teffinger a feel for the size of Rainer.

He wanted to experience the man's power.

He wanted to appreciate what he was up against.

He found parking at Coors Field and hoofed it over two blocks to where the steel framework of a high-rise was under construction, currently twelve or thirteen or fourteen stories up, flanked by the black webbing of a crane that rose another hundred feet still.

A chain-link fence wrapped the site.

Inside, two men sat in the shade of a construction trailer, eating sandwiches and drinking from thermoses.

"Have you guys seen Danny Rainer around?"

One of them pointed up to where four or five

men were working at the highest levels of the steel, not much more than tiny silhouettes against the sky, aligning a post being lowered by the crane.

"He's up there."

"I'm talking about Danny Rainer the owner," Teffinger said.

"That's him."

"He does physical work?"

"Every day."

Teffinger looked up.

"That's a good place to not lose your balance."

The man swallowed what was in his mouth and said, "You'd never catch me up there, not in a hundred years. I don't care what they pay. They can keep the money."

Teffinger swallowed.

He was a wimp when it came to gravity.

He used to climb at Red Rocks back in the days before they clamped down. One day he and a friend had to jump over a chasm, which was easy since it was only eight feet across and the other edge was three feet lower. Then bad news came. There was no way out on the opposing ridge. They had to jump back, this time going up three feet instead of down.

That made a difference.

It made him look down.

It made him sweat.

It made him picture things that weren't all that pretty.

He'd seen people drop from the rocks before. Two girls dropped out of the hatchet lady's cave once. They didn't appreciate that the pigeon poop on the front ledge was slippery.

They landed not more than thirty feet away from where Teffinger and Heather White were feeling each other up in the shade of a boulder.

They splattered all the way over to him.

His shirt ended up with so much blood on it that he took it off and left it there.

Trisha Bolton and Mary-Ann Swanson.

He never met either of them but their names were indelibly etched in his brain even now.

The sky beat down.

He wiped his forehead with the back of his hand and said, "Where can I catch Rainer at the end of the day?"

The man pointed to a Harley, an older model, not tricked out, not chromed out, just an ordinary ride with tassels hanging from the handlebars and leather saddlebags draped over the rear fender.

"That's his, right there."

"Thanks."

22

At the end of the day Teffinger hung across the street where he watched the boxer descend a rickety side-elevator to earth, disappear into a construction trailer for a meeting, and finally head for his Harley, the last bike left. Teffinger tailgated the man through thick traffic, getting more and more glances from the Harley's rearview mirror as the blocks clicked off.

On Colfax the bike jerked to the curb and fishtailed to a stop.

The boxer was off, staring Teffinger down, daring him to do something stupid.

Teffinger pulled up alongside, powered his window down and said, "Let me buy you a beer."

The man's face contorted.

"I don't know who you are but you're fucking with the wrong man."

Teffinger raked his hair back.

"My name's Teffinger," he said. "I'm a homicide detective. All I want is a few minutes of your time. It'll be off the record."

A car behind honked.

Teffinger's rearview mirror showed three male figures in a low rider, not amused at being blocked. He waved them around and turned his attention to the boxer.

"Beer or not? Your choice."

The boxer hesitated and then pointed to a blue tavern across the street. "Over there." Teffinger knew the place. He'd pulled bodies out of there on two occasions, one a drunken fight over twenty-five cents and the other a married man from Central City looking to get some tranny lipstick on his cock.

They sat at the far end of the bar with cold bottles of Bud, Teffinger's treat, a whole $2.00. He took a long swallow and smacked his lips. "I admire you for being able to work high. I couldn't do it. It would kill me in about ten minutes."

The boxer's ice didn't melt.

"You learn," he said. "Why are you talking to me?"

Teffinger pulled the victim's photo up on his phone and said, "Her name's Portia Montrachet. She got murdered downtown Wednesday night. We're in possession of a security tape from that night. It shows that you were in the vicinity." He took a short swallow. "I was hoping you might have seen something."

"No, nothing."

"You sure?"

"Wish I had," he said. "She's a nice looking lady."

"Agreed. Did you know her?"

"No. Did you?"

The words hit Teffinger with the power of a tire iron.

"Me? Why do you say that?"

"She just looks like your type."

"How do you know what my type is?"

"Just a guess."

Teffinger leaned forward on his elbows and stared at his reflection in the mirror. He closed his eyes and could feel Portia's body under his, he could taste her sweat and feel her soul from the way she moved her muscles. He opened his eyes. A young woman in street clothes slipped into a barstool three down and ordered a Coors Light.

She was in ordinary clothes, jeans and a T.

He looked at the boxer and said, "There was a time when the pros all wore short red dresses and blond wigs. Things have changed."

"I can't argue with that."

"I used to drink Coors Light," Teffinger said. "There was a joke about it. They said that drinking Coors Light was like making love in the bottom of a canoe. Do you know why?"

The boxer shook his head.

"No, why?"

"Because they're both fucking close to water."

The corner of the man's mouth turned up.

Then he swallowed what was left in the bottle, threw a ten on the bar and left.

Teffinger sat there. He could feel Portia in his blood. Outside, the Harley fired up and rumbled down the street. The young pretty with the Coors Light slid over and said, "Hi there."

Teffinger focused on her.

Her face had a smile just for him.

It was big.

It was friendly.

It was intimate.

She'd learned how to force it on at will and give it to a stranger. She rubbed his arm and said, "You're a nice looking man."

Teffinger pulled a business card out of his wallet and handed it to her. "If you ever get in trouble or need someone, I want you to call me," he said. "Day or night, now or five years from now. Keep this card with you. That's my cell phone number right there. I answer it no matter when it rings."

Then he was gone.

23

Back in the Tundra Teffinger called homicide to find Sydney still there. "The boxer is a man named Danny Rainer," he said. "He's a richer-than-bitch business man. I just had a beer with him."

"Don't tell me this stuff."

"What do you mean?"

"You drank a beer with a suspect," she said. "And you drank on the job. What's next? Oh, yeah, wait. The question isn't what's next? It's, what was before. That brings us to your little touchy-feely session with Portia Montrachet, another suspect if I recall right."

"I need you to do something for me," Teffinger said.

"Teffinger, did you hear anything I just said?"

He smiled.

"I'm sorry, were you talking?"

"Teffinger, I'm serious. You're on the edge. Reel yourself in. I'd do it for you but I don't want to get my hands all gross."

He exhaled.

"Are you done?"

Yes.

She was.

"The boxer killed Portia," he said.

"Why? What'd he say?"

"He said he didn't do it."

"So why are you saying he did?"

"Because I was looking in his eyes when he said it. He was lying."

"Here we go—"

"Trust me," he said.

"So what was his motive?"

Good question.

"I have two possible theories," he said. "The first is pure and simple carnal kicks. This guy isn't getting where he needs to go just by spending his money. He owns a development company that's building a high-rise down in LoDo, the one right near Coors Field."

"I know the one you're talking about."

"The guy could spend his days sipping Margaritas but he works on the site as, get this, an iron worker. I was watching him. Most of the time those guys up there are tied off to a lifeline. Sometimes they unfasten to do something or move around but it's not often. Our guy, the boxer, never ties off. He didn't tie off one time the entire time I was watching him."

"So he has a death wish?"

"No, I think the opposite," Teffinger said. "I think he wants to experience life so fully that he won't let the possibility of death dilute him."

"And he decided to experience Portia?"

Teffinger nodded.

"Exactly," he said. "It was a chance encounter and he made a split-second decision."

"I get it."

"Does it make sense?"

"Obviously there's a lot of speculation in there but it's all possible."

"Good, then I'm not crazy."

"I didn't say that," Sydney said.

He smiled.

"Point taken."

A beat then, "What's your second theory?"

"Huh?"

"You said you had two possible theories," Sydney said. "What's the other one?"

"No, I only have the one theory."

"You said you had two."

"Yeah."

"So what is it?"

"I've reconsidered it," he said. "It's too far-fetched."

"Why, what is it?"

"Just forget it."

"How can I forget it? You're making it into too big of a thing—"

"I'm not making it into anything; you are."

"Only because you brought it up."

"Well, now I'm taking it down. Do me a favor and work the keyboard tonight. Find out everything you can on the boxer. I want to know where his dark side has taken him in recent years."

"Why?"

"Because if we only concentrate on his latest adventure we're limited," he said. "We need to find his other crimes and start building a bigger case."

"You think he has other crimes?"

"I'm positive."

"Murders?"

"The man who killed Portia didn't even blink," he said. "That takes practice."

24

Friday night after dark a vicious thunderstorm rolled out of the mountains and monster-punched Denver with mean heavy fists. With a beer in his gut and a second in hand, Teffinger watched it from a lounge chair on Del Rey's patio under the shelter of the upper level deck. Jagged flashes of lightning ripped across the sky, whipping like a downed power line. Wild thunder ricocheted through the clouds with the power of a thousand maniac drums.

It was raw.

It was powerful.

The force of it all worked its way Teffinger's blood.

It made him alive.

It made him an animal.

Del Rey stepped to the edge of the patio and stood under the water cascading off the upper deck. Her hair matted down and her blouse soaked to the skin. She swallowed what was left of her drink and threw the glass into the backyard.

Then she went into a sensual, trancelike dance

Her arms went up.

Her hips swayed.

Her lips opened.

Her eyelids dropped.

Every fiber of Teffinger's being screamed for him to take her, right now, this second, before the universe ticked even the smallest tick.

He resisted.

Instead he watched.

He drank her in with his eyes.

He let her into his blood.

She stepped over and straddled him. The wetness of her thighs and her drenched shorts worked its way through his pants and onto his skin.

It was good.

It was right.

It was destined.

Her lips came to his, stopping just short, so close

that the warmth of her breath filled every pore of his body. She licked his neck and pushed down with her body.

Electricity ripped across the sky.

In that split second Teffinger's peripheral vision detected something out in the field, a long ways off, eighty or a hundred yards, possibly a dark silhouette, possibly a man. Before he could focus on it the world defaulted back to blackness.

A heartbeat later another bolt of lightning flashed.

The silhouette wasn't there.

He stared at exactly where it should be.

It wasn't there.

There was only prairie grass whipping with a voodoo curse.

"Teffinger, what's wrong?"

"I don't know," he said. "I thought I saw something."

"What?"

"I don't know."

He kept his concentration on the location and waited for the next explosion of lightning. It came quickly. Nothing was there that shouldn't be. Still, his gut churned and he shifted to get up.

"Get in the house, turn off all the lights and lock all the windows and doors," he said.

"Teffinger—"

"Do it. Hide somewhere and don't come out until I tell you to."

"Teffinger, this is crazy."

"I'm not taking any chances," he said.

"There's nothing there," she said. "It's just a trick of the night."

"Get inside. I'll be back."

He ran towards the mark.

The weather immediately assaulted him with thick heavy pelts driven by a horizontal wind, working its wicked way into his eyes in spite of his best squinting. The world under his feet was black and uneven, twisting his ankles and stressing his knees.

The rain soaked through his clothes.

It made them heavy.

It made them grip.

He forced more power out of his body to compensate.

His speed didn't slow.

With every pounding step he got closer and closer to whatever it was that was out there.

He took another step, and another and another.

His heart pounded.

His chest heaved.

Suddenly something was in front of him, low to the ground as if waiting, not part of the topography. It caught his foot on the upswing and sent him in a violent trip. He tried to brace before he smacked face-first into the ground but wasn't fast enough. His forehead hit something hard and unforgiving. Fireworks shot through his brain. He got to his feet, staggered and then fell to the side.

Everything went black.

The next thing that happened was gunfire.

It pulled him out of a deep unconsciousness long before he was ready. It made him stagger to his feet. Then a voice shouted, "Don't move!"

He instinctively dived.

It did no good.

The gun went off again before he even hit the ground.

25

Teffinger rolled when he hit, not sure if he'd been shot or not. The gun fired again. Something directly above him made a painful sound and landed with a horrific weight on his legs, pinning him down.

He scrambled to wedge out.

His hand pushed against something sharp and jagged.

He immediately knew what it was and jerked back before jaws clamped down.

Lightning flashed.

For a fraction of a second the world lit as if the noon sun was out. It was long enough for Teffinger to see he was under a mountain lion. The animal's face had been destroyed into a gooey mess by a bullet.

Del Rey was two steps distance.

Her arms were down.

In her right hand hung a limp gun.

What Teffinger tripped over was a small deer, just a baby, separated from the pack by the storm, now deader than dead with a ripped throat and a number of vicious bites torn out of its body.

In that split second Teffinger realized just how lucky he was.

The animal could have killed him a hundred times.

He'd be dead beyond help if it weren't for Del Rey.

He got out from under the animal, muscled to his feet and took Del Rey in his arms.

"I owe you one," he said.

"One?"

26

At exactly seven o'clock Friday evening, Jori-Lee wiped a D.C. sweat from her brow, pulled her cell phone from her purse as she sat on a bench near the Smithsonian, and punched in the numbers the mystery jogger passed to her yesterday evening.

Her heat pounded.

A woman answered, "Hello?"

The voice belonged to the runner.

"This is Jori-Lee Kent."

Silence.

"Your little boss Nelson Robertson is supposed to be making this call, not you. Did you tell him?"

"No."

"You didn't?"

"No."

"Well that was a big fucking mistake."

The line went dead.

Jori-Lee redialed.

No one answered.

She paced next to the street, second-guessing the sanity of everything she'd done, everything she was for that matter. Outside the day's shadows were getting longer but the air still had the city in a stranglehold of humidity and heat. A passing bus sprayed diesel fumes at her.

She choked them out of her lungs and almost headed home.

Instead she redialed.

The connection went through.

Before the woman could even answer Jori-Lee said, "Don't hang up!"

"You didn't follow directions."

"I will," she said. "First tell me what you want to talk to him about."

"It's personal."

"In what way?"

"You're playing a dangerous game, lady."

Suddenly a strange pop came through the line, one that made Jori-Lee picture the phone falling to the floor. Then frantic sounds came through. The more Jori-Lee concentrated on them the more she pictured the woman being attacked.

"Stop!"

The word was laced with fear.

Stop!

Stop!

Stop!

Then the words got muffled, as if a hand went over her mouth.

"Shut up bitch!"

Smack!

Smack!

"Don't fight me!"

The words were gruff.

They belonged to a man.

Jori-Lee didn't know the speaker.

He was a stranger to her.

The struggling stopped, just like that, with the force of something absolute, not a gunshot, maybe a knife. More sounds came but they were from motion rather than fighting.

What was he doing?

Was he making sure she was dead?

Was he turning her body face up?

A moment passed.

Jori-Lee concentrated.

The sounds were faint, barely perceptible.

She couldn't figure out what any of them belonged to.

Then a very disturbing noise came through, as if someone or something was physically touching the phone.

"Who's there?"

The words pounded into her blood with the force of a drug.

DAY FIVE

July 12
Saturday

27

Teffinger woke Saturday morning when the first strokes of dawn bent around the edges of the window coverings and washed the room in a soft watercolor glow. Next to him, half covered and half not, was the incredible being of Del Rey, motionless and breathing deeply. Seeing her made Teffinger feel sorry for every man in the world who wasn't him.

It wasn't just the woman's body.

She was more than just one of the interests he'd let parade in and out of his life.

He could see her popping out little Nickies.

He could see them together when they were older and slower and no longer playing at the edge.

He rolled onto his back and closed his eyes.

The events of last night briefly flashed in his brain. The jaws snapped again at his face. The gunfire rang again in his ears.

He squeezed it out.

It was interesting but not productive.

Today he needed to be productive.

The boxer Danny Rainer killed Portia, possibly for kicks and possibly as nothing more than a chance encounter gone bad. The evidence wasn't there, not yet, but evidence is always just a matter of time. As much as Teffinger wanted to take the boxer's smirky face down right now this minute, his more immediate problem was the lawyer, Jack Colder.

The lawyer was the one who hired Portia in the first place.

He was also the one who would hire—or, more likely, had already hired—Portia's replacement.

He was the one who would see that the job got completed.

He was the one still in motion.

Plus, going back, he was the one who killed or hired someone to kill Seth Lightfield, the man who filled his place in bed. Taking the lawyer down would close a cold case; and there were few things in life as sweet as closing a cold case.

Teffinger showered, towel-dried his hair until the drip was gone and headed for the kitchen, wearing jeans but no shirt or shoes.

Del Rey had her back to him, making coffee.

She wore a black muscle shirt and white panties that said Love Pink on the back.

He cupped her stomach from behind and nibbled her neck.

"Did I say thanks for saving my life?"

"I don't remember."

"Well, if I didn't, I will."

She turned and pressed her stomach to his.

Her face was serious.

Something was on her mind.

"You're thinking," Teffinger said.

She nodded.

"I had a weird thought. I keep telling myself that it's too crazy to be true but I can't shake it."

"Go on."

"Okay, well, Susan Smith knew that Portia was in town and after someone named Susan Smith, because you told her," she said.

"Technically Sydney told her."

"Right, but the fact is that she knew."

"True, she knew."

"So, what if she knew something else, namely that she was in fact the Susan Smith who was the target. What if she got already knew Danny Rainer and had some type of history with him. What if she got Rainer to lay in wait for Portia and take her out when she showed up?"

Teffinger shook his head.

"Even assuming all that," he said, "killing Portia would only buy her time. Someone hired Portia. She was nothing more than a human knife. Getting rid of her wouldn't solve the problem at the source. The only way to really get rid of the problem would be to kill the person who hired Portia. Right?"

"Correct."

Teffinger frowned.

"When someone says Right, and it is right, the answer is supposed to be Right, not Correct."

"They're the same thing."

"Yeah, I know, but it still needs to be right. Otherwise you upset the balance of the universe. Right?"

She ran a finger down his chest.

"Teffinger, stay focused," she said. "I agree that killing Portia would only buy her time. So, what would be her next move? It would be exactly what you said it would be—kill the source."

"Meaning the lawyer, Jack Colder."

"No."

"No?"

"No," she said. "What she told you about Colder being a jilted lover probably has a lot of truth to it, otherwise she wouldn't have dragged it out. But if her goal is to kill the source and Colder really was the source, she wouldn't tell you about him because then you'd be in his shadows. If you ask me, Colder is a misdirect."

"A misdirect?"

"Right, the source is someone else. While you're focused on Colder, that's where she's going to strike."

Teffinger shook his head.

It was too farfetched.

"Here's what I need from you," he said. "Colder hired Portia. He did it through that P.I. out in D.C., Oscar Benderfield. The P.I., in turn, had an off the grid meeting with a D.C. lawyer named Leland Everitt as soon as he got back from hiring Portia in Denver.

That means Leland Everitt is in the chain. He's in a firm called Overton & Frey. In fact, Leland Everitt might be the person that Colder hired, then Everitt in turn hired Benderfield."

"Right. You already told me all this."

That was true.

He had.

"What I need to do is to confirm that there is some type of connection between Colder out here in Denver and someone in D.C. on the other end, be it Benderfield or Leland Everitt or his law firm or, in fact, anyone else. Once I have that connection I'll know my theory is solid."

"Well, work on your connection then," she said.

"I already have."

"And?"

"And, I can't find it."

"So why are you clinging to this theory?"

"Because it's the right one," he said. "What I need is your help. You're a lawyer. You run in the same circles as Colder. Find out if he has any connections to D.C."

She pondered it.

"There are a couple of things I can do," she said. "I can find out all the cases where he or his law firm have appeared as the attorney-of-record. I can see if any of those cases were in D.C. courts or had D.C. attorneys on the other side. I can also get the names of the parties on both sides of the case. I can feed those names to you and you can run background checks on them. Maybe one of them has a D.C. connection."

Teffinger kissed her.

"That's what I'm talking about."

"I'll do it but not with any enthusiasm," she said. "Like I said, Colder's a misdirect. Susan Smith is the one you should be focused on."

"You want to make a dungeon bet on it?"

She shook his hand.

"You're on."

Five minutes later Teffinger was in the Tundra heading for the office with a cup of coffee in his left hand.

His stomach churned.

Until this morning he'd never realized exactly how intelligent Del Rey was. Sure, he knew she was a lawyer and was a reputable one, which obviously took some horsepower in the smarts department, but he never appreciated her depth until they had a common ground. Not one in a thousand people could have come up with the theory she had.

Even Teffinger hadn't come up with it.

To her face, he'd dismissed it.

Deep down, though, it was starting to vibrate.

28

Del Rey's theory that Susan Smith killed Portia clawed deeper and deeper into Teffinger's brain in spite of his every effort to dismiss it. By mid-morning it was so intrusive that he had to get around the woman to take a closer look.

When he knocked, the woman answered the door in workout clothes.

Her chest heaved.

Her body was moist with sweat.

"Come on in."

He followed her to a treadmill next to a large window and watched the numbers as she worked the dial, stopping at 8.

"I'm impressed," he said. "That's about double what I do."

Her feet pounded.

She looked his way.

"I doubt that."

"In my defense, though," he said, "I don't go that fast but I even it out by not going that far."

She smiled.

"Are you here to protect me?"

"Maybe a little."

Her lungs sucked deep. "It's times like this I actually think about quitting cigarettes."

"You should."

"Can't."

"Why not?"

"I like them too much."

Teffinger frowned.

"Nothing personal but I wouldn't touch one with a ten-foot pole."

She glanced his way.

"They don't make ten-foot poles any more. In fact

I doubt that they ever did."

The corner of his mouth went up.

"You're probably right."

"I mean, what would you do with one if you had it? Touch an ugly girl? No, that's what you wouldn't touch her with. So why even have them?"

He nodded.

"I have to admit, I've never seen one."

The woman's face grew serious.

She said, "So what do you have on Colder? Anything yet?"

He explained how he'd made an excuse to meet with the lawyer, the excuse being a lie, namely that the firm's phone number was found in Portia's purse.

"I'm impressed," Susan said.

"With what?"

"That you lied. I didn't think you had it in you. So what was your impression of him?"

"He fits."

"Meaning what?"

"Meaning he has the arrogance, the hate, the strength, the money, the whole package."

"Okay. So now what?"

"Now I tie him to Portia."

"How?"

"By first tying him to D.C."

"How?"

"I have a few things in progress," he said. "Tell me about Seth Lightfield?"

"Why?"

"Because Colder killed him too, right?"

"Right."

The woman focused on the distance, as if gathering distant thoughts. Then she said, "Seth was pure sex. Every inch of him oozed it, from his eyes to the way he walked. He picked me up down at the D-Drop one drunken Saturday night. I was under a table blowing him within the first half hour."

Teffinger pulled up the image.

"Lucky guy."

"Actually, he was," she said. "I wasn't looking for an angle with him, either."

"What about Colder? Was he someone you had an angle with?"

"He had money. He had power. He had stature. What do you think?"

"I don't know," Teffinger said.

"Yes you do. Seth was totally different from every-thing that had been going on in my life for the last ten years. He wasn't work. He was candy."

Teffinger swallowed.

"How'd you feel when he got killed?"

Susan's eyes flashed.

She punched the Stop button with the palm of her hand and ground to a halt.

"How did I feel when he got killed? Do you want the truth?"

Yes.

He did.

"I felt like Colder figured out a way to do it and get totally away with it. I felt like the justice system would be a joke. I decided to kill him myself. I walked Colfax at night until I was able to buy an unregistered gun. I stalked Colder for over two weeks."

Teffinger exhaled.

"You didn't kill him."

"No."

"Why not?"

"I don't know. I should have."

29

Late morning Del Rey called Teffinger sounding like she just stepped off a roller coaster. "You want a connection between Jack Colder and D.C.? Well, I've got one for you. I've got a big one for you."

Teffinger halted a coffee cup that was headed for his mouth.

"Go on."

"All right, it turns out that Colder won a big antitrust case in the U.S. District Court here in Denver four years ago. The other side appealed to the Tenth Circuit and lost. Then the other side filed a Petition for Writ of Certiorari with the United States Supreme Court."

"What's that?"

"It's basically a motion asking the Supreme Court to hear the case," she said. "Whether they take it or not is discretionary. They can hear it if they want or not hear it if they don't want. If they don't hear it then the decision of appeals court automatically stands. Anyway, when a party files a Petition for Writ, the opposing part has the right to file a brief in opposition, if you will, telling the Supreme Court why they shouldn't take the case. Colder hired a D.C. law firm to help draft the brief in opposition and co-sign it as attorney of record."

"What firm?"

"The firm's called Overton & Frey. It's big and it's hard-hitting. It does a good chunk of appellate work before the Supreme Court."

"What attorney did Colder work with?"

"Two attorneys actually signed the brief, one by the name of Molly Flagger and another by the name of Leland Everitt."

Leland Everitt.

Leland Everitt.

According to D.C. detective Randy Johnson, the black private investigator with the bleached hair, Oscar Benderfield, met with a lawyer named Leland Everitt when he got back into town from Denver.

The conclusion was inescapable.

Jack Colder hired Portia.

He didn't do it directly.

He contacted his attorney-friend Leland Everitt who in turn contacted his PI connection Oscar Benderfield who in turn hired Portia.

Colder got a twisted little chain reaction in motion.

"Nick are you still there?"

The words brought him back to focus.

"You done good," he said. "Who was the client Colder was representing in all this?"

"It's a company called Vistigo. They're into communication satellites and high-speed data transmission. All the appeals and briefs are public records. I'll email them to you if you want."

He wanted.

He wanted indeed.

He hung up, immediately called his counterpart in D.C., Randy Johnson, and brought him up to speed on the good news. The man wasn't as excited as Teffinger anticipated.

"Knowing it is one thing. Actually cracking a link is another."

"Start with emails and phone records," Teffinger said. "Get warrants."

"Easy to say."

"You don't think you can?"

"That's not up to me," he said. "That's up to the D.A. Just between you and me, I'm not sure he has the intestinal fortitude to go up against someone like Overton & Frey. A misstep in that direction can end a career."

"Well, try."

"I will," Johnson said. "I'll do it this afternoon and let you know what happens. All I'm saying is to not get your hopes up."

Teffinger hung up.

His gut was hollow.

Johnson wasn't going to get anywhere.

Johnson didn't want to get anywhere. It wasn't the D.A. who was going to be the roadblock; it was Johnson himself. He was scared of setting up a sequence that could swing back and knock him on his ass. The fear was there in his voice.

Teffinger needed a Plan B.

He needed it badly.

He needed it now.

30

Plan B wasn't complex. It was a simple trip to Jack Colder's law office to rattle the man's cage. "You have a relationship with a lawyer out in D.C. by the name of Leland Everitt," Teffinger said. "Leland Everitt rubs elbows with a black investigator with bleached hair by the name of Oscar Benderfield. Oscar Benderfield isn't a particularly nice guy. He hires people to kill other people."

Colder screwed his face into confusion.

"I know Leland Everitt," he said. "We worked a Supreme Court case together. I never heard of the other guy."

Teffinger frowned.

"Are you scared?"

"Of what?"

"Of being where you are right now, because it's a dangerous place."

"Here's my advice," Colder said. "You're pointed in the wrong direction. Go back to the drawing board and get whatever it is you're working on straight."

Teffinger raked his hair back.

It immediately flopped back down.

"Someone hired by Oscar Benderfield came to Denver to kill Susan Smith, who, ironically, is someone you're not particularly fond of. That's the drawing board I'm working from."

The implication hung in silence.

Then Colder said, "Get out of my office."

"I'm giving you a chance to cooperate."

Colder opened the door and motioned Teffinger towards it.

"Have a nice day."

Teffinger stood up.

"There are a lot of links in this twisty little chain," he said. "One of them will snap. It's the first one that does that gets all the breaks. This is your chance to be smart and cut your losses. Pass this opportunity up and it goes to another link. Then you get to curse yourself with hindsight."

Colder tensed.

"I don't know how you got pointed in the wrong direction but you did," he said. "Now let me explain something to you. A firm like this is built on reputation. If I hear even a whisper of a rumor that you're saying even the smallest thing out there in the world to hurt this firm's reputation, I'll slap a defamation suit on you so big that you'll think you're under attack by a pack of brainsick gorillas. Am I clear?"

Teffinger tossed his card on the desk and headed for the door. Halfway through he turned and said, "Call me. You have until five o'clock. Then I get on a plane to D.C. and have a little chat with Oscar Benderfield. I'll bet he ends up being smarter than you."

Down at street level under a bright Colorado sky he called Sydney and said, "I just put a serious rattle on Jack Colder's cage. What I need is for you to get down here to his law firm and see if he leads us anywhere."

"Why don't you do it?"

"Can't," he said. "I've got something else going on."

"Like what?"

"Rattling more cages. Colder might head home and put together a care package and then head for the airport. If he does, arrest him right after he buys a ticket."

"Okay."

"Be careful of him. He's a rat in a corner."

31

Jori-Lee tossed with a demonic possession all Friday night, hardly able to sleep, instead replying over and over the sounds of the mystery jogger getting murdered on the other end of the phone.

She didn't call the police, at least not yet.

She didn't need to be sitting in a room talking to them, not after breaking into Robertson's house. There were too many ways things could twist back on her. If she could give them some concrete information on the killer it might be different; but she'd only heard a few words. The voice could belong to anyone.

Tracing the dead woman's phone number wasn't hard.

It belonged to one T'amara Alder, a Miami woman.

Jori-Lee pulled the woman's house up on Google earth.

It was in a crowed Miami neighborhood west of downtown, just south of an airport. The more Jori-Lee stared at it the more she knew she should get down there before the police did. So far there was no news report of a local murder, meaning the police didn't know what happened, meaning they wouldn't be snooping around down in Miami yet. The window of opportunity was there.

She should take it.

She should take it now, this second.

She realization hit her so hard that she grabbed her purse, called a taxi and paced outside next to the curb until it came.

"Dulles," she said.

Two hours later she was in a window seat of a bumpy jet six miles above the earth, trying to figure out if the man who killed T'amara Alder perceived her to be a threat. He knew she'd heard his voice but it was only a couple of words.

Shut up bitch!

Don't fight me!

Would he be worried that she'd be able to recognize it?

Her incoming number would be indelibly etched in Alder's phone. From that the killer could figure out who she was and, in fact, probably already had.

She hardened her gut.

There was no time to think about it right now.

Right now she needed to concentrate on the task at hand once the landing gears touched earth.

At first she was scared to break into the dead woman's house.

The prospect still made her palms sweat but now she was equally resolved.

She'd rent a car, scope it out during the day and make her move after dark.

She'd need a flashlight.

She'd need dark clothing.

She'd need a hotel room.

She'd need an excuse for being in Miami in case it ever became an issue.

She'd need a fair share of luck.

Most importantly, she'd need to be invisible.

She'd need to be the ghost that never was.

32

Colder wouldn't crack. He'd flee the country, either that or lawyer-up and bide his time to make sure that fleeing was his only remaining viable option. He wasn't the weak link. That honor went to Oscar Benderfield.

That was fine.

In fact, that's the way Teffinger preferred it.

Benderfield was the smallest fish.

Strategically it would be more satisfying to use him to bring down the bigger ones.

Teffinger headed to DIA, bought a ticket for D.C. and paced in Concourse C next to the wall-to-ceiling glass with a nervous eye on the mountains of winged metal falling in and out of the sky.

Flying wasn't natural.

It was nothing more than an act of luck.

Luck was something that could run out at any random moment. He'd flown a number of times before and had only crashed once. That was on the Nile in a puddle-jumper so he wasn't sure if it really counted. Even if it did, at this point he was still pressing whatever few ounces of luck he had left.

His phone rang and Sydney's voice came through. "Colder just walked past Susan Smith's place and gave her apartment the finger."

"Her or her apartment?"

"The apartment," Sydney said. "Susan wasn't around as far as I could tell."

Teffinger chewed on it.

Colder's hate was so livid that he had to manifest it. He was unhinging. The hate was overpowering the need to stay concealed.

"Where is he now?"

"Walking towards the financial district. He has a leather briefcase in his hand."

"Stay with him."

"Okay but if he hasn't busted me yet he will soon. He looks over his shoulder every twenty seconds."

A calm voice dropping out of ceiling speakers announced the boarding of Teffinger's flight. People stood up, grabbed bags and kids, and headed for the gate.

Susan Smith would be murdered tonight.

Colder would either hire someone or do it himself.

The finger to her apartment was the final goodbye.

Teffinger cashed his ticket in and walked to the

Tundra with a brisk stride.

Outside the terminal walls the air was an oven.

He was almost to the Tundra, way at the west end of short-term parking on level E, when his phone rang.

"Teffinger, it's me."

Me was Del Rey.

Her voice sounded like a car crash.

"What's wrong?"

"Someone broke into my place," she said. "There's a dead magpie on my kitchen counter. Someone ripped its wings off."

Teffinger pulled up the image.

"Are the wings there?"

It was a stupid question.

It was also all that he could think of to say while his brain spun the possibilities.

"No, I don't see them."

He broke into a trot.

"Leave now," he said. "Get in your car and get out of there. Stay on the phone so I know you're safe."

"I don't think anyone's still here. I think they're gone."

"I don't care if they're gone or not. Get out of there right now."

Forty minutes later he met her down at 6th by the fairgrounds and held her tight. She was calm now. The initial shock was gone.

"I don't want a police report," she said.

"That's not smart."

"I don't want the dungeon becoming public knowledge."

"I'll keep a cap on it."

"You can't and you know it."

He frowned.

The words were true.

"Give me your key," he said. "I'll go up and have a look around. When I'm sure it's safe I'll give you a call and you can come up."

Five minutes later he was in her house.

No one was there.

The magpie was on the counter right where Del Rey said it was. The wings were ripped off and gone. The head was cut off and lying cockeyed with opened eyes next to the body. A kitchen knife was on the counter next to the head. Goo was on the blade.

He found the wings.

One was in the refrigerator.

The other was on Del Rey's pillow.

He left everything as it was and called her.

"It's clear," he said, "come on up but be prepared."

Four minutes later she walked through the front door to the kitchen and asked a question Teffinger didn't expect.

"Did you do that to the head?"

No.

He didn't.

"It wasn't like that before," she said. "It was on. The head was on. Do you hear what I'm saying?"

33

Teffinger's best arguing couldn't convince Del Rey to report the intrusion and get an official case on file. "This is Unincorporated Jefferson County," she said. "The sheriff's office is right across the street from the Taj Mahal."

"The what?"

"The courthouse. Every judge in the county would know about the dungeon within a week."

Teffinger wasn't impressed.

"So what?"

"So when I walk into a courtroom I need respect," she said. "I don't want anyone in the room with a trump card. Lawyers included for that matter."

Teffinger leaned against the countertop, almost on the bird.

The place hadn't been trashed.

Nothing of value had been taken.

A gold watch sat unceremoniously untouched on the bedroom dresser next to a stack of twenty-dollar bills.

He focused on Del Rey.

"So you don't have even the faintest idea who did this?"

She shook her head.

"Like I said, my best guess is that it has something to do with my law practice because that's the only thing in my life powerful enough to spin into something like this. But I can't think of a single case or client or opposing counsel or opposing client that fits."

"Well, someone's messing with you, that's for sure. Either that or this is some kind of a warning."

"A warning about what?"

He shrugged.

"I don't know."

He photographed the bird and the wings, getting several shots of each from different angles, and threw the parts out in the open space. Then he called Dr. Leigh Sandt, the FBI profiler from Quantico, and pulled up an image of a classy fifty-ish woman with step-master legs.

She actually answered.

"It's me," he said.

"Teffinger?"

"Yeah, don't hang up."

He explained the situation and said, "So what's your take on it?"

"To me it's a message," she said. "It's a warning. The guy is saying, There's death right here on your kitchen counter. You're next."

Teffinger swallowed.

"You really think it's that serious?"

"I do. If you had more information I might have a different conclusion, but looking at it with no more facts than what you told me, I'd lay my money on it being a foreshadowing of what's to come—especially since valuables were lying in plain sight and weren't touched. It's a statement that this isn't about money. She can't buy her way out of it."

Teffinger exhaled.

"Is there any significance to the placement of the body parts?"

"I don't know. As for the pillow, maybe there's nothing more behind it than the guy saw the Godfather at some point in time."

Teffinger smiled.

"Can you do what I'm going to ask you to do?"

"Teffinger, don't you dare. I'm slammed with fifty other things—"

"I'll take that as a yes," he said. "How soon can you do it?"

He didn't need to define it.

They both knew what he meant.

It was to see if any other files existed with a similar MO. It was to see if the creep was already implicated in a prior investigation somewhere, leaving body parts of an animal as a precursor to murder.

"God, I hate you," Leigh said.

"Hate and love are the same thing. You know that, right? Ciao."

"Hey, you still there?"

He was.

"There's one more option to consider."

"Which is what?"

"Maybe the guy isn't targeting Del Rey at all. Maybe he's targeting you. Maybe the warning is for you."

Teffinger shook his head.

"That's awfully indirect."

"Admitted."

"Personally I don't see it."

"It would have to be coming from someone who knows you're spending time with Del Rey. When I say that maybe he's targeting you, I don't mean that you're necessarily the one who the guy is going to kill. It might be you but it might equally be Del Rey. For hundreds of years people have been killing the warrior by killing the thing that the warrior loves. It's nothing new. I'll tell you one thing. Now that I realize the target may be you, I can take my time in digging into it."

Teffinger smiled.

"Not funny," he said.

"A little funny."

"Okay, a little."

"I'll be in touch."

The line went dead.

Teffinger's gut churned.

Del Rey put her arms around him and said, "You look like you just saw a ghost."

He kissed her forehead.

"Either that or the ghost saw me. Time will tell."

34

Jori-Lee landed uneventfully at Miami International Airport, rented a black Camry and checked into the Beacon Hotel on Ocean Drive in the heart of South Beach. She couldn't afford ten cents of it. It all went on plastic. She'd have to worry about that part of it later.

A salty breeze blew off an endless beach.

Friendly aqua waves lapped against the sand.

The hotel was art deco.

Her room was nice, on the ocean side.

Ocean Drive buzzed.

Palm trees swayed.

Life was good.

She didn't ever want to leave. She wanted to spend every day of the rest of her life right here. She wanted to run on the beach all day long and stay up all night gyrating to a nightclub trance with a man who couldn't keep his hands off her.

She could do it if she really wanted.

She had the looks.

She had the smile.

She could wear a bikini and, if she got a few months of time in a gym, she'd be able to rock it.

She knew how to make a man see nothing but her. She'd never exercised those particular skills, not yet, not to their fullest extent, but they were there. They were in the quiver of her fingertips and in the warmth of her breath and in the blood just under her skin.

She had the pedigree, too.

She had the Harvard law degree, not to mention her current law clerk position at One First Street, the golden ring itself, working under the coveted wing of Nelson Robertson, no less—the swing vote and by default the most powerful judge of the nine.

With that pedigree she could walk in any social circle, especially here in Miami, which was a rung or two down from D.C.

She should do it.

She should go out tonight, meet a man and make a new life happen.

She should simplify.

She should forget.

She should get a wild side.

She should change directions.

The thought was wine in her blood, so much so that she got a beach towel from the lobby, bought a white bikini and jaywalked her way across the boulevard to where the sand and the water and the bodies were.

She jogged at the water's edge, where her feet splashed and the sand was smooth.

She jogged until she had no more jog left.

She turned.

Her peripheral vision warned her of something approaching.

It was coming fast.

It was coming through the air.

Her head ducked.

A Frisbee swished past.

"Sorry about that."

The words came from a man trotting her way, a man who looked like he belonged on a surfboard, or in a rock band, or on the cover of a magazine.

His skin was golden.

His hair was blond and hung past his shoulders.

His arms and shoulders and chest were built for handstands.

His smile was without a worry.

She must have had a look on her face because the man slowed down, stopped just short and said, "Do you believe in fate?"

"Sometimes."

"Me too."

35

Teffinger got bad news late Saturday afternoon. It came from the FBI profiler Dr. Leigh Sandt who called and reported in a beaten voice that the bird ripper wasn't on their radar screen; if he was buried in a file somewhere, he wasn't coming to the surface.

He was a ghost.

Ten minutes later Randy Johnson called from D.C. homicide to report that the district attorney wanted more evidence before going for a search warrant against either the lawyer, Leland Everitt, or the investigator, Oscar Benderfield.

Until then everything was in stall mode.

When the phone rang a third time Teffinger didn't answer.

Instead he called Del Rey.

"Are you still alive?"

"Alive and billing hours."

"At the law firm?"

"Right."

"With the front door locked?"

"Yes, master."

Okay.

Good.

"I have my gun with me," she added.

Teffinger pulled up an image of the weapon firing a hot yellow explosion into the eye of a mountain lion in the thick of black night.

"I never asked you before but is that thing registered?"

"I don't know. It's not mine."

"Whose is it?"

"Someone left it here."

"Who?"

"Trouble."

"The woman from the dungeon?"

"Right. Your threesome friend."

Teffinger frowned.

"Well, don't kill anyone who doesn't deserve it."

"That's a person who would be hard to find."

When he hung up the office was too small, the walls were too close, the ceiling was too low and the chatter was too choked. He needed space, needed it fast and needed it hard. Five minutes later he was two blocks away, walking aimless on a cracked sidewalk with too many thoughts eating the tails of too many other thoughts.

That was the problem.

The monster had too many heads.

Teffinger couldn't keep them straight.

He needed to bring down the Harley-riding, iron-walking, money-bored boxer, Danny Rainer, for getting his kicks killing Portia Montrachet.

He needed to bring down the fancy-pants lawyer, Jack Colder, for setting a hit in motion against Susan Smith, as well as his prior work on the dancer, Seth Lightfield.

He needed to bring down the D.C. links, Leland Everitt and Oscar Benderfield, for their roles in the hit parade.

He needed to keep Susan Smith from being murdered.

And now, on top of it all, he needed to keep Del Rey out of the grasp of the bird ripper, whoever he was and whatever his motive might be, including the possibility that Teffinger himself might be the target.

It was too much.

He couldn't concentrate on one ugly face long enough to memorize it.

He was spread too thin.

He needed to prioritize.

Del Rey would be the priority.

Susan Smith was nice, she was interesting, she was too young to die, but she wasn't Del Rey. If Teffinger could save only one of them it would be Del Rey.

Not to mention he owed her one for saving his life.

His phone rang. He checked the number to find it belonged to the same caller as a few minutes ago, the third call, the one he didn't take.

He answered.

It was Bob Nelson, the coroner.

"I'm finding some suspicious post-mortem bruises on Portia Montrachet's body," the man said.

"Suspicious in what way?"

"Suspicious in that they could be read to suggest she was moved after she was killed."

Teffinger wasn't impressed.

"The guy probably dragged her back farther into the alley. That's what I would have done."

"These are more suggestive that she was carried and dropped."

"Same thing."

"You're right."

"Don't give me too much credit. Even a monkey at a typewriter spells a word sooner or later," Teffinger said.

Nelson laughed.

"Yeah, well, keep pecking."

"Got to. It's a volume thing."

Del Rey.

She was going to die tonight; either her or Teffinger.

He could feel it in his bones.

36

The beach god who believed in fate had a name, Sanders Tripp, which meant he was technically no longer a stranger, which was good because Jori-Lee wanted him to be anything but that. She let him walk her in the aqua froth of the waves and tell her jokes and stories until the white of his smile and the toss of his hair washed over her and made her pull up nasty flashes of the two of them together.

He wasn't real.

He couldn't be.

Yet every time she looked over, there he was.

He was a diversion, a fantasy, a quivering between her thighs, a moment in the sun, until he said something that suddenly made him three-dimensional. "At the risk of blowing my surfer-boy patina, I'm going to tell you a secret. You have to promise not to tell anyone though."

She pulled a zipper across her lips.

"I know you from Harvard."

"You do?"

Yes.

He did.

"You were a freshman in the law program when I was in my last year there. I tried to get your attention about a hundred times. It never worked. You always had your nose in a book."

"You're a lawyer?"

He nodded.

"Guilty, going on two years. In fact, I'm billing you for my time right now." He smiled. "Just kidding about that last part."

"You don't need to be. I'll pay."

"In that case I'll take it out in trade."

37

Early Saturday evening Teffinger had a thought that shook him to the core, namely that the ripped bird was a diversion rather than a warning. It was a strategic move perpetrated by the person who was going to kill Susan Smith; it was done to misdirect Teffinger in the wrong direction.

He had no proof of course, but the logic resonated with a thunder he couldn't ignore.

He called Sydney and said, "We're going to a Plan B for tonight."

"Which is what?"

"Which is, instead of my staying with Del Rey at her place, I want you to. Don't get too concerned though. Nothing's going to happen."

"Why not?"

He explained his diversion theory and the fact that Del Rey wasn't in any real danger.

He expected pushback.

She didn't give any.

In fact she said, "I can't believe that you figured this out when Leigh didn't. That's a first."

"And a last," he said.

"Does this mean you'll be with Susan Smith?"

"Every minute."

"Well keep the little guy down and your guard up."

"The little guy?"

"The Little Guy, Bob, Rolling Thunder, whatever it is that you call him and, please, don't tell me what it is."

"Andy Conda."

"I said not to do that."

He hissed his best snake hiss.

"I'm hanging up now," she said.

The line went dead.

He had half a mind to dial her back and hiss when she answered but didn't. Instead he called Susan Smith and told her his diversion theory and his conclusion that the man would probably strike tonight while the diversion was fresh.

She was silent.

Then she said, "I'm not running."

"I know."

"We already talked about it."

"Right, I know. I'm not asking you to. I'll be inside your apartment with you tonight unless you have an objection. We'll have people outside too, good people."

They talked about details.

Then he hung up.

The sky was in that magical stage between dusk and dark when the colors changed so fast that you never really knew what they were. Half the cars had their headlights on. A streetlight kicked to life right in front of Teffinger's eyes.

Everything was set.

He should feel good.

He didn't.

He felt like a mouse on railroad tracks.

38

Saturday night after dark an evil wind-whipped storm took revenge on Denver from out of a black-hearted sky. Teffinger leaned against the wall out of line of the windows with his legs stretched out and his weapon by his side, watching a spider crawl across the carpet. The lights were dim. The window coverings were open just enough for the killer to detect Susan Smith's movement inside and confirm that the sweet little target was home.

The woman walked to the window, pulled the

blinds to the side and looked out. She wore jeans and a long-sleeved pullover that rode just above a tanned navel.

"Can't really see anything," she said.

Teffinger grunted.

"I'd guess not."

He was a rubber band stretched to the point of snapping.

"It's a good night for killing someone," Susan added.

That was true.

The men outside were compromised, both visually and in terms of readiness.

They were soaked.

They were slow.

They were cold.

They couldn't tell a man from a dog at fifty yards distance.

Inside, Teffinger's eyes were heavy

His brain was slower.

His watch said 11:23.

He'd been on a dead run since 5:15 this morning.

He jumped when his phone rang.

Sydney's voice came through with, "I'm still here at Del Rey's. Everything's quiet but I could do without the storm."

"Same here."

"Hey, remember when I said before that Susan Smith might have been the one who killed Portia?"

He remembered.

"Well, it just occurred to me that the dead bird works into that."

"How?"

"Like you said, a diversion. It takes the spotlight away from her."

"It seems thin."

"Thin or not, keep your guard. That's all I'm saying."

He looked over.

Susan was in a chair, watching him with an unblinking stare, smoking a smoky smoke.

"Sure."

"I mean it, Nick. And by all means don't let her know you're onto her. She'll put a bullet in your head and make it look like you went down saving her from the killer. In fact, find out if she has an unregistered gun sitting around."

"The storm's working your imagination," he said. "How's Del Rey?"

"Alive."

"Keep her that way."

A beat then, "She showed me the dungeon, Teffinger."

He swallowed.

"She wants that kept quiet."

"I know. She made me promise before she showed it to me. We're going to put on some popcorn and watch a movie later."

"She should be in bed. She should be sticking to her normal routine."

"Do you know what the movie's called?"

No, he didn't.

"It's called Nicky Does a Threesome."

Susan mashed the cigarette in an ashtray and stood up. "Colder can't come for me here. It's too fortified. He has to get through a lobby, up to my floor, through the door, all the while avoiding cameras, not to mention physically getting to me before I can call 911. The outside's no better. What's he going to do, throw a grappling hook up to my balcony and then pull himself up with a rope? He's a lawyer, not Spiderman. We need to go out to a club or something. We need to give him an opportunity to stick a knife in my back."

"No."

"It's Saturday night," she said. "If he's really set on taking me tonight, he's out there in the storm somewhere waiting for me to head out. Do you want to catch him or not?"

Teffinger shook his head.

"It's too risky."

"So is sitting here and wasting our time," she said. "Tonight I have you. A week from now I won't. If he's going to make a move I'd rather it be tonight. Then at least I have a fifty-fifty chance."

Teffinger muscled to his feet and paced, thinking it through.

Neither option made him smile.

If she got murdered a week from now when he wasn't around, no one would blame him. If she got murdered tonight on his watch, however, well, the math was evident. It would be better for him to just sit tight.

It's not about you, he muttered to himself.

"What?"

He looked at her, brought his voice to speaking pitch and said, "Okay."

"Okay as in We're going out?"

He nodded.

"Yes. More accurately, you're going out. I'm going to be the invisible man."

She headed for the bedroom.

Over her shoulder she said, "I'm going to take a quick shower. Get rid of the backup guys. They'll just mess things up." She stopped, walked over and put her arms around him. Then she looked into his eyes and said, "Get your game face on."

"It is on."

"In that case, I'm going to die."

He smiled.

"I'm not kidding," she said. "You look like you're 20 seconds away from sleep. Let me put some coffee on."

Right.

Coffee.

Good idea.

39

They ended up at a beat-pounding club in LoDo jammed with a sea of dressed-to-kill bodies in motion. Susan was solo in a sin-white dress that showcased a tight body to perfection. Teffinger hung back, keeping her in sight as best he could as she wedged and twisted through a sea of drunken skin.

The woman's scent was in the air.

Eyes turned as she passed.

Hands and hips and legs brushed against her.

If someone was out to kill her tonight, this was his chance. He'd be here. He could drop her with a bullet to the side or a knife to the stomach before she even knew he was there. He could be three steps away before the woman hit the floor, and ten steps away before anyone noticed her. He could be out the door before anyone realized the woman was down from an assault as opposed to alcohol or exhaustion.

He might be a her.

Don't forget that.

Portia was a her.

Teffinger looked for the person who didn't fit, the one who was too old, too young, too sober, too focused, too alone or too dressed up or down.

No one held his attention for more than a heartbeat.

Everyone fit, even the ones who didn't.
He was here though.
Teffinger could smell him.

He lost line-of-sight of Susan, momentarily concerned but knowing she'd surface just as quickly. When she didn't surface, not in five seconds, not in ten, he pushed towards the last place she'd been.
From that vantage he still couldn't find her.
He moved through the crowd on the tangent she'd been heading.
The woman didn't materialize up ahead, or to the side, or behind.
He kept going and got more of the same.
He called her cell phone.
She didn't answer.
He got dumped into voice mail.
"Call me," he said.

It wasn't good but he wasn't ready to panic. The woman wouldn't leave the club without him. She was probably on the dance floor. There, the bodies gyrated with abandon, each blocking view of the next. Teffinger would have to push in. He'd have better luck squeezing into a can of sardines.
Suddenly something happened he didn't expect.
Arms wrapped around him from behind.
He turned to find an Asian woman, one he didn't know, one with sunset eyes and a dangerous body, one who would work not just fine but very fine in different circumstances. He opened his mouth to say

not tonight but before the words got out the woman was already dragging him into the motion.

Teffinger could do a lot of things but dancing wasn't one of them. His best move was a back and forth shuffle that had more wood in it than some entire lumberyards.

Right now he didn't care.

There were too many bodies for anyone to see him.

Getting into those bodies would give him a fresh vantage point.

He followed.

They ended up in the thick of it.

Teffinger leaned in and said, "Be warned, I can't dance."

The woman turned full circle and said, "You be warned, I don't care."

The beat grabbed him, first by the hips and then by the throat.

He gave into it.

A familiar face appeared in the crowd.

It was a rough, manly face.

It belonged to the lawyer himself, Jack Colder.

The man's hair was disheveled as if he'd been caught in the rain. That's how a man would look if he'd been staking out Susan Smith's building out in a storm.

The guy had guts to come here in the flesh.

Teffinger's chest tightened.

He leaned into the girl and said, "You're lovely but

I have to run. It's business."

"Wait, let me give you my number."

his nature was to say something polite.

Before he could, she was already gone.

He pushed through the crowd in the direction of Colder, not yet knowing what the plan was when he arrived, but knowing it would be something. The man was closing in on Susan Smith, only five steps away, as Teffinger approached.

He spun the man around.

Colder halted in disbelief then said, "Back off asshole."

"You stay right here."

"Fuck you."

When the man turned, Teffinger grabbed his shoulder.

A terrible fist swung at his face.

He twisted to avoid it.

He was fast but not fast enough.

The impact landed with the might of a baseball bat. His feet wobbled and his body tumbled. Colder was over him with fists cocked and an insane face. His jacket hung open. A gun holster came into view.

Teffinger acted like he was struggling to get to his feet and then kicked the man's legs out from under him. As he hit the floor Teffinger punched him in the face with every molecule of energy in his body.

The man's head snapped back.

Then all motion in his body stopped.

40

The beach boy Sanders Tripp didn't turn out to be the typical starving young lawyer. He came from money, lots and lots of money, and lived on an upper floor of the ultra-chic Paramount Bay Tower. On the terrace, Jori-Lee took in the killer view of Miami to the left and the sailboats cutting wakes through the bay across Ocean Boulevard.

"Something's wrong," Sanders said.

That was true.

They came from different worlds.

The man's closet was bigger than her apartment.

"This is nice," she said.

"But?"

She pulled a ten-dollar bill from her purse, put it in his hand and said, "I want to hire you as my lawyer. That's all I can afford though. The rest will have to be pro bono."

He twisted the paper in his hands.

"Are you in some kind of trouble?"

"I don't know," she said. "Maybe."

"In that case I'm your lawyer. Talk to me."

She hesitated, not knowing where to start, and then just jumped in, getting the salient facts out one after another, albeit not exactly in a straight line. When she graduated from Harvard law three months ago, she was fortunate enough to land one of the most coveted jobs in the universe, namely a position as a law clerk with a Justice of the United States Supreme Court, in this case Justice Nelson Robertson.

Sanders didn't believe her, not at first, then must have seen the expression on her face and said, "You clerk for Robertson?"

She nodded.

"Yes."

"In D.C.?"

"Yes."

"At the Supreme Court Building?"

"Yes."

"That's at One First Street, right?"

"Yes."

"Damn. How'd you get a job like that?"

"We can get into that later. For right now, what I have to tell you relates to my job," she said. "I'm going to have to tell you some things that are sensitive beyond belief. You have to absolutely promise me with every fiber in your being that you'll keep every word I tell you in absolute secrecy."

"Of course."

"That's why I'm officially hiring you as my lawyer," she said. "You're duty bound."

He stuffed the ten in his pocket.

"I've accepted the money. Your confidences are mine, by promise and by law."

"I'm serious about this."

"Trust me, nothing will get out." She studied him, looking for lies or exaggerations. None were obvious and, in fact, the opposite if anything. "Go on," he said. "Tell me what's going on."

She did.

Two weeks ago she went to Robertson's chambers to tell him about a new case out of the Ninth Circuit that was on point with a pending case. "He was on the phone talking to someone, so I held back just outside the door to wait until he was finished," she said.

"Okay."

"He didn't know I was there."

"All right."

"He was talking low and I could barely make out what he was saying. But as the conversation went on, it became clear that he was talking to someone who was blackmailing him about something."

"Something, as in what?"

"I don't know," she said. "It was something serious though. The nature of the discussion was that he was to vote a certain way in an upcoming case."

Sanders shook his head.

"No," he said. "That kind of stuff doesn't happen."

"I wish you were right," she said. "I don't know how long it's been going on or how deep it is. The conversation was clear though. He was talking about throwing a case."

Sanders focused on a water-skier carving a white line in the sky-blue water of the bay, then turned back.

"What was the case?"

"It's called Davidson v. Fifty."

"Which is about what?"

"It's basically a First Amendment freedom of speech case," she said. "It involves a comment posted on an Internet blog. The person who posted the comment was an American who was in France at the time he typed the comment. The person who was allegedly defamed was an Australian woman who was in Australia at the time the comment was made. She's a public figure in Australia but not in America or France. She later sued the defendant in a California court and the issue before the Supreme Court is whether she has a cause of action in the state court or whether such an action would be in violation of the First Amendment."

"So which way is Robertson supposed to vote?"

"Basically to protect the right to freedom of speech and deny the plaintiff's claim as non-cognizable. You have to keep all this quiet."

"I will, I will. Has the case been decided yet?"

"No. It's still pending."

"Okay. So what happened next?"

She gathered her thoughts and said, "That night I slept on it. Robertson was clearly in some kind of trouble and I didn't see any way that I could help him. The whole thing was so much bigger than me. But I didn't have the option to sit by and do nothing. The integrity of the court had been breached. Whatever damage had occurred so far, it couldn't continue, not even for one single case. I suppose I could have gone to the FBI and blown the whistle at that point but that didn't sit well with me. For one, Robertson would fall. He's a great man. His legacy would be ruined. Right or wrong, I felt he deserved a right of redemption, so long as it was immediate and forever. With that goal in mind, I came up with a plan."

"Which was what?"

"I became obsessed with finding out more," she said. "Tuesday night Robertson was slated to speak at a fundraising function. I took the opportunity to break into his house."

Sanders leaned back.

"That was pretty gutsy."

"Not really," she said. "What would he do if he found out? Go to the police? In his master closet I found a black briefcase. Inside that briefcase was a MacBook Air. I copied the files from that computer." She pulled a flash drive out of her purse and passed it to him. "Take a look at this under the file called Photos and then we'll talk some more. Share this with no one and don't make any copies."

41

Colder didn't move, not in five seconds, not in ten, not in thirty. His eyes were open, unblinking, staring at nothing. Teffinger knew the look, he'd seen it before, and didn't need to check for vital signs although he did.

He got no pulse.

He got no breath.

He got no reaction.

He got no life.

The insane beat of the club continued to drop out of amped-up speakers as if nothing had happened. A crowd pushed in, tighter and thicker and deeper than the second before. Teffinger couldn't breath. He busted through and didn't stop until he got outside.

There the storm fell, pushed by a demonic wind, and Teffinger didn't care. He braced against it in the open near the street and sucked the wet air into his chest.

It felt like voodoo.

It felt right.

The drumming in his veins softened.

He'd just killed a man.

Legally it was self-defense; he had no question about that. There'd be a thorough investigation of course but in the end he'd be cleared. That wasn't the issue. The issue was whether he could have held back, whether he could have countered without so much intent, without so much power, without so much re-action.

Did he kill the man on purpose?

No.

That's what he told himself, no.

Deep in his gut though he wondered if he was just tricking himself.

Either way, what was done was done.

It couldn't be undone.

It was his.

He owned it.

The investigation, headed up by detective Richardson in conjunction with Internal Affairs, dragged into the small hours of the night. Witnesses saw the dead man strike Teffinger first and then stand over him with clenched fists. Security videotapes confirmed it.

Teffinger cooperated but didn't care.

He cared about one thing and one thing only, namely that Susan Smith hadn't yet shown her face and still wasn't answering her phone. It shouldn't be an issue, not with Colder dead, but her absence minute after minute after minute grew more and more palpable.

Teffinger broke loose at the first crack and headed into the storm to find out what in the hell was going on.

42

Needing to be the ghost that never was, Saturday night after dark Jori-Lee drove past the dark lifeless house of T'amara Alder one final time and found it exactly as coffin-quiet as before. She parked a block over and doubled back on foot, dressed in shades of black. An image was back in her head, an image of the woman being killed on the other end of the phone, followed by the killer's voice in Jori-Lee's ear.

She made her way through the dark to the back door.

It was locked.

The windows were equally locked.

With her elbow, she busted the door glass and then stood still, listening for a barking dog or nosy neighbor.

Nothing came.

The world stayed the same.

She reached through, unlocked the bolt and entered.

The only sound was the motion of air passing in and out of her lungs. She was in a small kitchen, a place of no interest, and made her way to the living room. There she closed all the window coverings. Creaking stairs led her to the upper level where the bedrooms were. She closed all the coverings, took a pillowcase off a pillow and then headed back down.

In a small study she flicked on the flashlight.

Papers came into view on a wooden desk—bills, handwritten notes, coupons and the like. She stuffed the cell phone bill into the pillowcase. A telephone book sat folded opened to the Hs. No numbers were circled. She ripped out the two facing pages and stuffed them in the pillowcase. In the upper drawer was a stack of business cards cinched in a rubber band. They went into the case.

She needed to find the woman's computer.

That's where the secrets would be.

There was no desktop computer, printer, fax machine or home phone.

She headed upstairs.

Next to the bed on an end table was an iPad.

She took it.

In the master closet on an upper shelf was a box of loose photographs.

She took them.

She checked the rest of the house including the basement and found nothing else of interest. Then she got the hell out of there.

She didn't know if the iPad had a GPS tracking device but wasn't about to take any chances by bringing the thing back to the hotel. Instead she headed west out of the city and pulled over in a dark enclave of a raggedly industrial road.

There behind the wheel she brought the screen to life.

As she hoped, the woman's email account displayed without requiring a password.

A recent message confirmed a flight to Hong Kong with a departure set for 8:30 Tuesday morning. A second confirmed a three-night stay at the Kowloon InterContinental.

Hong Kong.

Why did that strike a cord?

She dug but couldn't bring it up.

It would come to her later.

In any event, the woman was getting out of town.

Why?

Was she trying to escape?

Was she going to shake Robertson down for money and then retire in comfort?

Was she meeting a friend or a lover or a co-conspirator?

There were too many messages for her to process. Even the inconspicuous ones might show relevance later on closer scrutiny, meaning the device was too valuable to abandon.

She shut it off, cranked over the engine and pointed the front end towards Paramount Bay.

She needed to find a dry safe place to stash the device.

Then she needed Sanders.

DAY SIX

July 13
Sunday

43

Susan was nowhere to be found, not all night, not at the club, not at her condo, not at the other end of her phone, not at a single point in the universe. The club's security tapes showed her milling around in the early goings and then dancing seductively with a hypnotic young woman who looked like she belonged sipping margaritas in a Mediterranean beach cabana. That was the last sighting, recorded ten minutes before Colder made Teffinger do what he did.

Teffinger's best hope was that the woman left the Mediterranean beauty, couldn't find him to tell him her plans, and figured no harm done since she'd be safe.

That was his best hope.

It didn't come from his gut; it came from his brain.

His gut didn't have a best hope.

His gut was a lot more cynical than his brain.

At four in the morning Teffinger checked the woman's condo one final time, found her not there again one final time, and slumped down on her couch.

He closed his eyes just to rest them for a second.

The darkness felt like cool water.

It felt good.

It felt right.

His phone rang, initially as an abstract barely-audible sound and then growing louder and louder as his brain kicked out of unconsciousness and into reality. He flipped it open just before the last ring.

It was Sydney.

"Where are you? It's ten-thirty."

He muscled against the cushions into a vertical position.

His tongue was sandpaper.

His face was leather.

His eyelids were glue.

He stood up, got his balance and headed for the bathroom. "I'm at Susan's," he said. "Is Del Rey okay?"

"Yeah, not a bird-ripper in sight."

"Good," he said. "Close your ears or you're going to hear something you'd rather not." He took a piss, not talking, not holding back, watching the water splash and using the seconds to wake up. "Okay I'm back."

"That was disgusting."

"Good because that's how I feel."

"So what's the plan for today?"

"The plan is to find Susan."

"You may want to change it."

"Why?"

"A call came in a half hour ago," she said. "It was a guy who said he saw a man stab a woman in the stomach with a big knife and stuff her into the trunk of a car."

"Where?"

"Out in that industrial area near the BNSF switch-yard."

"When? Last night?"

"No, no, Wednesday night," she said. "By the description he gave of the woman, plus the method of murder, it actually sounds like Portia Montrachet. That's how and when she was killed."

"Couldn't be her," Teffinger said. "She was killed in the alley."

"Not if you believe this guy."

Teffinger kick-started the shower and unbuttoned his shirt.

"Did he describe the killer?"

"He didn't get a good look at the guy's face," she said, "other than in a general way. Get this, he said the guy reminded him of a boxer."

Teffinger unzipped his pants and stepped out.

"So what's our little friend's name?"

"He wouldn't say."

"He's anonymous?"

Yes.

He was.

"What do you think?" Sydney said.

Teffinger grunted.

"I think someone knows we're investigating the

boxer as a suspect and is trying to put the squeeze on him through us, rightly or wrongly."

"Why?"

Good question.

"Maybe he has a grudge, or maybe he really did see the boxer do it and tried to shake him down but it didn't work, which is why the guy didn't call us all this time. Either way I'm not impressed."

"Me either."

"Why not?"

"Because Susan killed Portia."

"Just because you keep saying that doesn't mean it's going to turn true. I'll be at the office in half an hour. Then we're going to look for Susan. In fact, see if you can figure out who that Mediterranean woman is that she was dancing with."

"She's probably dead somewhere, compliments of your little friend," Sydney said.

44

A body showed up Sunday morning at the BNSF switchyard, ironically in the same area where the anonymous caller said he saw a boxer stab a woman in the stomach Wednesday night. The body no longer moved because the head that was attached to it had a bullet hole in the back.

The man's wallet was intact.

Inside that wallet were sixty hundred-dollar bills and two condoms.

Also inside was a driver's license that identified him as one Benjamin Fisher.

He was in his late thirties, heavily tattooed and pierced in all kinds of painful places. Up top was hair too long with a bald spot in the back. He looked like the kind of guy who had learned how to bring trouble into his life.

It was detective Katie Baxter's scene.

Teffinger only came because she called him.

"Listen to this," she said.

This was the man's cell phone.

"This is Colder," a voice said. "I want to call off the project. Everyone still gets their money but I want the project called off. Call me as soon as you get this and let me know you got it."

Teffinger knew the voice.

It belonged to the lawyer, Jack Colder, the man he killed last night.

"There are ten more messages just like it," Baxter said. "We traced the number to Jack Colder."

"When was the last call made?"

She checked.

It was ten minutes before the man's last breath.

"Play it," he said.

She obliged.

It came from the club, heavy with background music. Teffinger recognized the song. It was pounding down right around the time he lost sight of Susan.

"Thanks." He nodded towards the body and said, "Do you have a timeline of where this guy was before he got himself all dead?"

"Not yet."

"Let me know when you get it, please and thank you."

"He's a private investigator," Katie said.

"The dead guy?"

"Right."

"Maybe Colder had him working on a case."

Teffinger considered it.

It fit.

"Yeah."

Walking back to the Tundra, a dark thought descended on him. I want to call off the project. The project was the murder of Susan Smith.

Colder must have used the investigator as a middleman to hire a third person to kill Susan Smith.

Colder must have changed his mind.

That's why he was calling the investigator, to call off the hit.

He must not have known who the hitman was.

Colder wasn't at the club last night to kill Susan Smith.

He was there to protect her.

Teffinger doubled back to the scene and said to Katie, "I'm going to be assisting you on this investigation if you don't mind."

"Great."

"Does our investigator friend have an office somewhere?"

He did.

She gave him the address.

It was south on Broadway.

"I'll head over and see if there's anything there worth knowing."

She nodded.

"Sure." She wrinkled her forehead and said, "Teffinger, are you okay?"

Good question.

He killed an innocent man last night.

Susan Smith was either dead or in the throes of getting dead.

"I'm fine," he said.

Then he was gone.

He headed to Broadway and then south. Pieces fell into place as he bobbed and weaved through traffic. The investigator must have eventually gotten a hold of the man he hired. It was too late at that point, though. The man had already killed or abducted Susan Smith. At a maximum she was already dead and at a minimum she was alive but had seen his face.

Aborting the project was no longer an option.

The hitman got worried about an unraveling project.

He got worried about too many loose lips.

He took the investigator out with a bullet to the brain.

He would have done the same to Colder except Teffinger spared him the need.

One fact was clear.

Whoever killed the investigator was the same person who already had killed, or would soon kill, Susan Smith—probably the former.

His phone rang and Sydney's voice said, "I found the Mediterranean woman. Her name is Sanapella Seffrada. She lives at 1352 Delaware."

Teffinger's brain spun.

Maybe the Mediterranean woman saw the hitman.

"Meet me there."

"When?"

"Now."

He called Katie.

"I want to know every number your little dead investigator friend called or got a call from yesterday," he said. "Make a list from his cell phone. Get me the associated names and addresses too."

"Ouch."

Ouch?

Ouch wasn't what he wanted to hear.

He wanted to hear anything except ouch.

"What do you mean, ouch?"

She told him.

It wasn't good.

It involved the cell phone and gravity, a lot of gravity, gravity and a train rail.

"Okay, get the information from the phone company."

"That will take a warrant."

That was true.

He knew that.

The D.A. would have to draw it up and then find a judge on a Sunday who would sign it. The phone company would have to have their legal department review it. Then they'd have to gather the information, be sure that it was accurate and complete and complied with the scope of the warrant, etcetera. The process typically took days.

"Get it going," he said.

The delay wasn't the big issue.

The big issue was the probability that the records wouldn't be useful in any event. If the investigator had half a brain he would have either used a payphone or met with the third party in person, most likely in connection with delivery of a retainer. He wouldn't be dumb enough to leave an electronic trail.

The Mediterranean woman was Teffinger's best immediate hope. If she turned out to know nothing, the world would be ugly.

He called headquarters to see if any more bodies had shown up since last night, if not in Denver then elsewhere in the region.

None had, just the guy Katie Baxter was working down at the switching yard.

That was good.

Susan might be alive.

She might be dead and unfound, but she might also still be alive.

45

Jori-Lee woke Sunday morning in a dawn-washed bedroom next to a naked surfer. The animal lust that made their bodies collide last night still resonated between her thighs. She could feel his touch on her body and his tongue in her mouth. Roll over and take me again, do it now. The man didn't move. He didn't respond to her voodoo spell. She kissed his cheek, eased out without waking him and took a long hot shower. When she got out, Sanders was in the kitchen working up omelets.

He handed her a cup of coffee and said, "Morning, glory."

She took a sip.

"You're a bad boy."

He raised an eyebrow.

"Why?"

"Lawyers aren't supposed to sleep with their clients," she said. "Or harbor criminals."

"Or make omelets?"

She smiled.

"Omelets are okay."

"In that case I'm violation-free so far today. Are you impressed?"

"I am but it won't last," she said. "You'll be back to your old ways before you know it."

"You think?"

"I'm counting on it."

He tapped her coffee with his and said, "In that case, here's to bad lawyers."

"To very bad lawyers."

Sanders's face got serious.

He picked a flash drive off the counter, tossed it up and down in his hand, looked Jori-Lee in the eyes and said, "We need to talk about this."

"Yes we do."

The file at issue, labeled Photos, contained hundreds of photos and videos downloaded from the web, porn photos and videos to be exact, porn photos and videos featuring men under extreme domination to be even more exact. Most of the tops were women; taking the man with a strap-on, or sitting on his face, or pissing on him—that kind of thing. Some were gay, depicting dungeon scenes where a leather-clad master or panty-clad transvestite was working over a helpless male slave.

"So Robertson's a closet freak," Sanders said. "That's pretty much what we have here."

"Right."

"He must have been at it a long time. You don't get that twisted in a weekend. Imagine having that kind of decay way down inside while sitting on the Supreme Court. Every time he opened his mouth it was another lie. Personally I couldn't live like that. I'd explode." He exhaled and added, "At least we know why he's being blackmailed. Someone found out about his little fetish and threatened to out him.

Granted, it's not illegal, it's not like it's kiddie-porn or a snuff film or something like that. But it has all the shame and embarrassment to take him down. If it ever got out, every church-going do-gooder in congress would be clamoring for his impeachment. The fall from an office that high would kill anyone, including him, and he knows it."

Jori-Lee nodded.

"What I don't get is how someone got the goods on him," she said. "Someone has proof; otherwise he wouldn't be engaged in talks to throw a case."

"Someone," Sanders said. "You act like it's a mystery. Someone is your little friend, T'amara Alder. That's why she's dead. She was blackmailing Robertson and he had her killed."

"It doesn't fit."

"Sure it does."

She shook her head.

"T'amara Alder has no clue what cases are before the court, much less care who wins them. If she had something on Robertson she'd be going after money. If you ask me, she was a messenger for someone else."

"Who?"

She shrugged.

"I don't know, maybe someone who has a stake in the case."

"One of the parties?"

"Possibly one of the parties, or maybe someone downstream who has some kind of financial gain or loss on the line."

"Such as who?"

"I don't know."

Sanders frowned.

"It's not a big money case," he said. "It's a freedom of speech case. Plus, if she was only the messenger, why kill her? Why not go after the real thing?"

"I don't know. To send a message?"

"I don't know either," Sanders said. "The only thing I know is that you were on the line when the Alder woman got murdered, not to mention you're in possession of Robertson's computer files. If there's a list out there of people to kill, you're on it; maybe it's still a Jane Doe at this point, but you're on it, make no mistake about that. And sooner or later someone's going to figure out who Jane Doe is."

Jori-Lee already knew that.

Still, the words felt like a spider crawling up her leg.

Ten minutes later Sanders had a strange thought and said, "One thing we haven't considered is that maybe T'amara Alder wasn't a blackmailer or a messenger."

Jori-Lee wrinkled her brow.

"Meaning what?"

"Maybe she knew who the blackmailer was and was going to tell Robertson," he said. "Maybe she was killed by the blackmailer rather than from Robertson's direction."

"So she was trying to help Robertson?"

"Precisely."

46

The Mediterranean woman, Sanapella Seffrada, didn't answer when Teffinger knocked, because that's the way his life worked. He pounded the door with a frustrated hand, still got nothing, and huffed off. Halfway down the walkway, "Hey," came from behind him. He turned to see a sleepy dark beauty with disheveled hair in the doorway.

He walked towards her.

"Are you Sanapella Seffrada?"

She studied him.

"You're the guy who killed that other guy last night down at the club."

Teffinger shifted his feet and explained he was with Denver homicide, looking for a missing woman. "You were dancing with her last night," he said. "She was wearing a white dress. Her name is Susan Smith."

The woman held the door open.

"You want some coffee?"

He did.

He did indeed.

The woman wore a T and black panties.

"Your eyes are two different colors," she said. "I had a cat exactly like that once, white fur, all white except for one foot which was black. His name was Alley."

"What happened to him?"

She shrugged.

"He went off to Hollywood to become a star."

Teffinger smiled.

"He's probably waiting tables."

"Probably." She pushed hair out of her face. "I never got the woman's name last night. Susan, you say."

He nodded.

"She deserves something more exotic."

"Anything you could tell me would be appreciated."

She got a vacant look.

"There's nothing to tell, really. We just bumped into each other and had a few dances. That was it. To tell you the truth, I don't even remember her that well. I was pretty high."

"With more than alcohol?"

She nodded.

Teffinger took a long sip of coffee.

"With what, exactly?"

"Ecstasy, exactly."

Teffinger was familiar with the name but didn't know much about its properties, particularly its effect on short-term or long-term memory.

"So you didn't leave with her then?"

"No."

"Okay."

"I left with someone else. She's up in bed."

A sound came from behind.

Teffinger turned to find a woman coming down the stairs, a striking woman in a turquoise T, groggy with sleep. Her hands went up to ruffle her hair, raising the T up just enough to disclose an absence of panties. She gave him a peck on the lips and said to Sanapella, "Your man's nice. I'll help you do him if you want."

Sanapella swallowed what was left of her coffee.

"Sure, why not?"

Teffinger shifted his feet, focused on Sanapella and said, "How is it that you and Susan stopped dancing?"

"Let me think ... okay, I remember now, a guy cut in."

"For you?"

"No, her."

Teffinger's chest pounded.

"Describe him."

"That would be pretty hard considering I never saw his face?"

"You didn't."

No, she didn't.

"He stepped between us and was facing her," she said.

"So you only saw the back of his head—"

"Right."

"Describe it."

"The back of his head?"

"Right."

"It was just the back of a head. Oh, wait, now I remember something, he had a ponytail, it was black."

Teffinger smiled.

"Good, what was he wearing?"

"I don't remember."

"A shirt? A jacket?

"I don't remember."

"Was he tall or short?"

"He was tall enough but not overly, if that makes sense."

"How was he built? Thin, bulky?"

"I don't remember. The whole thing was just a flash."

He turned to the other woman, the one with the T. "Did you see him too?"

"No."

Back to Sanapella, "When the man cut in, what happened next?"

"They danced."

"Did the man flash her anything, something that could have been a knife or a gun?"

She shrugged.

"I didn't see anything like that."

Teffinger exhaled.

"Okay, that's fine. What I want you to do is come down to the station and look at some videotapes of the crowd from last night and see if you can spot him."

"Like I said, I didn't see his face—"

"I understand but maybe you'll see something that will spark a memory, a body posture or clothes or something like that. All I'm asking is that you take a look. Will you do that for me?"

"Sure, why not?"

47

The dead PI who Colder repeatedly called last night to abort the project had an office on south Broadway in a standalone building that was an affront to every building code known to man. Surprisingly the front door was cracked open a couple of inches. Teffinger knocked and shouted, "Anyone here?" No one answered. He tried again, got more of the same, and thought briefly about getting a search warrant before going any further. Instead he decided to follow the directions on the door:

Benjamin Fisher, Private Investigator

Confidentiality Guaranteed

Walk-Ins Welcome

Inside the place was a throwback to an old black-and-white TV show, replete with garage-sale furniture, mismatched metal filing cabinets and a large wooden desk with enough food mashed into the scratches to live on for a week.

A smaller desk was to the right.

On it was an ashtray overflowing with butts, each smudged with pink lipstick, meaning the dead man had a secretary or assistant.

Teffinger looked at the papers on the desk, not touching them, not going beyond the invitation on the door. None of them related to the hiring of a hitman to kill Susan Smith. Most were handwritten notes relating to small matters—follow a husband; follow a woman receiving workmen's compensation to see if she was doing anything that would prove her claim of physical injury was fabricated or exaggerated; figure out if a judgment debtor had a secret bank account in the Caymans; that kind of thing.

Teffinger frowned.

He couldn't snoop further, not legally.

He needed a search warrant.

Suddenly the door opened and a woman walked in, a bleach-blond with pink lipstick that matched the butts, cute in a trashy sort of way. She wore a cheap yellow sundress with a stain on the hem and over-sized white sunglasses, the latter of which she took off as she said, "Who are you?"

Teffinger went to answer but his lips didn't move. His brain was too busy processing the fact that the woman looked exactly like what he would have expected her to look like, had he done any expecting before she walked in.

"I'm Nick Teffinger," he said, "I'm a homicide detective. Do you work here?"

She did.

"Good," he said. "Your boss Benjamin Fisher got killed last night. He hired a guy with a ponytail to kill a woman named Susan Smith. I need to know who that guy is."

Her name was Danielle Westchester and she knew nothing about anything, not for the full ten minutes

Teffinger grilled her, but she did give him permission to search the place and even directed him to where things could be found.

Minutes passed, then halves of hours, then hours, and none of those things were helpful.

Not one of them gave shape to the elusive ponytail man.

Then something happened that Teffinger didn't expect.

He found phone records that showed numerous calls between Bennie on the one hand and a Washington, D.C. area code number on the other.

The number turned out to belong to another private investigator, none other than Oscar Benderfield, the black man with the bleached hair who first hired Portia to kill Susan Smith.

The two investigators were connected.

"This is why you don't know anything," he told Danielle. "Bennie didn't hire the guy with the ponytail, not directly anyway. He passed the assignment on to a buddy in D.C. They must have some kind of network in place."

Del Rey called and said, "Are you okay?"

An image flashed in Teffinger's brain, an image of her dancing in the storm, so perfect, so seductive, so absolutely right.

The answer was no; he said, "Yes."

"I need to see you."

"Why?"

"Because I'm going to explode if I don't."

He played it out.

He deserved it.

It wouldn't take much time.

Still, it would take some time, and some was something he didn't have, or more to the point, Susan Smith didn't have. "Right now I have zombies coming at me from every direction," he said. "I'll see you tonight."

"Zombies," she said. "Now there's a word I never thought I'd hear coming out of your mouth."

"Yeah, well get used to it."

"Come on, Teffinger, just ten minutes—"

"Tonight, I promise."

"You promise?"

He did.

He did with every fiber of his being, then he got off the line before his weakness betrayed him.

He headed to homicide where Sanapella Seffrada and her little no-panties friend were reviewing the club tapes under the guidance of Sydney, who pulled Teffinger into the adjoining room, closed the door and said, "Not good so far."

"Great, another zombie."

She wrinkled her face in confusion.

"Private joke," he said.

"Whatever. We found at least a dozen guys with ponytails. None of them are ringing bells. With the cameras coming from the ceiling, their faces are at an extreme downward angle. Plus the film's grainy beyond belief when you try to zero in on something that small."

Teffinger slumped in a chair.

The lack of sleep from last night was a wet blanket around his brain.

"Keep trying," he said.

"I will but don't expect anything."

He closed his eyes.

His head bobbed.

The next thing he knew Sydney was helping him onto a couch.

His feet were up.

His shoes were off.

The fluorescents went out.

The door closed.

The air got quiet.

Then everything disappeared.

48

Someone had proof. Someone had proof that Robertson was way down deep into the freaky stuff; otherwise he wouldn't be getting ready to throw a vote.

Who had it?

Who?

Who?

Who?

Jori-Lee rattled the question inside her gray matter hour after hour without coming an iota closer to finding the answer. Then something struck her. Just having the proof wouldn't be enough to make Robertson act.

He'd need to see the proof.

He'd need to be sure someone wasn't just trying to fake him out.

Early Sunday noon, out on the terrace overlooking the bay, Jori-Lee pulled up the "Photos" file from the flash drive and opened the porn videos, one after another, watching them for thirty seconds and then going to the next. Sanders came out, handed her a glass of iced tea and said, "What are you doing?"

"Chasing a long-shot."

"Meaning what?"

"Meaning that I don't think Robertson is the kind of guy to go to the extreme of throwing a case unless someone had him totally by the balls," she said.

Sanders shrugged.

"You know him better than me."

"The more I think about it," Jori-Lee said, "the more I'm persuaded that it wouldn't be enough for someone to just have evidence that the man was downloading porn, or even evidence that he was addicted to it."

Sanders shook his head.

"You're wrong," he said. "The shame and ridicule would be a bullet to his brain. The inevitable impeachment process that would follow would be a torture rack."

"No."

"No?"

"Well, not no, yes, but if he admitted he had an addiction or got off course, and then entered into some kind of program to get help, people would forgive him," she said.

"Wrong."

"Why?"

"That might work with rock stars or athletes, but when it comes to the law, particularly the highest echelons of the law, the integrity and thought process needs to be clean and un-decayed. There can't even be an appearance of impropriety."

She took a sip of tea.

"What I'm thinking is this," she said. "I don't think Robertson would bend all the way to the dark side if only watching things was the issue. I do think he could bend that far, though, if doing things was the issue."

"Doing things?"

"Yeah, getting dominated, actually living out the fantasy, not just watching other people do it. If he did that, and someone had proof of him doing that, say by way of a videotape of something like that, then I could see him getting desperate enough to throw a case."

Sanders didn't disagree.

"If that happened, whoever is blackmailing him would have shown him a copy of the videotape," she added. "They might have emailed a digital copy to him. When I looked at the videos before, I only looked at a handful of them, which was all my brain could hold without imploding. The long-shot I'm chasing is that Robertson actually received a videotape of himself in action."

Sanders cocked his head.

"If that's the case, after he watched it he would have hit the delete button so hard his finger would have broken."

"Not necessarily," she said. "He'd keep it as proof he was being blackmailed, if everything eventually hit the fan; it would be a way, at a minimum, of taking the blackmailer down with him. He'd also want it up the road to refresh his memory as to what his new friend exactly had. If that's true and he kept it then the question becomes, where would he keep it?"

"You think he buried it in there with all the other videos—"

"That's where I'd put it."

The corner of Sanders' mouth turned up ever so slightly.

"I'm glad you're on my side," he said.

49

Teffinger woke on a couch in a conference room and vaguely remembered Sydney closing the window coverings, giving him a soft kiss on the cheek and saying, "Nightie-night little angel." He bolted upright, not needing to waste even one more precious second of the day. The oversized industrial clock on the wall, the one with the twitchy second-hand, said 3:03, meaning he'd been out for more than two hours.

For a brief second he raged at himself.

Then he calmed.

On the outside glass of the door was a yellow post-it. It said, "Beware of animal. Do not feed."

He headed down the hall to the main homicide room, poured a cup of coffee, took a seat in front of Sydney's desk and tossed the post-it on her desk.

"That's your handwriting," he said.

She nodded.

"Feel better?"

"Actually, yes." He pointed to his cheek and said, "You kissed me just before I fell asleep. Right there."

She soured her face.

"In your dreams."

"Are you saying you didn't?"

"Do my lips look like they've touched acid? Are they falling off?"

"No, they look fine."

"Okay then." With a serious face she added, "I got the best still photos I could from the videotape footage of the men in the club who had ponytails. Then I emailed them to every contact we have at the club, including the manager, the doorman and the bartenders. Except for one person, a bartender named Brank, everyone's gotten back to me. A few of them recognize a few of the ponytails—three total to be exact—as regulars, but no one knows them, as in a name or anything. My assumption is that if the ponytail followed Susan to the club then he's not a regular. So we can probably scratch three off the list which still leaves nine, nine grainy ghosts."

A dead end, that's what it was; deader than dead, even.

"Okay."

"So, stay on it?"

Good question.

"Like you said, the guy's probably not a regular there. Even if we found someone who saw him there that night, they wouldn't know him." He exhaled. "Let's expand the scope. Get every security tape in a two-block radius. Maybe we'll get lucky and see him walking to the club or parking a car."

"Remember, it was storming."

He remembered.

"Get the tapes around Susan's building too."

Two hours later he was in a window seat of a big metal beast with his hands in a death-grip on the arm-rests and sweat dripping into his eyes, sweeping into menacing clouds at a speed man was not meant to go. He listened for noises, the kind that mean that some stupid two-dollar bolt somewhere was coming loose and perfecting an evil plan to throw the aircraft into a death spiral.

Seconds passed, then minutes.

The plane didn't fall out of the sky.

The bumps lost their bite.

The wings smoothed out.

The ground got farther.

Strangely, the more distant it got, the safer Teffinger felt.

The nose of the plane was pointed towards D.C.

Don't do anything too stupid, he warned himself.

No promises, he answered back.

50

The long-shot struck payday, sick, sick payday; payday in the form of a video buried deep in the file, a video in which Robertson himself played a demented little role right there in his own demented little flesh. There was no question it was him.

His face was clear.

It was clear as he lay on his naked back on the carpet with his privates in some kind of metal device, obediently sucking a woman's toes. It was clear as he got bent across a table, strapped down and then rammed from behind by a woman with a strap-on. It was clear in the next twisted little deal, and the next, and the next.

The woman's face, by contrast, wasn't clear.

It rarely came before the camera.

When it did, a black leather mask concealed it.

"So who's the woman?" Sanders asked. "T'amara Alder?"

"It has to be."

"It's a hidden camera," Sanders said. "It never moves. Robertson didn't know he was being filmed."

True.

Sanders got a look on his face.

"You're thinking—"

He nodded.

"I'm thinking that Robertson doesn't belong on the bench, not at that level."

"That's not our call."

"If it's not ours then whose is it?"

"Stop it."

"At this point we should just do what it takes to get him off," he said. "I'm not saying go public and embarrass the man. Try it private first. Let him know what we know. Let him resign for whatever reason he wants to come up with. Get a void in his position and let it get filled with someone who deserves it."

"No."

"Why not?"

"Because I'm not perfect."

Sanders shook his head.

"That doesn't even make sense."

"I'm not perfect, you're not perfect, he's not perfect, none of us are perfect," she said. "He's got issues but if they're not interfering with his duties then they're nobody's business."

"But they are interfering," Sanders said. "He's going to throw a case, remember?"

"That's the future," Jori-Lee said. "The future may or may not come to pass."

"We should get him out now," Sanders said. "If we just wait until he actually throws a case then things will be worse, not just for the reputation and integrity of the court but for him personally as well. He'll be facing jail time. We both know what he'll do to avoid it." He put a finger to his head and pulled the trigger. "Let's get him out, mitigate damages all around and let everyone go their merry way. Don't think of it as ratting him out. Think of it as saving his life."

Jori-Lee considered it.

It made sense inside her head.

It didn't make quite so much sense inside her gut.

Sanders was too eager.

Why?

Was he picturing himself making the rounds on the talk shows and nonchalantly dropping in a bookstore with his latest squeeze and showing her his new bestseller sitting on the shelf?

"Remember one more thing," he said. "T'amara Alder is dead. Who do you think is behind that?"

Jori-Lee swallowed.

Only one answer made sense.

She wished there was another but there wasn't.

There was only one.

Nelson Robertson.

"He's coming for you," Sanders said. "You're the last person on the face of the earth who ought to be protecting him. What you ought to be doing is yelling to the world about the monster you found."

She studied him.

His eyes were experience.

His skin was sunshine.

His face was a magazine cover.

His body was a Greek statue.

His hands could cradle a baby or swing a sword.

"I can't think," she said.

51

D.C. was sloppy with drizzle when Teffinger touched down late Sunday night. By the time he rented a car, got his bearings and made the actual drive to Oscar Benderfield's house it was almost midnight.

The structure was dark as death.

Teffinger rang the bell, then again and again, in rapid succession, while simultaneously rapping powerful knuckles on the wood.

An interior light went on.

The porch light went on.

Teffinger stood there, getting increasingly wet and increasingly inspected, feeling the man's thoughts on the other side, whether to open the door or not.

The entry swung in a few inches and got snagged by a chain. Benderfield's confused face and bleach blond hair appeared in the crack.

"I'm a homicide detective from Denver," Teffinger said. "We need to talk."

"About what?"

"About lots of stuff. This is off the record but if you don't open the door we'll continue this tomorrow and I guarantee you things will be ugly."

Silence.

"Are you here to arrest me?"

"No. We're going to talk and then I'm going to leave."

The door closed.

The chain came off.

"Come on in."

The interior was out of a magazine, with perfect textures and perfect colors and perfect attitude and perfect swagger and perfect proportions. The man was living large, too large given his craft.

The place was built on coffins.

Teffinger felt dirty just being in it.

They ended up in the kitchen on opposite sides of counter, Benderfield with a glass of orange juice in hand and a face that was growing ever more awake. The man was bigger than Teffinger expected, six-three or more. He wore loose silk pajamas that mostly but not totally belied the muscle underneath.

"I'm going to make you a deal," Teffinger said. "Before I do, though, let me tell you why you should take it. You should take it because I know all kinds of things about you."

"Like what?"

Teffinger laid it out. Benderfield came to Denver and hired Portia Montrachet to kill Susan Smith. The only reason the hit didn't go through was because Portia got murdered minutes and feet before the attack.

"Recently you got a call from a friend of yours in Denver, a man named Benjamin Fisher. At his bequest you hired a second hitman, a guy with a ponytail," Teffinger said. "That's what I want to know about. Who was he?"

"As a hypothetical, even if you were right, why would I tell you anything?"

"Because that's how you get the deal."

Benderfield took a calculated sip of the OJ.

"Explain this so-called deal."

"It's simple," Teffinger said. "I'm going to give you a 48-hour head start."

"To do what?"

"To get to the bank, transfer your money to the Caymans, sneak across a border, slither under a rock, whatever it is your going to do to keep the needle out of your arm. You get 48-hours of totally uninterrupted and untracked time."

"Then what?"

"Then I hunt you to the ends of the earth," Teffinger said.

"You? Hunt me?"

Teffinger nodded.

"Forty-eight hours is a good deal," he said. "To get it though you need to talk, you need to talk now and you need to talk fast. Everything you say is off the record. I'm not reading you your rights, I'm not recording this, I'm not trying to pull anything funny."

"So what are you trying to do?"

"Save Susan Smith's life."

52

Seventy-two hours. That was Benderfield's demand. Teffinger could care less whether it was 48, 72 or 59.7. He checked his watch and said, "Deal, starting now. So talk. Tell me who has Susan Smith."

Benderfield took a long swallow of the orange juice.

"Ordinarily I don't talk about my associates," he said. "But putting a cap in my buddy's head, that was over the line."

"Your P.I. buddy."

"Right, Fisher. He called me the other night and said he had a client who wanted someone dead. The client was a lawyer. The money was solid."

"Who was the lawyer?"

"Someone named Colder."

Colder.

The answer was the one Teffinger expected but, still, it forced a feeling into his gut, the same feeling he had when he first spotted the man in the club, before he killed him.

"Go on."

"Fisher and me go back," Benderfield said. "He knows I have connections. That's why he called me. He doesn't have those types of connections. He's never been involved in anything like this before. To put it politely, he's small-time."

"So you hired someone for him?"

Benderfield shook his head.

No.

No.

No.

No.

No.

"I already had too many things going on," he said. "I gave him a very good piece of advice and told him to back off and shut the deal down. I told him to just walk away." A beat then, "He was weak, though. He couldn't let go of the money. That was his mistake. That's always been his mistake."

Teffinger's throat was sandpaper.

"Do you have any more of that orange juice?"

Benderfield did.

He got a glass, poured and then continued.

"Like I said, I already had too many things going on, but even more to the point, I didn't want to get involved. Fisher's okay as far as small things go but he's not really someone you want to be around if things get turbulent. He's not built for rough seas. He's built to leak. Anyway, after I got him convinced that I wasn't going to hire anyone, he said that was fine, he'd do it himself. All he wanted from me was a number to call. Ordinarily in a situation like that, I'd turn the person on to Portia. That wasn't exactly an option any longer."

True.

"There's only one other guy I know in that business. He goes by the name of Rail. I only used him once and that was enough. He did the job and did it well and did it on time, but there was something about him that made me feel as if a spider was crawling up my back."

"Rail—"

"Right, Rail."

"Does he have a first name?"

"That's all I know him by, Rail, and I'm sure that's an alias. Whatever his real name is, I don't know it and I don't want to know it. I told Fisher I had a number but didn't want to give it to him; the guy was too intense. He pressed me and I finally caved him. I told him to be careful. I told him to be positive that he didn't do anything to ignite the guy. If money was due at a certain time and place, he better be damn sure that money was there at that time and at the place."

"So you gave him a number?"

"I did."

"Give it to me."

"It's at my office," Benderfield said. "I have it written on a piece of paper stuffed in a book." He frowned. "It won't do you any good. Someone obviously pays the phone bill every month but I can guarantee you that Rail has more than enough safeguards in place so that it could never be traced to him, or if it could, it would be so complicated that he'd know it was going on and be a million miles away before you ever reached him."

"You'd be surprised."

Benderfield shrugged.

"Maybe I would. Should we go to my office?"

Teffinger stood up.

"Let's go. What does he look like?"

"Rail?"

"Right."

"Unknown," Benderfield said. "I've never met him. All my contact has been by phone. I never knew he had a ponytail until you just now told me. All I have is a name and a number."

"That's not true," Teffinger said. "You also have a prior kill with him. You know the name of one of his victims."

"Yeah, I suppose I do."

"Who was that victim?"

"Are we still off the record?"

"Trust me."

Benderfield hesitated and then said, "A woman named Kelly Nine."

The words were a bullet to Teffinger's brain.

"Kelly Nine? From San Francisco?"

"Yes. Do you know her?"

He nodded

"Yes."

"Small world."

Teffinger hardened his face.

"Who hired you to get Kelly Nine killed?"

Benderfield got a distant look.

"That's a big question," he said.

"Then give me a big answer."

Benderfield swallowed what was left of the juice,

turned to the sink, got the fancy brushed-nickel faucet flowing and rinsed the glass, taking his time, getting every last drop of orange juice out of it. He opened the dishwasher door, put the glass inside and closed the door.

For a heartbeat he stood there, frozen in time, with his back to Teffinger.

Teffinger's chest tightened.

He wanted an answer and wanted it now, not in ten seconds, not in five, not it two, not in one.

"I said, who hired you to get Kelly Nine killed?"

Suddenly the man twisted with a cat-quick lunge and swung a knife at Teffinger's face.

53

It took ten minutes to kill Benderfield, ten terrible minutes, ten minutes that left Teffinger drained of every ounce of strength and left him limp on the floor, too beaten to even raise a hand to his face to feel the damage. He didn't want to kill the man, not at first. He gave him every opportunity to back off.

Then the tipping point came.

It came as the man landed furious fists to Teffinger's face with the power of a pit full of wild banshees.

It came as the man's eyes burned insane with murder.

It came and didn't leave until the man's head

whiplashed back from a horrible blow to his face, a blow that resonated from Teffinger's knuckles all the way to his spine. Benderfield teetered for a heartbeat, drunken in time, and then dropped unceremoniously to the floor.

His head bounced once off the tile.

No more movement came from any part of his body.

He was dead.

Teffinger didn't need to check.

He recognized the silence all too well.

What happened next was a blur. He remembered staggering to his feet, making his way to the man's bathroom, getting the shower going and then stepping in and letting the water wash blood down his face and his chest and stomach and legs. He remembered watching it pool briefly at his feet before it twisted down the drain. He remembered staying there until the water became clear.

He dressed in fresh clothes, Benderfield's.

Then he left.

Every bit of it was wrong.

He should have called 911.

He should have stayed put until the cops arrived.

He should have been there to give a statement.

Doing right though wasn't an option.

Doing right would slow him down.

So instead he did wrong and drove to Benderfield's office, broke in and went through every book he could find, looking for a piece of paper with a phone number on it, Rail's number—the number of the person who snatched Susan Smith, the number of the person who killed Kelly Nine.

Kelly Nine.

Even to this day Teffinger's chest pounded when he thought about her out on the grass behind the bleachers on a warm summer night with her skirt hiked up and the beauty of her body glowing in the moonlight and her easy laughter filling every molecule of Teffinger's being.

Kelly Nine.

He didn't intend to love her, or anybody for that matter. He was just a high school boy looking for what every high school boy was looking for. By the time different college lives pulled them in separate directions, though, she was the only girl in the world and always would be.

Kelly Nine.

Time passed and she faded but never completely. They stayed in touch, flirty and sometimes intimate touch, even to the point of occasional booty-calls and sin-filled drunken nights in LoDo clubs. Then she moved to San Francisco.

Last year she was back for her niece's graduation from C.U.

Teffinger took her out drinking.

It was dark.

A wicked storm beat its wicked way down.

They ended up back at his place.

She kissed like high school.

In the morning, she was gone. Teffinger's lock had been jimmied from the outside.

No one heard from her the next day or the day after that or the day after that. She was gone from the face of the earth.

The longer Teffinger was away from Benderfield's house the clearer it became just how wrong it was to leave the scene. He should at a minimum call his counterpart, Randy Johnson, and explain what happened. He didn't have the man's number but called Miami homicide, told them he was a Denver detective with an emergency situation and asked to get patched through to Johnson at home.

The man answered with sleep in his voice.

"Randy, it's me, Teffinger. I'm in town. I went over to Oscar Benderfield's house tonight to have a little chat with him. He ended up attacking me with a knife and I ended up defending myself. He's dead. I should have stayed there and called 911. Instead I did something stupid and left the scene."

"Where are you right now?"

"I can't say."

"You mean you don't know?"

"No, I know, I just can't tell you."

The man exhaled.

"Meet me back at Benderfield's but don't go in, just wait for me at the curb."

"I can't."

"Why not?"

"I'll call you later and explain everything better.

Right now I have to run."

Teffinger hung up and called the FBI profiler, Leigh Sandt, pulling her out of a deep sleep.

"Have you ever heard of a guy named Rail?"

"Teffinger?"

"Yeah, me. Rail's a hitman. Have you ever heard of him?"

"Do you know what time it is?"

"Yes."

"It's the middle of the night."

"I know."

"What's going on?"

"I need to know who Rail is."

"Well you're asking the wrong person."

"You never heard of him?"

"No."

"Can you check your system?"

"Now?"

"Yes."

"Can it wait until the morning?"

"I don't know and I don't want to find out."

Silence, then, "Tell me what's going on."

He told her.

Her told her about how he knew that Rail was the person who killed Kelly Nine. He told her that Rail currently had his hands around the throat of another woman, Susan Smith. "He likes to play with his prey before he kills them. That means she might actually still be alive."

So far no book with a phone number inside had shown up. Maybe there wasn't one. Maybe Benderfield had been leading him on.

He kept checking.

He needed to get it done before Randy Johnson figured out where he was and pulled him downtown for questioning.

Come on Rail.

Show your ugly face.

54

Sunday evening Jori-Lee and Sanders drank wine on a blanket in a deserted section of beach thirty feet from the ocean's edge. A sunset flamed above with neon colors, then grew gray, then disappeared altogether as night pulled a blanket over Miami. Jori-Lee shifted onto her back and found a few stars already poking through.

She was torn.

Sanders straddled her stomach, pinned her arms over her head and said, "I'm not letting you up until you tell me what's going on inside that head of yours."

"Nothing."

"Wrong, something," he said. "I can smell it. You've been a zombie all evening."

He ran his fingers down her arms to her breasts, then under her T and across her stomach.

"God, Sanders."

"You can't resist," he said.

That was true.

"When I broke into T'amara Alder's house I found a bunch of photos and took them. One of them shows a small flowery tattoo on her right ankle. It's the same tattoo on the woman from Robertson's video."

"So there's no question T'amara Alder was the one working him over."

"None." A beat then, "I need to get back to D.C."

"Forget D.C.," Sanders said. "Call in and quit. Stay here with me."

"If you mean it I will, but after I figure out what's going on."

"So you're going back?"

"I have to."

Sanders exhaled.

"In that case I'm coming with you."

She almost said, That's not necessary. What came out was, "Okay."

DAY SEVEN

July 14
Monday

55

Rail's phone number never showed up. In the end Teffinger figured that the number was a lie designed to instigate a field trip during which Benderfield would find that nanosecond when Teffinger got off guard.

The man should have stuck to the plan.

It might have worked.

After the bust at Benderfield's office, Teffinger headed back to the scene and unruffled Randy Johnson's feathers to the extent possible by giving a statement, including the fact that he was coming back from the man's office, which he broke into.

Then he checked into the first fleabag he could find and slept.

That was last night, the middle of last night to be precise, the ungodly middle of last night to be even more precise.

Now it was morning.

The window coverings were vinyl pull-shades,

ten-dollars new, now worth about a buck fifty. Day-light squeezed around the edges, not sunlight, thick gunk.

Teffinger took a peek outside.

The morning was late.

The sky was a Simon & Garfunkel gray.

The sun, if there was one, was somewhere on the other side of the gray.

He took a long heaven-sent piss, got the shower up to temperature and stepped in. Before he got the curtain closed his phone rang, faint, coming from his pants over by the bed.

He got it, stepped back in the shower and stayed at the far end where the spray was less likely to kill it.

Del Rey's voice came through.

"It's me."

"How are you? Any signs of the bird ripper?"

"No bird rippers. I'm fine except for you not being here."

"Then you're doing better than me."

"Why? Why happened?"

"I ended up in a little tiff with Oscar Benderfield last night," he said. "He ended up dead."

"You killed him?"

"Don't say it like that."

"That's two in one week, Teffinger."

He knew that.

He knew that only too well.

"They were both self-defense. Benderfield actually attacked me with a knife." He pounded his hand on the shower wall. "They were both scum. Did I take things too far when they gave me a chance? I don't think so but I have to admit, deep down, I honestly don't know."

The words hung.

Del Rey said, "You didn't. I know you Teffinger, you're not like that. When are you coming home?"

"Today."

"Good."

He kissed the phone and set it on the edge on the tub on the safe side of the curtain.

The soap was some cheap rectangular thing that felt like waxy sandpaper and barely lathered.

Teffinger didn't care.

It was good enough to wash off the stench of last night.

He was working that waxy sandpaper through his hair when his phone rang. He stuck his face under the spray long enough to clear his eyes, then stepped to the back of the water and answered.

"Teffinger, it's me."

The voice belonged to the FBI profiler, Dr. Leigh Sandt.

"Tell me something good," he said.

"Something good."

He smiled.

"Not funny."

"A little funny."

"Okay, a little, what do you got?"

"You must have done something good in your prior life because Karma's coming back at you," she said. "I'm pretty sure Rail is a man from Portugal named Javier Arcos."

"Pretty sure?"

"Yes, as in ninety percent, not a hundred."

"Good enough. What's his story?"

His story was one Teffinger didn't expect. Javier Arcos, born in prison, grew up in the Lisbon ghettos before he eventually made his way at age eighteen to Monte Carlo, where his perfect face and perfect body got him entry to the beautiful people.

They scrubbed him up.

They took him in.

They showed him off.

In return he did favors; sexual at first, then the kinds that his street savvy was particularly suited to, none of which were legal. The life was okay but not what he wanted. What he wanted was his own money and his own rules. He got into black-market art, relics and ancient collectables.

His network grew.

His reputation grew.

He learned languages.

Then he got into the murder game, working for the richer-than-rich who had enemies that could no longer be ignored. He was good at his craft, good enough to be the only man for the job when the target was a diplomat or a high-profile person of prominence and presence.

He met lawyers.

They fed him secret assignments for secret clients.

"Two years ago, at the height of it all, he vanished," Leigh said.

"To where?"

"Unknown," she said. "The best working theory is that one of his own clients took him out as a way of tying up loose ends."

"Then why are we talking about him?"

"Because the next best working theory is that didn't happen. What really happened is that INTER-POL was getting too close so he just decided to turn himself into a ghost. He had more than enough money at that point to live comfortably wherever he wanted for the rest of his life."

"So why do you think this guy is Rail?"

"Because that's the name he used in Europe, plus he has a history of getting assignments from lawyers."

Teffinger's chest pounded.

This was the guy.

He could smell him now.

That was the good news. The less-than-good news was that there were no photos of the man that IN-TERPOL had been able to access. The man could walk up to Teffinger and slap him in the face with a dead fish and Teffinger wouldn't know who he was.

Also, one thing didn't make sense.

Why would anyone hire him to kill Kelly Nine?

She was a minnow.

He was more equipped to slay sharks.

"I have to go," Teffinger said. "You done good."

"Wait a minute."

He waited.

"You wake me up in the middle of the night wanting me to do work, and I actually get stupid enough to do it even though you're not my boss or even in the same organization, and then I come up with all this, and all you have to say is, You done good?"

"You're right," he said. "What I should have said was, can you email me the INTERPOL files?"

"Do you know what your problem is Teffinger?"

"No, what?"

"You're always you."

He smiled.

Then he hardened his face and said, "I killed two men this week."

"I know."

"That's a lot."

"Do you feel good about it?"

"Not particularly."

"Then don't worry about it."

"I didn't reign myself in. Five years ago I would have at least tried."

"If I know you, you did try. But even if you didn't, the sad truth is that the more crap we see, the quicker we are to cut to the chase," she said. "That's just the way it works. Ten years from now you'll walk down the street and randomly shoot little old ladies just because their hair's so goofy."

Teffinger pictured it.

The corner of his mouth turned up ever so slightly.

"How many kills does Rail have in Europe?"

"He's a suspect in at least fifteen," Leigh said. "There are probably two or three times that that no one knows about."

"That's a lot."

"More than you. So be careful."

56

Rail got pulled out of sleep Monday morning by the ringing of his phone, not the regular one, the special one, the one few knew about and ever fewer called. He grabbed it as he swung his six-three frame out of bed and answered as he headed for the bathroom.

The caller was a woman.

"Do you still have the digits I gave you before?"

The voice belonged to Emmanuelle Le Monte, one of the deeper and more intricate cogs in the Paris division of INTERPOL. The digits referred to her bank account in Switzerland.

"I do," he said.

"The price is 200,000 Euros," she said.

His pulse raced.

The price had never been that high.

Still, she'd never led him astray. She'd never overplayed the value of the information she would provide. She had something big, and, if he gauged the tone in her voice correctly, something immediate.

"Give me an hour."

"Do it and then call me back at this number in two hours."

"Okay. Throw a stone in the Seine for me."

"I will."

"A big one. Make a splash."

They met four years ago. He was on the banks of the Seine just down from the Eiffel Tower, throwing rocks in the water, ostensibly just a guy out killing time on an all-too-rare sunny Parisian day, not a guy stalking his next target, who was on the right bank, up fifty meters.

She strolled by.

Their eyes locked.

Rail knew even before his first breath exhaled that he could never consider his life lived unless he knew this woman, what she liked, what she hated, where she grew up and most importantly what she felt like in the dark when her body trembled and sex poured out of her every breath.

She offered him a cigarette.

He took it but didn't light up and instead inserted it carefully in his shirt pocket.

"I don't smoke," he said. "I'm going to save this for you for later."

"There's a later?"

"Yes."

He handed her a rock and pointed to a plastic bottle floating down the river, twenty meters off shore.

"See that green guy?"

"Yes."

"First one to hit it gets to choose position," he said.

She studied him.

Then the corner of her mouth turned up ever so slightly. She twisted the rock in her hand until it was best positioned and then threw.

Her aim was terrible.

Rail's wasn't.

That was four years ago.

Now it was today. Payment made, Rail called at the appointed time and said, "Give me 200,000 Euros worth of words."

"No problem," Emmanuelle said. "An FBI profiler by the name of Leigh Sandt has been asking about you. She thinks you might be connected to two cases in America; the murder of a San Francisco woman named Kelly Nine a year ago, and the abduction of a woman named Susan Smith from a Denver club a few nights ago."

Rail paced.

"How did she connect me?"

"Unknown, other than she was looking for someone named Rail," Emmanuelle said. "Although she's with the FBI, it's technically not an FBI investigation. She's helping a Denver homicide detective by the name of Nick Teffinger. He's the one who wants you."

"Nick Teffinger?"

"Yes, do you know him?"

"Let's just say we have some history together."

"Well, he has the whole INTERPOL file on you," she said. "So watch your back."

"You sent it?"

"No, not me personally, I would never do anything like that," she said. "Blanc is the one who talked to the FBI woman. He's the one who sent the file. So, was the price fair?"

"Unfortunately, it was. Call me if anything else comes up."

"You know I will."

He almost hung up when muffled words came from the phone.

"Rail, you still there?"

"Yes."

"I have a question."

"Go ahead."

"After you went to America, did you meet a woman? You know, someone like me?"

He focused on the distance, deciding whether to lie or tell the truth.

His instinct was the former.

She deserved the latter.

"I met someone but no one's like you and never will be," he said.

"Are you still with her?"

"No. I didn't work out."

"Maybe you should come back to Paris some day."

He nodded.

"Maybe I will."

His eyes narrowed. Only a handful of people knew he killed Kelly Nine. The people who knew he abducted Susan Smith were likewise limited.

Only one person knew about both.

That person was Oscar Benderfield.

57

Jori-Lee and Sanders caught the first available flight Monday morning from Miami to D.C., a pre-dawn deal so pre that it was almost a red-eye. Jori-Lee went straight to work from the airport, which got her to One First a mere forty-five minutes late, hardly enough to raise an eyebrow, although one did come up. It belonged to Robertson's secretary, a Marilyn Monroe type actually named Marilyn—the third of that genre to occupy that space if the rumors were true.

"Morning," she said.

"Back at you."

Robertson's door was closed.

Jori-Lee nodded at it and said, "Is he in?"

"Yes. He was in your officer earlier."

"About what?"

"I don't know. He's in one of his moods though; so be warned."

"How much of a mood?"

The woman leaned forwards and lowered her voice. "I've already got my asbestos underwear on."

Jori-Lee walked down the all-too-familiar paneled corridor, past the closed-door offices of the other two law clerks to her space, which was just before the kitchen and across from the library. The carpet was thick, pure wool and imported from England— green, the color of money. The static buildup never went away. She left the door open, plopped down in the worn leather chair behind her desk and touched a brass banker's lamp to get rid of the electricity.

Files were everywhere; on the desk, on the credenza, on the windowsill and on the floor, all patiently awaiting justice.

Her phone rang, not the desk phone, the cell.

It was Sanders.

She closed the door.

"Did you see the morning paper?" he said.

"No."

"Page eight. A woman's body was found yesterday in a dumpster."

"T'amara Alder?"

"That would be my guess," Sanders said. "The article doesn't give a name. Now that I'm physically in D.C., I'm getting more concerned that the guy who killed her will see you as a threat. I'm going to stake out your place today from across the street and see if anything weird happens."

"Be careful."

"Don't go there under any circumstances. When you're ready to leave at the end of the day call me and we'll make arrangements."

Suddenly a knock came at the door.

It opened and Robertson's face appeared.

He was intense, no play, all business.

"Got a second?" he said.

58

The flight back to Denver gave Teffinger the opportunity to get all the bark and bite out of his brain. Viewing things with a new calm, however, didn't bring a calm conclusion; in fact, the opposite. Given that someone hired Rail to kill Kelly Nine, and given that someone ripped apart a magpie and spread it out at Del Rey's house, Teffinger couldn't help but think that something personal might be going on.

Someone might be trying to make him suffer by killing his girlfriends.

Del Rey might be in more danger than he initially thought.

Admittedly the theory didn't fit perfectly. There had been lots of lovers between Kelly Nine and Del Rey who hadn't been harmed or threatened. Still, even without a perfect fit, the theory continued to stab the inside of Teffinger's head with jagged little blades.

Who hated him that much?

It could relate to a past case, although when he

tried to pull them up they were all shadows and none emerged with a commanding clarity.

It could relate to a past woman.

Maybe someone who portrayed herself as single really hadn't been. Maybe Teffinger inadvertently replaced someone and that someone didn't take too kindly to it. If he couldn't have a lover then neither could Teffinger. Maybe he was out there in the shadows taking his revenge.

Again though, when Teffinger tried to color in the lines, no color came. All he could get was the outline of a theory without any weight.

Outside, the plane's jets droned.

Other than that, Teffinger might as well be in his living room. The wings didn't roll, the nose didn't pitch, and not a single erratic wisp of wind touched the aircraft in any way that it shouldn't. Outside the window, insanely far below, rectangular farms and string-thin roads slowly came into view and then slowly disappeared behind.

It was calm.

His palms didn't sweat.

His chest didn't pound.

He closed his eyes.

His thoughts drifted to Kelly Nine.

Kelly Nine.

To this day Teffinger still couldn't figure out how her killer—Rail—got her out of Teffinger's bed without him hearing it, feeling it, sensing it or knowing a thing about it. Sure, he'd had a few beers that night, plus rock-star sex, but he wasn't passed out. He was sleeping, deeply albeit, but only sleeping.

However the guy did it, he had guts. It took a special kind of fortitude to abduct a woman right out of another man's bed.

How did he keep Kelly so quiet during the whole thing?

The logical answer is that he knocked her out with a chemical soaked cloth to the mouth. No forensic residues were found, however, which they would have been had that been the case. No did he stab her in her sleep and lift her out. That would have left blood on the pillow and sheets and probably even Teffinger. There was no such blood, not in the bed or anywhere else in the house.

To this day he didn't know how she died.

The body had yet to be found.

He exhaled.

These were old thoughts.

He'd been through them over and over and over and over.

They were always the same.

The plane bumped, barely a hiccup.

The motion was an electrical charge to Teffinger's heart.

His pulse quickened.

His breaths came quicker.

He opened his eyes.

Everything in the cabin was normal. That didn't mean the plane hadn't started to unravel. It didn't mean they wouldn't be in a death spiral five minutes from now. He concentrated. Nothing weird came.

Turbulence, that's probably all it was.

He closed his eyes.

Then something happened, something he didn't expect. A vision jumped into his brain, a new vision. In it, Kelly Nine was sleeping peacefully on her back. Suddenly Rail's hand came to the woman's throat and tightened with a python hold. She woke and looked up. Rail waved a gun in front of her face and looked hard into her eyes.

She knew those eyes.

She knew the ponytail.

She didn't move.

He motioned for her to get out of bed.

She did, quietly.

Then they left; she in front with Rail's gun jabbed in her back.

The plane dropped, twenty or thirty feet, and then crashed on an invisible floor of air.

Teffinger's eyes sprang open.

The pilot's voice came over the intercom. They were going to experience some turbulence. Everyone should return to their seats and fasten their seat belts.

Teffinger's belt was already on.

He cinched it tighter and put the armrests in a death-grip.

Kelly Nine knew Rail.

That's why she left voluntarily with him.

59

Kelly Nine knew Rail. That's why she left voluntarily with him. She stayed quiet because she knew how dangerous he was and that he'd kill Teffinger without so much as a blink if she woke him. That's the theory that twisted around inside Teffinger's head as the plane dropped out of swirling charcoal skies and landed fitfully but intact on a long skinny patch of DIA asphalt.

Twenty minutes later in the west-parking garage he eventually remembered what level he parked the Tundra on and found it intact and without door dings.

He slipped inside and turned the key.

The engine fired.

The radio kicked on.

> I don't care if Monday's black,
> Tuesday, Wednesday heart attack,
> Thursday never looking back,
> It's Friday I'm in love.

He sang along, yet again in awe that anyone could write a song so perfect. It was right up there with Duran Duran's Rio or The Beach Boys' Don't Worry Baby. He knew the name of the group at one point but couldn't get it to the front of his brain. It would come to him later when he didn't want it any more.

Wait, The Cure.

That's who sang it, The Cure.

Kelly Nine knew Rail. She stayed quiet because she knew how dangerous he was and that he'd kill Teffinger without so much as a blink if she woke him.

It made sense but wasn't a perfect fit. That's because Rail was a man at the top of his game. If he'd been hired to kill Kelly, why would he show his face beforehand? Why would he let her know him? If there was any order to the universe, that's the last thing he would have done.

Maybe she didn't know Rail.

Maybe she simply looked into his eyes and detected how dangerous he was.

Confusing, that's what it was.

The Colorado sky was crystal clean and filled with a light that injected straight into Teffinger's blood. He could never live in a place like D.C., not in a million years. He'd rather live in a box.

The Cure left the radio.

Junk came on in their place.

Teffinger punched the buttons a half-dozen times before closing it down altogether.

Then, heading up Pena Boulevard, a thought came to him.

It was a strange, strange thought.

There was no way it could actually be true.

So why did it beat like a city full of tom-toms inside his chest?

He knew the reason.

It was because Kelly Nine was an attractive woman.

It was because Rail was an attractive man.

It was because nature always took its course.

He called Nadia Nine, Kelly's sister, who answered on the third ring, and said, "It's me, Teffinger."

"Teff? Is that really you?"

"Yes," he said. "I have a quick question for you. Did Kelly ever mention a man named Rail to you?"

A beat then, "No."

"How about Javier Arcos?"

"No."

"Are you sure?"

"Yes."

"Was she dating anyone before she got killed?"

The woman exhaled. "Teff, no. You've already asked me that a hundred times. What's going on? Who's Rail?"

"Did she know a man with long hair? Someone who may have worn it in a ponytail?"

"I don't know."

"Think."

"Nothing's coming to mind."

"Did she know anyone from Portugal or from Europe?"

Silence, then, "It's strange that you ask that. She was talking about maybe going to Paris."

"With who?"

"I don't know," she said.

"With somebody?"

"She didn't mention anyone."

Teffinger exhaled.

Kelly wasn't one to do anything by herself.

"Do you still have her personal effects?"

Yes, she did.

They were in the garage.

An hour and a half later Teffinger was in Fort Collins going through box after box of Kelly's personal effects, down to his last ounce of hope and doubting the sanity of his theory.

Then he found something interesting.

It was a shoebox full of photos.

One picture stood out.

It was taken in an apartment at night, possibly a San Francisco apartment. A man was holding a stiff-arm and open hand in front of his face to block the shot. His head was turned 90-degress, as if jerking away. His eyes and nose and mouth and cheeks and forehead and in fact his entire face was out of sight behind the hand.

What wasn't covered was a ponytail.

It stuck out clear as sin.

Rail, Teffinger said.

60

Back at homicide Teffinger scanned the photo and emailed it to Leigh Sandt with a short explanation where it came from and the fact that the face behind the hand belonged to Rail. Leigh called almost immediately and said, "What have you done so far to enhance the reflection?"

"What reflection?"

She told him.

He pulled the image up on his phone and took a closer look. Sure enough, the man's face reflected ghost-like in the hollows of a black window, barely noticeable but noticeable nonetheless.

"That's why I'm sending it to you," he said. "To get that enhanced."

"Then why'd you say, What reflection?"

"Just to see if you really noticed."

"Whatever. Just for the record, though, your nose is growing."

"That's not unusual."

An hour later she called and said, "Check your emails."

He did.

One was from her.

Attached was a JPEG of a face, a chiseled manly face that was built to break hearts and take the world by storm; a face that was in Kelly Nine's apartment at one point.

"I'm going to send a copy to INTERPOL and have them run it past their contacts," Leigh said, "just to be sure it's him."

"No."

"No?"

"Yes, no," he said. "It's him. You can already count on that."

"So what's the problem with getting verification?"

"The problem is Susan Smith," he said. "INTER-POL is too big. They're going to get all excited and start chasing the guy like an elephant after a mouse. If he's the one who took Susan Smith—and I'm pretty sure he is—and if by some miracle she's actually still alive, he'll kill her the minute he hears the elephant coming and, trust me, he will."

"Okay."

"Okay what?"

"Okay, our secret, at least for a few days."

The corner of his mouth turned up.

"I owe you one."

"Add three zeros and you're halfway there."

He smiled.

The minute he hung up the smile fell from his face.

Every word he said about Susan Smith was true. Deep down where the dark devils lived though, he had to wonder if it was equally about getting a legitimate opportunity to kill Rail for what he did to Kelly Nine.

Sydney suddenly appeared in front of his desk and slipped a cup of coffee to him as she eased into a chair.

"There, the order of the world is restored," she said.

Teffinger took a sip.

It was hot.

It was good, not as good as the first four or five cups in the early morning, but what was?

He showed her the photo and said, "That's Rail."

She studied the face.

"Don't ever stand next to him," she said. "You'll be ugly."

Teffinger grunted.

"Good, because I feel ugly. He actually took her out at least once in San Francisco before he came to Denver and killed her," he said.

"Why?"

He shrugged.

"A cat playing with a mouse? I don't know—"

"It doesn't make sense," Sydney said. "Getting involved with a victim-to-be, even if just for a night or two, makes the risk go through the roof. If he really is the professional he's supposed to be, he wouldn't do that, not in a hundred years, not even in cat-years." A pause then, "Unless—"

Teffinger cocked his head.

"Unless what?"

"Unless that was part of his orders," she said. "You said someone hired him, right?"

"Right."

"Maybe that person not only wanted her dead but wanted to break her heart in the process. Maybe Rail's mission was to win her over, then show up one night with a serious face and tell her he was going to kill her, and why. Not only would she be facing death at that point but it would be coming from the very person she trusted and loved. The pain would be double."

"Who'd want to break her heart? An old boyfriend?"

Sydney shrugged.

"Could be. Tit for tat or something like that," she said. "Listen to me, I'm a poet and don't know it."

Teffinger downed what was left of the coffee, glanced out the window at the sky and said, "Your theory assumes she was the target. I've been wondering if maybe I was the target."

Sydney smiled, amused, and then realized he was serious.

He made his case.

She wasn't impressed.

"If you were the target you'd be the one dead, not her," she said. "She was the target. Everything's not about you, Teffinger."

The sky was beginning to cloud up.

"I hate planes," he said.

He called Del Rey at the law office. The tone in her voice indicated everything was normal; no bird rippers were at the forefront. "Tonight's going to be problematic," he said.

"Teff, don't you dare cancel on me."

"Trust me, it's the last thing I want to do. Unfortunately I have to make a run to San Francisco."

"Why?"

He explained.

Rail had been there.

Hopefully he'd left tracks.

"I'm coming with you," she said.

"I'll be back tomorrow, Wednesday for sure."

"Repeat, I'm coming with you."

He went to argue but suddenly had an image of the bird ripper grabbing her by the throat in the middle of the night, knowing that Teffinger was a light-year away. He said, "Okay."

"Really?"

"Really. We're leaving right now though. I'll swing by."

61

Got a minute? The words were plain vanilla as they came out of Robertson's mouth but they ricocheted like a hundred crazy yells inside Jori-Lee's head. Something was up, something bad. They took a long, endless walk down the corridor and ended up in his chambers with the thick, seven-foot oak door shut, which was a rarity even when the most delicate of discussions were at issue.

He ran his fingers through his hair and frowned.

A fierce litigator in his early years, he quickly outgrew the commonality of private practice and found himself a rising star in the district attorney's office in Denver, Colorado. There he sat first-chair for an uninterrupted string of first-degree homicide convictions and got known within the bar and bench as Junkyard, short for the Dog version. From there his white smile and firm handshake and favor-trading served as a springboard to the governor's chair.

He made friends.

He made enemies.

He made more of the first than the second.

His footprint spread outside Colorado, far outside.

That got him the Supreme nomination.

Now, ten years later, his presence still filled any room he was in. He could turn on the charm with all the force of a waterfall when he wanted to and, in most moments of the day, he did. Those who knew him better, however, were familiar with his more abrasive side. Those who knew him even better had learned how to avoid that more abrasive side.

Right now, sitting at his desk, that abrasive side was just below the surface, so close to busting through that it was almost a third person in the room.

"This isn't going to be easy for me," he said. "Allow me to show you something."

With that he fired up something on his computer.

It was Jori-Lee dressed in all things black, sneaking her way through Robertson's mansion during a dark night, obviously shot from security cameras she knew nothing about.

"I've been debating long and hard how to handle this," he said. "There are two ways we can do it. One, I can turn this over to the FBI, you can get disbarred before you even get admitted to practice, and you can spend a few nice years learning what jail food tastes like." He exhaled. "I'm assuming that's not your life goal. Am I right?"

Her breath didn't come.

Her body didn't move.

She nodded.

"I didn't think so," he said. "The other way we can handle this is first and foremost for you to return the flash drive and any and all copies you made of it. Did you make any?"

She nodded.

"I thought so," he said. "Who's seen them besides you?"

Sanders Tripp, that was the answer.

It was also an answer she would never give.

"No one," she said.

"No one?"

"No one."

He studied her with lawyer eyes, looking for lies. She wasn't sure whether he saw them or not. She could only hope they were masked by the sweat on her face and the tremor of her fingers.

"Do you agree to give them back?"

She nodded.

"Say it!"

"Yes."

"That's a smart answer," he said. "You're going to get a call today from an attorney by the name of Leland Everitt, who's with Overton & Frey. You've heard of that firm, I assume."

Yes, she had.

Everyone had.

It was one of the most powerful firms in D.C. and had offices all over the world.

"He's going to offer you a job," Robertson said.

"It's going to be very lucrative. It's going to be for a lot more money than you get here. You can't resist the offer. You're going to tender your resignation to me by the end of the day. I'm going to accept it." He leaned forward. "Now, here's the important part. My name is to never cross your lips again. You don't say anything about me to anyone for any reason. So now the choice is yours. One or two, which suits you better?"

Something snapped

Lightning filled her blood.

She stood up.

"You killed T'amara Alder," she said. "Either that or you hired someone to kill her which is the same thing. You did it so she wouldn't tell the world about all your sick little pervert nights." She hardened her face. "You want to go to the FBI? Really? That's what you want to do? Well then let me tell you something, go ahead and do it."

She walked calmly to the door, paused halfway through and said over her shoulder, "I was trying to help you. That's all gone now. Have a nice life."

She closed the door gently behind her.

Marilyn Monroe stared at her.

"Please tell Mr. Robertson that I'm quitting, effective immediately," Jori-Lee said.

Then she left.

62

The lights of San Francisco were just beginning to twinkle when Teffinger and Del Rey touched down at SFI. They took a jerky cab ride into the heart of the concrete, checked into the InterContinental and ended up dangling their feet over the water at the end of Pier 39 as they passed a bottle of wine back and forth. Deep shadows were quickly morphing into a black, black night. The air was still and unusually warm.

"I grew up here until high school," Teffinger said. "All my kid years were here."

"I didn't know that."

"I think in a way that may be why Kelly Nine moved here. She always asked me about it. I built it up probably more than it deserved."

Del Rey took a swig of wine.

"Do you miss it?"

He shrugged.

"San Francisco's a watercolor. Denver's an oil painting. They're both good in their own ways." A beat then, "I will admit though, when I lived here things were a lot simpler. I was a lot more innocent back then. I miss that. I miss baseball caps and hanging around Fisherman's Wharf and seeing everything through eyes that didn't understand much yet."

Del Rey squeezed his hand.

"Are you going to kill Rail, assuming you find him?"

"That'll be up to him."

She hesitated and then said, "Did you love Kelly?"

"Kelly's in the past."

"So was I once."

"Yeah but you're not now."

"No, I'm not. Actually, I think it's kind of romantic."

He cocked his head.

"What's romantic?"

"You hunting down the person who killed Kelly," she said. "I wonder if you'll do the same thing if someone kills me."

"No one's going to kill you."

"What about the bird ripper?"

Teffinger frowned.

"I still can't figure that one out."

"You said before he was someone from your past, maybe out to get you by getting your lovers."

"I know."

"And?"

"I've busted my brain a hundred different ways and still don't have a clue who could be crazy enough to hate me that much."

"Someone though."

He shrugged.

"Maybe, maybe not."

A pause, then Del Rey said, "Well, if you are right and Kelly was the first and I'm going to be the second, then the person who hired Kelly is the same one who's after me now."

"True."

"So, if that person hired Rail the first time, there's a good chance he hired him this time too. Why mess with a formula that's already worked fine once?"

"Are you saying Rail's the bird ripper?"

"I think I am."

Teffinger brought the bottle to his lips and took a swallow.

"Interesting," he said.

Few people were around.

Fifty steps away, leaning against a pole in the deep shadows up the pier, someone was lighting matches and tossing them to the ground.

He was alone, not much more than a black silhouette framed against a slightly less-black background.

"How long has that guy been there?" Teffinger said.

"What guy?"

She looked in that direction, seeing nothing until a match struck.

"Weird," she said.

"I can't tell if he has a ponytail," Teffinger said. "Can you?"

She studied the shape.

"Maybe if he moved—"

Teffinger got to his feet.

"Wait here."

"Teff—"

"I'll be right back."

With each step electricity arced deeper and deeper into Teffinger's body. The man was Rail. Teffinger could smell him. He could hear the man's jagged heart beating. He could taste the man's disease.

It didn't make sense that Rail would know where they were.

They just got into the city hours ago.

Still, it wasn't impossible.

He might have been staking out either Teffinger or Del Rey. He might have followed them to the airport. He might have even flown out on the same plane.

Teffinger didn't have his gun.

He didn't have a knife.

He didn't have anything.

That didn't stop him.

He kept walking, picking up the pace faster and faster.

When he got to the mark no one was there. A black hole hung where the man should be.

A feint patina of burnt sulfur hung in the air.

On the ground was a shape.

A closer look showed it to be a dead seagull.

The bird's wings had been ripped off.

The gooey blood was still fresh.

The man was nowhere to be seen.

Teffinger ran.

Fifty sprints later the man still hadn't come into

sight.

He ran faster.

No one appeared.

The man was a ghost.

Suddenly a dark, dark thought bit Teffinger's brain.

Del Rey was alone.

She was alone in the dark.

He turned and sprinted that way.

63

When Jori-Lee told Sanders what transpired in Robertson's office, he frowned and said, "You played it all wrong."

"What do you mean?"

"You burned your bridges."

"I don't care," she said. "Fuck him and fuck all the freaks he rode in on."

"I'm not talking about the bridges to staying there," he said. "I'm talking about the bridges to bringing him down."

The words made no sense.

She scrunched her face to prove it.

"Look," Sanders said, "obviously this lawyer who was going to call you and make a job offer—"

"—Leland Everitt—"

"—Right, Leland Everitt, obviously he's in bed with Robertson. He's covering the man's ass."

That was true.

"So what?"

"So, if he's in bed with him as to you, he was probably in bed with him as to T'amara Alder."

The words landed with an electric bite.

She flashed back to that terrible moment when the woman was murdered while Jori-Lee listened to it through her phone.

"Are you saying Leland Everitt killed T'amara?"

Sanders shrugged.

"What I'm saying is that you had a chance to get close to the man and find out."

She retreated in thought.

Sanders was right.

She'd been so wrapped up in the fear of being turned over to the FBI and the rage against being forced out of her job that she didn't think it through.

She looked at Sanders and said, "I'm going back to One First."

"What for?"

"To reverse it."

"How?"

"I'll tell him I've reconsidered," she said. "I'll take the original flash drive with me. I'll tell him that it's his as soon as Leland Everitt calls me. We'll part friends." A beat then, "Do you think he'll figure out what I'm up to?"

Sanders faded off.

Then he focused and said, "He didn't get to where he is by being stupid. Still, he's the one who opened the door. We'll just have to wait and see how it all plays out. What you need to be sure of is that you really want to put your life on the line. If my suspicion is right, Leland Everitt is an even bigger snake than Robertson. He's the one with the guts to get the dirty work done."

DAY EIGHT

July 15
Tuesday

64

Teffinger twisted and gyrated his way through an evil fitful sleep Monday night, dropping in and out of a frantic dream where the bird ripper made his way back to Del Rey before Teffinger could intercept him. In hindsight, that was the man's plan—to get noticed flicking matches, to draw Teffinger away, to circle back and do whatever sick little thing it was that he had planned for Del Rey, right under Teffinger' nose—just like Kelly Nine.

Teffinger fell for it but not for as long as he should have.

He made it back before the ugly jumped.

At the hotel they were so glad to be alive and unharmed that they took each other with the energy of an apocalypse.

That was last night.

Now it was morning.

Del Rey put on a no-big-deal face and did her best to hide that she was shaking with apprehension down at the core. She showered first, stepped out with a towel around her waist and said, "So what's the plan for today?"

Teffinger dropped to his knees and kissed her stomach.

"I'm thinking we should break up," he said. "We should go down to the lobby and have a fight. You slap me like the bastard I am, tell me to screw off forever and jump in a cab to the airport. You go somewhere you've never been. You hire a bodyguard and keep your head down."

She ran her fingers through his hair.

"And then what?

"And then you wait."

"Wait for what? Wait for him to kill you? Wait for him to find me?"

"Wait for things to get safe."

"Which is how long? For all we know he'll go on vacation for a year and then show up when we've forgotten all about him."

Teffinger frowned.

"All I know is that right now the most dangerous job in the world is being my lover."

She pulled him up, hugged him tight and said, "In that case I want hazardous duty pay. But whether you give it to me or not, I'm not quitting and I'm certainly not going to let you fire me."

He exhaled.

She was right.

The plan could backfire as easily as it could work.

The distance could be the worst thing, not the

best.

"Promise me one thing," he said.

"Which is what?"

"Which is at some point down the road, you'll let me win at least one argument."

She smiled.

"We'll see. You were a little rough last night—"

"Sorry."

"That wasn't a complaint."

Outside a blanket of fog floated over the city and blotted out everything nice. It forced a song into Teffinger's brain, a haunting song he played over and over back when he was an angst-filled teen trying to learn how to work a cheap guitar.

I see a red door and I want to paint it black.

No colors anymore I want them to turn black.

They ended up on Market in the heart of the financial district, winding through revolving doors into an opulent lobby with modern art on the walls that looked as if it had been thrown there. At the elevator bank Teffinger said, "Meet me on fifteen."

"Why, where you going?"

"I'm taking the stairs."

"To fifteen?"

He nodded.

"Why?"

"I like stairs, that's all."

"Well if you're taking them so am I," she said.

The climb wasn't as bad as Teffinger envisioned. At thirteen he said, "There's a lot more air here than in Denver."

"Tell that to my thighs. They're on fire."

Teffinger grunted.

"You said before it was romantic that I was hunting down Kelly's killer," he said. "I should have corrected you. I never did what I should have."

"What does that mean?"

"She got taken from my home in Lakewood," he said. "Lakewood had jurisdiction over the case, not Denver. I wasn't officially involved in the investigation, although they kept me in the loop. They never flew to San Francisco where Kelly lived at the time to personally talk to anyone. They only interviewed people by phone."

"So?"

"So, I could have flown out and done that in an ad hoc capacity," he said. "I didn't do it."

"Yeah but they did talk to everyone, right?"

"As far as I know," he said. "But phone and face are two different things. I should have come out when they didn't. I was drowned in work and convinced myself that's why I wasn't going. That wasn't the real reason, though. The real reason is that it just hurt too much. Instead of manning up and taking it, I let the pain turn into a wall. Then I hid the wall behind my work."

"You're human Teffinger," she said. "We all are. Don't apologize for it. Plus, you're here now."

He nodded. That was true.

"Just out of curiosity, is the pain still there?" she said.

He considered it.

"Yes but not as much. That's the problem with time. It robs you of things. I work too hard to get those things to have them robbed."

Floor thirteen held the offices of b.Box-Media, the advertising firm where Kelly worked at the time she was murdered.

They pushed through an ornate copper door embedded in an illuminated block-glass wall. Inside a too-cute receptionist with a too-white smile sat at a too-contemporary desk.

A narrow rectangular vase held one flower, a yellow rose.

A folded card was tucked under the base.

Perfume punctuated the air, more in the nature of vanilla strawberries than burning tires.

"Kelly Nine used to work here a year ago," Teffinger said. "I'd like to talk to whoever it was that was her best friend here at the time."

The woman studied him.

The smile dropped from her face.

"You're Nick Teffinger," she said.

"Right."

"There's a rumor you're the one who killed her," she said. "They said it was a lover's spat. Being a detective, you knew how to cover it up."

Teffinger tossed a photo of Rail on the desk.

"That's the guy who killed her. His name is Javier Arcos but he goes by the name Rail. He's from Portugal. Have you ever seen him before?"

The woman rose.

"No. Wait here."

She disappeared around a corner.

Teffinger hesitated for a heartbeat; then he swept after her.

65

In the flesh Leland Everitt didn't turn out anything like what Jori-Lee expected, which was a chiseled-faced alpha-male wolf pouncing at some helpless prey with barred yellow fangs. He was the opposite—shorter than average, a body that would be lucky to crank out five push-ups, a face made for radio, a forehead that was slowly creeping up his skull and a slightly-crooked tie. His manner was timid and unassuming, almost shy.

His office was large, opulent and old school, replete with mahogany built-ins, lush patterned carpeting and expensive oil paintings.

In that office with the door shut Tuesday morning. he told Jori-Lee, "I'll be honest, I have a lot of pull within the firm, but it's more of a democracy around here than a dictatorship. What that means is that I don't have carte blanche authority to hire lawyers. There's a process that has to unfold. So, the way we're going to have to proceed is to say that you contacted me. That's because I can't have a perception on the street that we're robbing One First of its talent.

The story is that after you contacted me we met, I liked what I saw and I'm bringing you in to meet the crew as a prospective addition to the firm."

"I was supposed to have a job," Jori-Lee said. "That's what Robertson said."

Lee nodded.

"And you will, and you will. We just have to stay within the structure. At the end of the day tomorrow, you'll have an offer. You can accept it if you want and, if you do, I look forward to having you around here and watching you mature into a partnership position. Or you can reject it. The choice is yours. My secretary, Anabella, will be taking you around today to meet some of the lawyers. You'll be joining six of us for lunch at The Palm at 11:30. Are you up for all of that?"

"Yes."

"Good."

The day turned into a blur of rotations in and out of offices populated with faces that were all etched to one degree or another with competence, a high work ethic and, to a more hidden degree, exhaustion. It wasn't until the end of the day that one of those faces broke the mold.

It belonged to Zahara Knox, a petite black-haired beauty with golden island-girl skin and no wedding ring on her finger.

Behind a closed door she leaned forward and said, "You look like a nice person so I'm going to do you a favor. Don't join this firm. Run like hell. Go anywhere you want but don't come here. Trust me, you'll be better off."

Jori-Lee cocked her head.

"Why? What's so wrong?"

The woman stood up, escorted Jori-Lee to the door said, "I've already said too much. Be a friend and don't tell anyone what I said."

"I won't."

"Thank you."

66

Tuesday morning Rail woke to find San Francisco encased in fog and the streets already neurotic with headlights. He pulled his hair into a ponytail, tucked it under a baseball hat and headed out for a jog down Haight Street. The salty air filled his chest like medicine. He needed to do what needed to be done and then get out of town before anyone recognized him.

The concrete was hard under his feet.

It jolted up his shins and into his knees.

He didn't care.

Pain was good.

Pain was nature's way of reminding you that you were still alive.

He passed a flower shop, the same one where he bought a yellow rose for Kelly a year ago. The thought of her popped an image into his brain, an image so clear and detailed that it was if he was right there.

———

A terrible storm pounded down on Denver. Jagged rips of lightning shredded the coal-black sky again and again and again, slamming shut with monstrous explosions that rumbled all the way to infinity. Rail took shelter as best he could, in the dark, hunched in a ball against the backside of Teffinger's house.

The Rocky Mountain air was thin.

Even though it was the middle of summer the night was cold. The rain was an onslaught of chilly little needles working their way into Rail's skin and then drilling deeper into his bones.

He shivered.

He willed himself to stop.

It didn't work.

In his hand was a pink SIG with a silencer. Ordinarily he wouldn't let a piece of art like that get wet in a million years.

This was no ordinary night.

The storm was actually a good thing. It kept the neighbors inside. It kept the dogs and coyotes away. It kept the rattlesnakes away.

Minute after minute passed, followed by a half-hour, followed by an hour.

Nothing happened.

Teffinger didn't show up.

No one else showed up.

Everything stayed frozen in time.

Then time changed.

Headlights punched up the street and pulled into Teffinger's driveway. The garage door came up, the vehicle entered, the door swung down.

The interior lights turned on.

Rail wedged back into a deeper shadow.

Teffinger went to the kitchen, got a beer for himself and a glass of white wine for the woman—Kelly Nine—and then turned off the lights as they headed for the couch.

They were visible at first, two black silhouettes raising drinks to their mouths and fondling each other. Then they dropped horizontal and molded into one indiscernible shape.

Rail crept closer to the window and waited for lightning.

It came.

The flash lasted only a bite of a second but was long enough to bring the shapes into clear view. The woman was naked now, stretched out on the couch with her arms up above her head. Teffinger had his lips and tongue on her stomach, making her hips gyrate.

Rail's heart pounded.

He waited for the next flash.

It took forever but when it came, the shapes were on the carpet now. Teffinger was on his back. The woman was straddling his hips and riding him for all she was worth. Her face was pointed away from Rail but he could picture it.

He'd seen it before from the other angle, many times in fact.

67

Kelly Nine's best friend at b.Box-Media turned out to be to a contemporary, late-20s Chinese woman named Dandan Phon, who Teffinger remembered talking to on the phone at one point but couldn't remember about what. Her face was confident, her dress was urban-chic, her facial expressions were quick and her eyes were focused.

Teffinger explained who he was and why he was in town. He handed her the photo of Rail and said, "Have you ever seen this guy?"

"No, never."

"Are you sure?"

"Crystal."

"Did Kelly ever mention seeing someone—a man, I mean, romantically?"

"No."

"No one?"

"If she was seeing someone she never mention it to me." She focused on the photo, looked into Teffinger's eyes and said, "Is this the man who killed her?"

He nodded.

"Yes."

"He would be her type," she said. "Sort of like you."

Teffinger asked her questions from every angle

and on every possible tangent, got not a bit of useful information, then gave his cell phone number in case anything came to her later.

He talked to four other people equally without knowledge of anything and then left.

Five minutes away he got a call.

It was from her, Dandan.

She wanted to meet for lunch.

She told him where and when.

"Come alone," she said. "Don't bring anyone with you. Can you do that?"

"Yes."

Shortly after noon, with Del Rey safely tucked back in the hotel room, Teffinger stepped off a trolley in the heart of Chinatown and made his way to Chef Jia's, a hole-in-the-wall looking place on Kearny Street between Jackson and Columbus. Dandan waived at him from a back table.

"I already ordered for you," she said.

He sat down.

"So what am I having?"

"Egg rolls."

"Sounds reasonable."

She smiled and then got serious. "There's something I'd like to tell you, something that might help you," she said. "But I'm going to need you to keep it absolutely confidential."

He nodded.

"Sure."

"I'm serious about the confidentiality," she said.

"What I'm going to tell you is partly about me and some things I've done, some illegal things. If word ever got out I'd be ruined. My family would be shamed. So what I need you to do is convince me that you really mean it when you say you'll be confidential."

Teffinger poured tea from a spout into a little ceramic cup.

He took a sip.

It was hot, coffee-like, but way short.

"Let me put it like this," he said. "I don't give a shit what you did, what you're doing or what you're going to do in the future. The only thing I care about in the whole world is finding the man who I showed you in the picture. And it's not just to avenge Kelly, although that's a large part of it. He took someone else and she may still be alive, a Denver woman named Susan Smith. On top of that, he may be after me and/or my lady friend Del Rey, who you met back at the agency. So, rest assured that anything you may tell me about yourself is thoroughly and utterly trumped. Your sins or lack thereof are not on my radar and never will be, unless you're selling kids into slavery or something like that. Give me even a grain of sand that helps me and I'll be eternally thankful. But even if what you tell me doesn't help, rest assured that your words will end at my ears. Nothing will come back to haunt you, ever, as least not as a result of me." He cocked his head. "Was that convincing enough?"

She smiled.

It was slightly crooked, very sexy.

"Yes."

"Good, because I usually don't talk that long."

"I can tell."

The food arrived.

It was in bags.

Dandan grabbed hers, stood up and said, "Let's go."

"We're not eating here?"

"No, we'll eat in the car. I have something to show you."

In the alley behind the building Dandan slid behind the wheel of a red 911 Porsche Targa of the mid-80s era, back when the styling was still exceptional. She hiked up her skirt far enough to wedge the bag between her thighs.

"You're a car girl," Teffinger said. "I like that."

"I hate cars, especially this one. Put your seat belt on."

68

They headed north out of Chinatown with something always in their way, either the hundredth red light or a car or a construction crew or a diesel-stained bus or some hit-me-and-I'll-sue-you fool crisscrossing this way or that. Dandan worked the clutch and the bag of eggrolls, not saying much, rarely getting out of second gear. Teffinger tried to keep his eyes on the cityscape and off Dan-dan's thighs, succeeding most of the time.

"I'm still deciding if I'm going to do this," Dan-dan said.

"Do what?"

"Show you something," she said. "It's against my better judgment."

"It's too late now," Teffinger said. "You already bought me eggrolls."

She looked over.

The corner of her mouth turned up ever so slight-ly.

"Good point."

"There's no turning back," he said, "not with the eggroll rule in effect."

She smiled.

"I get trapped in it every time."

"It's a sneaky thing."

They crossed the Golden Gate Bridge, wound through the tourist-soaked shoreline of Sausalito and killed the engine in the parking lot of a large marina on the north end of town. Five minutes later they stepped aboard a 30-foot Island Packard sailboat at the far end of the third dock.

"Yours?" Teffinger said.

"Yes."

"I never pictured you as a sailor."

"Good because I'm not," she said. "I hate boats."

She inserted a key into a formidable padlock at the cabin door, led Teffinger down teak stairs into the guts of the vessel, closed the door behind them and turned on the lights. She unlocked a storage door near the floor under the front berth, pulled out sail repair material, then reached farther in and retrieved an aluminum case, 2-feet by 3-feet and half a foot thick.

It was heavy.

She wrestled it onto the galley table.

"What do you know about art?" she said.

"Actually I paint a little."

"Really?"

He nodded.

"Plein air landscapes, mostly."

"Are you any good?"

"I'm in a few galleries."

"Well, you may find this interesting, then."

She opened the top. Inside was a painting, an impressionist painting depicting a black sailboat near a beach. Heavy rolling clouds filled the sky, mimicking in size, tone and scale the waves below. Several black-silhouetted figures in a wavy foreground field were doing something, possibly approaching the boat or coming from it. The piece was set in warm tones.

"This is called View of the Sea at Scheveningen. It was painted in 1882 by a man named Vincent Van Gogh," she said. "You've heard of him, I assume."

Teffinger recognized the style.

"Are you saying this is an original?"

She nodded.

"It was stolen in 2002 out of the Van Gogh Museum in Amsterdam, together with another one of his paintings called Congregation Leaving the Reformed Church in Nuenen. If you believe the Internet, the two together are worth over 30 million dollars. This one, in my option, is the much nicer of the two."

"So what's it doing here in your boat?"

"That's a long story, a long dangerous story."

"You've officially gone from having my curiosity to having my full attention," he said.

"The story relates to Kelly Nine."

Teffinger nodded his head towards the painting.

"Is this why she's dead?"

"No."

"No?"

"No."

"Then why do I care about this?"

She exhaled, unscrewed a bottle of white wine, filled two plastic glasses half way and handed one to Teffinger. He was more in the mood for beer but took a sip.

It wasn't bad.

"You're still going to be confidential, right?" Dandan said.

"Nothing's changed."

She studied him, looking for lies or exaggerations. She must not have found any because she said, "Okay then, here's what's going on."

69

Zahara Knox, the associate who so darkly warned Jori-Lee to stay away from Overton & Frey, lived on the 18th floor of a contemporary high-rise smack in the heart of the matter. Tuesday night after dark, Jori-Lee knocked unannounced and unexpected on the woman's door. Zahara answered dressed in jeans and a T, with a glass of white wine in her left hand, not her first. Her look of surprise fell off quickly.

"Come in."

"Thanks."

The interior wasn't overwhelming by square footage, probably less than a thousand, but was open, ultra-contemporary and played to a wall of floor-to-ceiling windows that had a view all the way to London. A lady-day 33 LP spun on an honest-to-God record player, weaving a scratchy lament of love gone wrong. The vinyl had a slight warp as it spun. The needle rocked up and down as if was riding an ocean swell.

Zahara topped her glass off, poured one for Jori-Lee and said, "You're still thinking about Overton & Frey but what I said has you spooked. You want to know why I said what I said."

Jori-Lee took a sip.

"Something like that."

"Sorry but I can't help you."

"Why not?"

"Because I don't know you."

"Whatever you tell me remains between us," Jori-Lee said. "I promise you that."

The woman wasn't impressed.

"Like I said, I can't help you more that I already have."

Jori-Lee looked around.

"Nice place."

"It's a golden handcuff," Zahara said. "My advice is to not put one on."

Jori-Lee hesitated, not sure she should say was she was about to, and then said it. "The warning you're giving me relates to Leland Everitt, doesn't it?"

The woman's lips said nothing.

Her expression said plenty.

"You know something about him," Jori-Lee added. "What is it? What exactly is he up to?"

Zahara stood up, took the wine out of Jori-Lee's hand and said, "It's time for you to leave."

Jori-Lee walked to the door, turned halfway through and said over her shoulder, "See you at the firm tomorrow. Thanks for the wine."

Then she was gone.

Outside in the car she told Sanders, "The woman's scared to death to talk but whatever she knows definitely relates to Leland Everitt. If we can get what she knows, I think we'll be in a position to take him down."

"Together with Robertson?"

She nodded.

"He made his bed, so screw him."

Sanders exhaled.

"Will Zahara open up?"

Jori-Lee nodded.

"Eventually," she said. "She liked me well enough even at the first to give me a warning, albeit cryptic. Whatever it is she has inside her, it's dying to get out. Where else, if not to me? I just need to get her confidence level up that I won't betray her trust."

"That will take time."

"It better not. That's something we don't have."

70

Okay then, here's what's going on. With that, there in the wooden guts of the Island Packard with an original Van Gogh sitting on the galley table, Dandan took a sip of wine and said, "Kelly met a man."

"Rail," Teffinger said.

Dandan nodded.

"Yes, Rail. She'd been with him for three or four weeks before she told me about him, although there was a spring in her step that hadn't been there before so I already knew something was going on. Anyway, he made her promise to never tell anyone about him. He told her he was involved in black market art. IN-

TERPOL was after him as were a number of more nefarious characters relating to transactions that went less than perfectly smooth. To prove what he did, he showed her the Van Gogh. She did research on it and confirmed that it really was an original that had been stolen in 2002 and had never been recovered. It was on a number of stolen art registries."

"So she didn't care that he was a criminal?"

"No."

"That's not like her."

"To tell you the truth, I think she actually liked it," Dandan said. "She wasn't herself doing anything illegal but suddenly had this portal into a whole different world that hardly anyone ever saw. He gave her details."

"Did she ever tell them to you?"

"No."

Teffinger took a sip of wine.

"So what did she tell you, exactly?"

"She told me about him, she told me about the Van Gogh, she told me I was the only one who knew and that I had to promise to keep her trust."

"Did you?"

"Yes, I told no one," she said. "You're the first person I've breathed a word of this to. Anyway, I was worried about her, getting in with a criminal and all that. The whole thing just sounded so dangerous to me. When I asked her where the guy lived, she didn't know. She said he didn't ever want her over there in case someone came for him. He didn't want her to ever get caught in the crosshairs. They usually only met at her apartment. He would crisscross all over town and be absolutely sure no one was following him when he came over. After dark they'd go for walks but they'd stay in the shadows. They never went out to restaurants or bars or anything like that."

"Big spender—"

"Money wasn't the issue," Dandan said. "She loved the man."

Teffinger wrinkled his face.

"Goddamn it."

"I decided to do a little snooping around on Kelly's behalf," Dandan said. "One night when he left her apartment, I followed him."

"Did Kelly know?"

"No, she knew nothing. He led me to a shipyard way down south, past the airport. Hundreds of boats of all sizes were propped up on blocks either being stored or renovated or gutted for parts or whatever. It must have been okay to sleep over on them because a few people were, although not many. It turned out that Rail was staying on an old rusty tugboat that looked like it hadn't seen water in twenty years. It didn't totally shock me given what Kelly said about INTERPOL being after him. It was actually a good hideaway with a lot of escape routes."

"Did you tell Kelly?"

"No," Dandan said. "A week later, though, she mentioned that Rail was coming over that night. I took the opportunity to pay a visit to his place."

———

Dressed in a black hoodie and even blacker jeans, Dandan parked the 911 a full half mile from the shipyard and closed the distance on foot under a dark moonless sky. The wind was strong, rattling and whistling everything stupid enough to be in its path. Dandan hunched against it with the hood up and her hands in the pockets.

She hated cold.

She hated wind.

She hated dark places.

She hated grungy places.

She pressed forward with increasingly faster steps, determined to get the whole thing over with as quickly as possible now that she was actually going through with it. She didn't know what she expected to find.

Her blood raced.

She worked her way between ghostly hulls and menacing shapes, memorizing each one, focused on keeping her bearings and sense of direction. The wind smelled like rust and diesel and dried seaweed and abandonment. The ground was rock and gravel and scraps and rutty dirt, good enough to twist an ankle if she let it.

Rail's vessel was dark and dead when she got to it.

She threw a rock against the hull.

No one came out.

No voices shouted.

Propped against the side was a tall wobbly ladder made of two-by-fours. She pulled a flashlight out of her back pocket, ran the beam quickly up and down the wood and then killed it. She climbed up slowly in the dark, testing each rung and working to not get splinters.

Then she was up.

The deck was higher than she thought.

It was a long, long way down if she had to jump.

She brought the flashlight out and turned it on long enough to get oriented. Then it went back out. The cabin door was firmly locked. There were windows, lots of them, but breaking one was out of the question. A hatch near the front of the boat was propped open a couple of inches, enough to get her fingers under.

She pulled.

It didn't move.

She squatted and put her entire strength into it.

It fought her but eventually came up.

She crossed her chest, wedged her legs in and dropped down. The fall was farther than she expected. She powered on the flashlight and found herself in a windowless cavity of the vessel. The hatch was above her head by a considerable amount. If she jumped she might be able to grab an edge and hang on. She wasn't sure if she'd be able to muscle out from that position or not.

She swallowed.

The cavity was full of old junk on fabricated metal shelves—dinghy ropes, grimy chains, and rusty parts. Behind a metal door was a shallow cavity. Inside that cavity was a shiny aluminum case. She brought it out, set it on the floor and opened it up.

Inside was an impressionist painting.

It was the Van Gogh that Kelly told her about.

She ran the beam over it.

Her chest pounded.

This could change her life.

It could change her life forever.

She closed it up and put it back exactly as she found it. At the end of the cavity was a bulkhead door.

It was locked.

The only way out was through the hatch.

She turned the flashlight off, wedged it in her back pocket, positioned herself under the hatch and jumped for it.

She fell short by a good six inches.

She tried again.

She fell short again.

She was trapped.

She made a platform of junk, tall enough to let her jump and actually get a grip above.

It didn't matter.

She was able to hang but that was it.

She didn't have the strength to muscle her way up and out.

She was trapped.

Time passed.

Then the inevitable happened.

Rail came home.

Dandan wedged her body into the narrow cavity

with the Van Gogh and closed the door all but an inch, fearing it would latch and entomb her.

There was no darker blackness anywhere on earth.

The air passing in and out of her lungs sounded like a hissing snake bobbing its fangs in front of her face.

71

As Rail jogged up Haight he suddenly felt predator eyes drilling into the back of his head. He could be wrong. He'd had a number of false flashes in the past. He'd also had some that saved his life. His heart pounded. His instinct was to turn but he didn't. He kept jogging with his face pointed into the fog.

The important thing was to stay normal.

The important thing was to not drive the predator back into the shadows.

He continued at a steady pace for two blocks, crossed the street and continued in the same direction. A quarter mile later he turned left around a corner and ducked behind a parked van.

Nothing happened for thirty seconds.

Then a black sedan turned the corner.

Its lights were off.

It moved slowly.

Two figures were inside, one male and one female,

neither in good enough focus to make out features. The figure in the passenger seat—the female—brought a cigarette to her lips and took a deep drag.

The vehicle stopped at the first crossroad and hung there as if deciding which way to go.

Then it did a quick 180 and headed back.

72

Luckily, Rail never came into that part of the boat that night. In the morning I got smarter. I found a scrap piece of metal somewhat shaped like a hook. I tied it onto the end of a rope and tossed it time after time after time out the hatch until it finally caught on something. I was able to pull myself out, barely, but I did it. I untied the hook, threw it and the rope back into the boat and then pushed the hatch back down to where it had been originally. It was light out at the time but I don't think anyone saw me."

Teffinger frowned.

"You came back later and stole the painting," he said.

Dandan nodded.

"I did, but that didn't happen until after Kelly got taken out of your bed," she said. "It's not that I didn't want to steal it before then, I did, but I refrained myself. I thought Rail would think Kelly took it. I was afraid he'd kill her. After she died, though, I acted quickly, before Rail got scared and decided to leave town."

Teffinger took a long swallow of wine.

He smelled lies.

The more likely scenario was that Dandan took the painting before Kelly went to Denver. Rail thought Kelly was behind it, followed her there and pulled her out of Teffinger's bed to interrogate her. She knew nothing about it.

He killed her.

After all, that's what he'd been hired to do all along.

"So why are you telling me all of this now?" Teffinger said.

"I didn't say anything before because Kelly was already dead and there was nothing I could do to help her," she said. "Telling anyone about the painting would only risk my losing it."

"That's still true," Teffinger said.

The woman exhaled.

"I saw Rail on the street yesterday," she said. "I think he got onto me somehow."

"So you're looking for protection—"

"To a point," she said. "You're looking for Rail and he's looking for the painting. I figured you could use that information to your advantage somehow."

Teffinger swallowed what was left of the wine.

"Take me to his tugboat," he said.

"Right now?"

He nodded.

"Yes, right now."

Traffic was thick and talk was minimal as they headed south. En route Teffinger called Del Rey to be sure she was safe in the hotel room, which she was. Not only was the door locked but she'd pulled a couch in front of it. On the table in front of her was Teffinger's gun, fully loaded with the safety off.

"Don't let anyone in," Teffinger said. "No room service, no nobody."

"I won't."

"Promise me."

"Cross my heart."

"And hope to die?"

"No, and hope to live."

"Fair enough."

Teffinger turned his attention to Dandan.

"Look," he said. "I don't know if you told me the truth about stealing the painting after Kelly got murdered or whether you did it beforehand. There's something you should know though. If you did do it beforehand, that wasn't the reason Kelly got killed. Someone hired Rail to kill her. She was as good as dead from the first moment she met Rail."

The woman cast a glance his way.

"Nice to know but I didn't take it beforehand," she said. "I might be a greedy bitch but I don't put my friends in danger."

The words sounded sincere.

"What was Kelly up to before Rail entered the picture?"

"Meaning what?"

"Meaning someone wanted her dead badly enough to hire Rail to do it," he said. "If I knew who that person was, I'd be a giant step closer to Rail."

"She wasn't up to anything that I was aware of."

"I'm thinking that she either saw something she shouldn't have or learned something she shouldn't have," Teffinger said. "For some reason she became a threat to someone. It could have happened all of a sudden, by some freak accident. Did you ever notice a change in her behavior? Did she get withdrawn or overly serious or concerned about something she wouldn't talk about?"

"Wow—"

"Is that a yes?"

It was.

"Like I said before, Kelly had been seeing Rail two or three weeks before she ever mentioned anything about him to me," she said. "There was a day when she missed work. In hindsight, if I'm remembering it right, it was in that time period a week or so before Rail came into her life. It was a Wednesday. Tuesday everything had been fine, Kelly was just her normal old Kelly self. Then she called in sick on Wednesday. On Thursday, when she got back to work, she was different."

"In what way?"

"I don't know exactly," she said. "But it wasn't exactly her that came back. It was a different version of her."

"Where'd she go that Tuesday night?"

"I don't know."

Teffinger took out his phone, pulled up the calendar, clicked back to last year and then worked backwards from the time Kelly got murdered. "If I'm doing this right, the Wednesday she missed was in the first or second week of April."

"That seems right."

He called Sydney in Denver.

"I need you to do me a big favor," he said. "See if anyone got murdered in San Francisco on the first or second Tuesday night of April last year. If someone didn't get murdered, figure out if something happened that, if someone else saw it, someone would want that person dead."

Silence.

"Who is this?"

"Funny," he said. "This relates to Kelly Nine."

"I already figured that out. How soon do you need it?"

"Let me put it this way," he said. "Do you have it yet?"

"Teffinger—"

"Please and thank you."

A pause then, "How's Del Rey?"

"She's alive."

"That's almost a first for you," she said. "If I ever get in danger, remind me that I don't want you guarding me."

Back to Dandan, "The man who hired Rail did it

through a private investigator in Washington D.C. by the name of Oscar Benderfield. Have you ever heard of him?"

"No."

"Do you know anybody who knows him or who has ever mentioned him?"

"No."

"How about any lawyers in D.C.? Do you know any?"

"No. I hate lawyers."

"Does that mean you know some?"

"No, I just hate them on general principle."

Five minutes later they were at the shipyard. They parked a half-mile away and headed in on foot, weaving through a graveyard of rusty hulks that were at the wrong end of their useful lives.

"That's it over there," Dandan said.

Teffinger studied the vessel.

It was a dilapidated piece of junk.

"It looks like it came here to die," he said. "Stay here."

Then he headed that way.

En route he picked up a stray piece of rebar.

It was dirty and rusty in his hand.

It felt good.

It felt like it could crack a skull if it needed to.

73

The tugboat showed no signs of recent habitation. There were still distant remnants of prior life but they were from a time long past. Several unopened cans of food were in the galley, thick with dust. A box of cereal was tipped on its side. The cereal was gone, replaced with mouse droppings. The batteries in a flashlight were deader than dirt.

Spiders owned the place.

Still, Rail was back in town and might have the place in mind as a source of refuge. He might show up at some point. With that in mind, Teffinger scrounged around until he found a pencil. He looked for paper, couldn't find any, then ripped open the cereal box and used the inside cardboard. On it he wrote, Van Gogh, followed by his cell number. He put it on the counter next to the sink and left.

Back at the Porsche Teffinger told Dandan, "Rail left a long time ago, probably right after you took the painting."

"What about evidence?"

"I didn't see anything of use."

"What about fingerprints?"

"INTERPOL already has his fingerprints."

She cranked over the engine, shifted into first and took off.

"So now what?"

"Now you go back to work."

"Are you going to stake the place out?"

"No."

"I saw him on the street," she said. "He's in town. He might end up back there."

Teffinger scratched his head.

"If he does he'll call me."

"Why would he do that?"

"Because I left him my number."

Dandan frowned.

"Nothing personal but you don't seem like a real detective half the time."

"You're generous. Most people put my real time no more than ten percent."

Dandan knew she should smile but didn't. Instead she said, "I'm going to stake the place out tonight."

Teffinger swung his eyes at her.

"No."

"I'll be way off," she said. "He won't see me. If he shows up I'll call you."

"No."

"Why not?"

"Well, for starters, you'll end up dead and then I'll have one more thing to kick myself in the ass about for the rest of my life."

"But—"

"No buts. So what are your plans for the Van Gogh?"

"Sell it."

"How?"

"I found someone."

"Someone in the black market?"

She nodded.

"Is he shopping it?"

"He is a she and the answer is yes."

Teffinger shook his head.

"That's how Rail got onto you."

"I doubt it."

"Trust me," he said. "If I was you I'd drop out of sight, right here right now. I wouldn't go back to work, I wouldn't go back to my apartment, I wouldn't do anything I normally do, I'd get cash out of the bank and throw my credit cards away, I'd stay off the Internet, I'd throw my phone away, and most of all I wouldn't tell my little black market friend where I was." She studied him. "Rail's killed for a whole lot less than the value of that painting," he added, "a whole lot less, not to mention it was technically his to start with."

Her normally confident eyes clouded over.

"I thought he was in town to kill you or Del Rey."

"He is but think two birds, one stone."

She swallowed.

"Will you help me?"

Suddenly Teffinger's cell phone rang and a man's voice came through.

"You left me your number."

"Rail?"

"Yes."

"That was quick."

"I'm right behind you in a black Mustang. Do you see me?"

Teffinger turned.

The man was there, almost on their tail, holding a phone to his ear.

"I see you."

"Have the good Miss Dandan drop you off at the first bar. I'll buy you a beer."

"That's not a good idea."

"Sure it is," Rail said. "We walk in, we talk, we walk out and go in separate directions. No funny stuff from your end and none from mine. We have a thirty minute truce."

Teffinger swallowed.

"No."

The Mustang dropped back, swung around a corner and disappeared from sight.

Rail said, "I didn't kill Kelly Nine but I know who did. I'll give you his name in exchange for the Van Gogh."

"Bullshit," Teffinger said. "You killed Kelly. You also killed Susan Smith."

"Susan Smith isn't dead."

"Then where is she?"

"I'll tell you. Are we going to meet or not?"

"Call me back in an hour."

He killed the line.

74

Late Tuesday afternoon Teffinger pushed into the guts of a corner dive off Haight Street called the Dusty Beat. Deep in the dim lighting, two half-clad hookers sandwiching a loud drunk in a cheap suit turned to check him out.

One blew him a kiss.

The other could care less.

Teffinger walked past them to the man in the last booth, the man with the ponytail, the man with the solid chest and python arms, the man with the GQ face and the white cotton shirt rolled up at the cuffs.

A draft sat on the table, waiting for Teffinger.

He slid in and took a long swallow.

It was his brand, Bud Light.

Rail extended his hand and said, "Rail."

Teffinger shook it.

"Teffinger."

The man's grip was a vice.

"The first rule of what I do is to never get attached to the target," Rail said. "With Kelly Nine, I broke that rule. You know her. You can understand how that could happen."

Teffinger nodded.

"Who hired you to kill her?"

"Oscar Benderfield."

"You know what I mean."

"I don't know the ultimate source," Rail said. "Benderfield never disclosed his clients. It was better for everyone that way."

Teffinger looked for lies.

He found none.

"I fell in love with Kelly," Rail said. "I knew from moment one that it was a problem and I didn't care. What I did care about was keeping it quiet. I told her about my involvement in the black market. I showed her the Van Gogh to prove what I was saying was true. There was a chance she would reject me at that point but it was a chance I had to take."

"You never told her you were a killer."

Rail shook his head.

"Of course not."

"Then she never loved you back because she never knew who you really were," Teffinger said.

Rail frowned.

"You're trying to hurt me," he said. "That's not productive. You have something I want and I have something you want. We need to focus on being productive."

Teffinger took a swallow of beer and hardened his eyes.

"The Van Gogh disappeared, you knew Kelly was behind it because she was the only one who knew about it, you followed her to Denver and killed her."

Rail shook his head.

"I didn't kill her."

"Sure you did. Just admit it, you'll feel better."

"Like I said, I was in love with her," he said. "The

problem was that I was hired to kill her. My falling in love with her didn't change the fact that someone out there in the deep dark world wanted her dead. Sooner or later my delay would be viewed as a default. The contract would be deemed terminated. At that point both she and I would be targets. So, I stayed around in the shadows waiting for my replacement to show up. I wanted to find out who was behind it all to get him to back off or kill him if it came to that. When Kelly went to Denver it was only supposed to be for a few days, to see her family and friends. I followed her there to protect her."

"So you still had the Van Gogh when you left?"

"Yes."

"You did?"

"Yes. It disappeared afterwards."

Rail pulled a pack of cigarettes out of his shirt pocket, tapped two out and extended one to Teffinger, who declined. Rail lit his from a book of matches, blew smoke and said, "She went out with you while she was in Denver. That was a shock to me. It was storming out. I waited outside in that storm in your backyard hour after hour and waited for the two of you to return." He hardened his face. "I saw the two of you on the couch. I saw you screwing her. I saw her riding you the exact way she rode me."

Teffinger remembered the night.

He remembered the storm.

He remembered the couch.

He remembered the sex.

He remembered every detail.

"So you got jealous and killed her."

"In a manner of speaking, yes," Rail said. "What I did was leave. I just pointed my face into the rain and walked away, right out of her life and right out of my life. I left her to my replacement. I didn't know that he'd actually show up that same night. That was a strange coincidence. But I knew he'd show up sooner or later and when he did, I wouldn't be there any more to protect her. She was as good as dead the minute I walked away."

"So who was your replacement?"

"I'll give you his name," Rail said. "First let's talk about the Van Gogh."

Teffinger shook his head.

"No, first let's talk about Susan Smith," he said.

Rail shrugged.

"Sure, why not? I was hired by a private investigator named Fisher to kill Susan Smith," he said. "He was a conduit, similar to how Oscar Benderfield played things, being paid by a lawyer named Jack Colder. I took Susan Smith out of a Denver nightclub. I danced with her and licked her ear and told her I wanted to do a lot more of that, except between her legs. That was the night you killed Colder, apparently thinking that he was the one after her when in reality he was trying to call the whole thing off. He was there to protect her. Life twists in weird ways, you have to admit."

"Then you killed Fisher," Teffinger said.

Rail nodded.

"He was a flake," he said. "I gave Susan the oral reward, by the way. Never lie to a woman. Later she told me something you might find interesting. She told me she killed a man named Seth Lightfield, a dancer, apparently. She said now I knew her darkest secret. It was her way of trying to convince me that if I let her go she'd never tell the cops about me because now I had something just as bad on her."

"Why'd she kill him?"

"They were lovers," Rail said. "She took up with him after she got out from under that lawyer, Colder. It turned out that he wasn't as true to her as she was to him. So there were are again, back to the world's oldest motive."

Teffinger processed it.

It could be true.

She said she suspected Colder of doing it but that could have been a ruse to keep the light off her. If that was actually true, it was more and more of a tragedy that Teffinger killed Colder.

"So what did you do with her?"

"I'll tell you after we talk about the Van Gogh."

"You said before that she's alive."

"She is."

"Then tell me where she is."

"I will but first we have to talk about the Van Gogh," Rail said. "I'm being more than fair here. So far I'm the one doing all the talking."

"First let's talk about one more thing," Teffinger said.

"You're after me or Del Rey or both of us. Tell me why and tell me who's behind it."

Rail looked confused.

"I'm not after either one of you."

"That's a lie. You were on the dock last night. You were smoking, just like you are now. You ripped the wings off a bird. You tried to draw me away so you could double back and take Del Rey."

Rail wrinkled his face in disgust.

"Someone ripped the wings off a bird? That's sick—"

75

Tuesday night after dark Teffinger and Del Ray by-passed the hotel elevator, took the fire stairs down to street level and disappeared out the back side of the structure into the service alley. They stayed in the shadows for two blocks, flagged down the first cab they saw, had the driver zigzag this way and that until they were sure they weren't being followed, and then got dropped off on Waverly Place, which was an alley in Chinatown between Stockton and Kearny, sometimes called the street of painted balconies.

From there they walked a block over.

Two doors down a green neon dragon hung over a wooden door. Scribed on that door were the words Green Dragon Oriental Massage.

They entered that door and found themselves in another time and place. Peaceful water trickled out of bamboo into a shallow pool. Soft music dripped out of hidden speakers. Lush red linens textured the walls. A vanilla scent perfumed the air.

A young Chinese woman in a tightly wrapped kimono emerged from behind a wall of hanging beads.

"This way," she said.

They followed her down a corridor where the woman opened a locked door with a key and then escorted them up a stairway where she unlocked another door.

They entered and found themselves in a small apartment.

The window coverings were drawn tight.

The lighting was soft.

A woman on a couch got up, walked over to Del Rey and said, "You're a lucky woman, to have him." Then to Teffinger, "This place belongs to a friend of mine. No one will ever find me here. Del Rey can stay here too if you want her to."

"We'll see."

They poured wine and then Teffinger got to the point.

"The Van Gogh doesn't belong to Rail," he said. "It belongs to someone else. Rail only had it because he was brokering a deal for the man. You took it at exactly the wrong time. Rail had already taken a $2,000,000 earnest money deposit from the buyer. He was supposed make the exchange the next week, meaning deliver the painting to the buyer, collect the full purchase price and then turn that money over to the seller, less his 20 percent commission. Needless to say none of that went down. The seller wasn't happy. To stop a bad precedent, Rail needed to be dead. His only option was to disappear off the face of the earth until he could get his hands back on the painting and just hope that he could make things right again."

Dandan frowned.

"What about the two million?"

"Rail kept it," Teffinger said.

"That was stupid."

"He needed it to stay hidden."

"I doubt that the buyer took too kindly to that."

"That's one way to put it. Rail's been looking over his shoulder for over a year now, both shoulders in fact. When the painting came back on the market Rail traced it to San Francisco."

"To me specifically?" Dandan said.

"To a point," Teffinger said. "You were on a short list. It probably would have been only a matter of days before he figured it out completely. Of course, after he got my note on his boat and then saw us leaving together in the Porsche, he now knows for certain that you're the one who has it."

Dandan frowned.

"What are my options?"

Teffinger walked to the window, pulled the curtain back a smudge and looked out. He saw nothing there that shouldn't be.

"Here's what Rail proposes," he said. "He still has one million left out of that two. He'll turn that over right now to you for the painting."

"It's worth twenty all day long," Dandan said.

"Hear the rest of the proposal. Once he gets the painting in hand, he's going to try to get a deal back on track. The sale price, ironically, is exactly what you said, namely 20 million. The buyer still owes 18. Rail will try to get it and then hand over 16 to the seller, which is the purchase price less his 20 percent cut, which comes to 4 million. That will leave 2 million in his pocket. He'll turn that over to you when everything is complete."

"So my total is 3?"

"Yes."

"That's bullshit."

"It's not your painting," Teffinger said.

"It's not his either. My broker has inquiries coming in at 21 and 22. I'd be crazy to settle for 3, especially when 2 of it is on the come. We both know I'll never see it."

Teffinger shrugged.

He couldn't disagree with the last part.

Then he narrowed his eyes and said, "When Rail gets the painting he's going to tell me who killed Kelly. He also says Susan Smith is still alive. He's going to tell me where she is."

"He's lying to you. Like you said before, he's been looking over his shoulders for over a year. He'll say anything to get out from under it all. He's lying right to your face. All he wants is the painting and he'll say anything to get it."

"I don't think he's lying. But either way keep in mind that if you don't do a deal he'll kill you sooner or later. That's the end game. My advice is don't let greed suck you into an early grave."

Dandan topped off her wine, took a long swallow and looked Teffinger in the eyes.

"I'll call you in the morning with my decision," she said. "It's too much to process right now."

"Fine. But have a final answer by nine o'clock."

"I'll call you at nine."

They left.

76

Outside a cold drizzle dropped down that hadn't been dropping down before. "Dandan's a greedy little bitch," Teffinger said. "She's not going to be thinking about anything tonight. She's playing us off until morning so she can move the Van Gogh to a new location. She's going to try to sell it herself and then disappear, even if it means she'll have to spend the rest of her life worrying about Rail."

"You think?"

He nodded.

"I can't let her greed get in the way of Susan Smith."

"Meaning what?"

"Meaning we need to get to the painting before she does."

Del Rey wrinkled her brow.

"You gave her your word before she ever told you about the painting," she said. "You wouldn't even know about it if it wasn't for her putting her trust in you."

That was true.

"You can't betray that trust," she said.

"I don't want to."

"But you're going to?"

"Pretend you're Susan Smith for a minute," he said. "What would want me to do?"

"Nothing because I'd be dead."

Teffinger shook his head.

"You'd want me to help you. You wouldn't care about an old piece of canvas."

Del Rey held Teffinger's hand. "You think she's alive because that what you want to think," she said. "I have to agree with Dandan on this one. Rail's lying to you. If Susan was still alive, why wouldn't she come forward?" A beat then, "This isn't about Susan Smith. This is about Kelly Nine. You want to avenge her death."

Teffinger went to deny it.

No words came out.

"It's about both," he said. "It's also about finding the source of the person who put a contact on Kelly. That same person might have one on you. So this is about you too if you want to get right down to it."

"I still think Rail's lying about that too," she said. "He's the one with the contract on me, or you, whichever."

"No, he's definitely telling the truth on that one," Teffinger said. "Think about it. He was initially hired by Oscar Benderfield to kill Kelly. He didn't follow through and a second person had to be hired. At that point Rail had burned his bridges with Benderfield. Benderfield would never hire him again, not in a million years."

"I wouldn't be so sure," Del Rey said. "Benderfield gave Rail's name to his P.I. buddy in Denver; Fisher, remember? Obviously the bridge wasn't totally burned."

Teffinger chewed on it.

He hadn't thought of that angle.

It wasn't totally crazy.

"We're not going to figure it out right now," he said. "Right now what we need to do is get the Van Gogh in our hands so we can keep all the options open."

"I still don't think you should betray Dandan's trust."

"I'm not betraying her trust," he said. "I'm saving her life. That's what she wanted me to do, protect her."

Del Rey wasn't impressed.

"There's a saying," she said. "To betray someone else is to betray yourself."

They took a cab to Avis, rented a white 4Runner and

pointed the front end across the Golden Gate Bridge towards Sausalito with the wipers swishing back and forth to a slow demonic beat.

Thirty minutes later they were at the marina.

"Wait here," Teffinger said.

"Nick, I still don't think we should do this."

"Just wait here."

He climbed around the security gate and took one careful step after another down the slippery docks. No one was around, or if they were they were sealed up in their boats doing whatever they did in there.

He made his way to Dandan's Island Packard without slipping into the water.

The vessel was dark and gently tugging at the ropes.

He stepped aboard.

The cabin door was padlocked.

He tugged on the front hatch to see if it was latched from beneath.

It wasn't.

He muscled it open and dropped down.

Inside he hunted around until he found a flashlight and a toolbox and then jimmied the storage lock off.

He pulled out sail repair materials and shined the light in.

The aluminum case didn't come into view.

He got down on his stomach and took a better look.

The case wasn't there.

At the 4Runner he told Del Rey, "It's gone. Dandan must have moved it earlier today, probably when I was meeting with Rail."

"So now what?"

"I'm betting she has it with her," he said.

They headed back to the Green Dragon Oriental Massage and pushed through the front door the same as before. The young beauty in the wrapped kimono came to greet them the same as before. Unlike before, though, the woman didn't say, "Follow me."

This time she said, "Dandan left."

"When?"

"Ten minutes ago."

"To where?"

"I don't know. She didn't say."

"Is she coming back?"

"I don't think so. She was carrying her suitcase."

DAY NINE

July 16
Wednesday

77

Wednesday morning Jori-Lee got a call from Leland Everitt who said, "You made quite the impression yesterday. I'm officially authorized to offer you a position at Overton & Frey. If you're interested and would like to come down, we can talk about salary and benefits and the like."

"Yes, I'm interested."

She arrived an hour later and ended up spending most of the morning with HR signing forms and going over employment policies she cared nothing about.

Then she got pointed to her new office.

Ten minutes later Zahara Knox came in and closed the door.

"This is the opposite of running," she said.

Jori-Lee nodded.

"I appreciate the warning and want you to know you don't have to worry about me ever mentioning it to anyone."

The woman studied her.

"Well, good luck to you."

"Thanks."

She was assigned to a mentor, senior partner Adam Black, who in turn temporarily assigned her to assist the litigation department, which in turn wasted no time in turning her into a billable-hour machine.

Mid-afternoon her phone rang.

It was Zahara.

"Adam Black is a spy for Leland Everitt," the woman said. "Be careful what you say to him."

The line died.

She reached into her purse and pulled out the key-card given to her by HR this morning, the one that would get her in and out of the firm after hours, plus activate the elevator.

It felt nice in her hand.

Then she made friends, played nice, and spent the rest of the afternoon trying to get as much work on her desk as she could.

The word spread.

Lawyers showed up with files, dogs they wanted to get rid of, dogs that barked because the case was a loser, or the client was a slow pay or no pay, or because the work was duller than dirt.

She didn't care.

She smiled and took it all as if it was gold.

By the end of the day she had more than she could do in a week.

She could justify being around after hours.

78

Dandan and her stupid little painting held the key to everything. Teffinger and Del Rey spent a good chunk of Wednesday morning trying to track her down, only to find that she was nowhere—not at her apartment, not at work, not at the Green Dragon, not at the Island Packard, not on the other end of her cell phone, not in the backseat, not anywhere.

Nine o'clock came and went and she didn't call.

She was on the run with her precious little treasure.

Her plan was obvious; sell the painting and retire to a life of luxury, someplace no one would ever find her.

Screw her job.

Screw her friends.

Screw her past.

Screw everything but the insane pile of money.

Where was she, right now, this minute?

Somewhere …

Would she leave San Francisco?

It was definitely possible but Teffinger's gut didn't feel it. The woman knew the area. She knew the haunts. She knew the escape routes. She knew where to run. Most importantly, she still had lots of contacts to tap if her back got up against the wall. On top of that, travelling with the Van Gogh would be problematic. It was in too nice of a case. Someone would cast an eye on it and wonder what little wonder was inside that deserved such a fine shelter.

No, she'd go to lengths to keep eyes off it.

That meant staying in San Francisco.

A hotel would require a credit card. She was too smart to use her own but might borrow one from a friend. Even then, though, she'd be too afraid to leave the painting alone.

"I think she's somewhere in Chinatown," Del Rey said. "That's where her roots are. That's where she'll feel the safest. That's where she'll have the most eyes protecting her. Plus it's easy to look down on street level and see who's there, meaning not just you and me, but Rail and whoever it is that's after him, i.e., after the painting."

Teffinger didn't disagree.

"I need coffee," he said.

Teffinger hated Starbucks. It was too expensive and too much of an ordeal to get a cup filled. There was always a line and the top two things Teffinger hated in the world were lines and lines. One popped up though, convenient as hell, so they stopped in.

The line wasn't that bad.

The coffee was hot.

The booth was clean.

"There's one person Dandan can't cut communications with," he said. "That's her black market friend, the one selling the painting for her."

Del Rey nodded.

"And?"

"And if we could find her—she said he was a she, remember?—we might be able to use her as a conduit."

"That's just swapping one impossible task for another," Del Rey said. "You're not going to crack into that code."

"True but Rail already has."

Del Rey considered it and then shook her head.

"Even if he knows, or could figure it out, why would he tell us? Why wouldn't he just follow the lead himself?"

"Because he doesn't know there's a problem yet."

"Right but he will as soon as we tell him."

"That's why we're not going to tell him."

Teffinger took a long swallow of coffee and then called Rail. "We don't have Dandan completely on board yet," he said. "She's still mulling over the prospect of selling the painting herself."

"Then she's dead," Rail said. "Tell her that."

Teffinger exhaled.

"She's working with a broker, a female broker. What I want to do is shut her down."

"How?"

"I need her name," Teffinger said. "Once I have it I'll flood the Internet with buzz about how the FBI and INTERPOL are closing in on her. No one will want to touch her. Dandan won't be able to find another broker. She'll have no option but to take your offer."

Silence.

"I don't like this," Rail said.

"Your call," Teffinger said. "Either help me or don't."

He hung up.

Fifteen minutes later Rail called back and said, "The woman's name is Savina Bandini. She works at Gallery Corsa, which is an art gallery in Rome. You didn't hear it from me."

"I'll be in touch."

"Don't let this drag out," Rail said. "Starting at five o'clock tonight our truce is forever off. At that point you do what you need to do and so will I."

"Fair enough."

79

Rome was ahead of San Francisco, time-wise; how far, Teffinger didn't know, but it could easily be the end of the workday there or maybe even evening. He got Gallery Corsa's number from the Internet and dialed from his cell.

Don't be closed.

Don't be closed.

Don't be closed.

A man answered in Italian. Teffinger asked for Savina Bandini and got put on hold for a full minute before a woman's voice came through.

"Ciao."

"Is this Savina Bandini?" Teffinger said.

The woman answered in English.

"Yes."

"I'm calling about a special painting that you may have for sale. It has a view of the sea in it. It was painted quite some time ago."

"Who is this?"

"My name is Nick Teffinger," he said. "I'm calling from San Francisco."

"I'm with a client right now," she said. "I'll call you back."

The line died.

Teffinger powered off, swallowed what was left of his coffee and said, "She's going to check me out."

"Why'd you give her your real name?"

"Because I'm going to play this one straight up."

"Do you think that's smart?"

"We'll find out."

Thirty minutes later Savina Bandini called back. Her voice was slightly different, possibly coming through a more secure line.

"No one knows you," she said.

"That doesn't matter. What matters is that your client, Dandan Phon, stole the painting."

Silence, then, "I'm aware of the history."

"Walk away from this one," Teffinger said. "If you don't, Dandan will be dead by the end of the week.

My suspicion is that you won't be far behind."

"Are you trying to scare me?"

"I'm just stating facts. Trust me, this one isn't worth the risk."

"That's interesting but it's also moot," she said. "The piece went under contract an hour ago."

"Call it off."

"That's not the way this business works."

She hung up.

80

Teffinger's head filled with bark and bite. Rail would never tell him where Susan Smith was, or who killed Kelly Nine, unless Teffinger delivered the Van Gogh to him. Now that was impossible.

"The exchange hasn't been made yet, right?" Del Rey said.

Teffinger nodded.

"That's my assumption. If it just went under contract, the buyer would still need to travel to San Francisco, or wherever the exchange is going to be. The buyer's also going to need to get the painting authenticated, meaning an expert will need to look at it."

"So Dandan still has it."

Teffinger nodded.

"That's my assumption."

"We still have time to find it then."

Teffinger frowned.
"And what, steal it from her?"
"If we have to."
He shook his head.
"She'll end up dead."
"So what do we do?"
"I don't know."

Out of Starbucks Teffinger maneuvered the 4Runner into thick traffic and went with the flow, needing motion but having no destination. He could deal with a lot of things but not knowing what to do next wasn't one of them. It clawed at him from under his skin.

He needed a plan.
He needed it now.
A block passed.
Del Rey powered up the radio.
A Nirvana song filled the air.
Here we are now, entertain us—
"We have Sirius," she said.
"See if they have a Beatles station."
"They probably do."
She leaned forward to work the knobs.

Suddenly the windows exploded with a violent impact so absolute that Teffinger's entire body jolted. His window vaporized. Noisy air rushed in where the glass should be. Del Rey's window was equally gone. A blue car to their side squealed to the right around a corner. It was then that Teffinger realized what happened.

They'd been shot.

Del Rey's face was contorted with fear but there was no blood.

She hadn't been hit.

Teffinger focused on the disappearing car.

It was getting away fast.

He slammed on the brakes.

Someone from behind rammed him.

81

A pale-faced detective by the name of Eric Blocker processed the scene. Teffinger co-operated to the extent necessary, letting him know about the ripped bird in Del Rey's house, the second one on the dock last night, and his theory that he might be the intended target. It was definitely an attempted murder, but attempted at to which one of them, he wasn't sure.

Teffinger didn't get much of a look at the guy in the blue car but the look he got was good enough to tell it wasn't Rail.

So he said nothing about Rail.

He also said nothing about Dandan, Kelly Nine or the Van Gogh. Those dominos were too close together and too unstable to have a stranger stomping around them.

He informed Avis that their vehicle was being temporarily held for processing. They understood and amazingly delivered a replacement vehicle right to the scene.

It was two hours before Teffinger was able to get in the new 4Runner and pull away.

"You're not impressed with that detective," Del Rey said.

"Actually he's perfect," Teffinger said.

"Meaning he's not smart enough to get in our way."

He smiled.

"Let's just say he processed an attempted murder scene right at the scene without removing the intended victims to a safe location. I didn't say anything because I was hoping the guy in the blue car would swing by to gander at all the stir he created."

"Did he?"

"Possibly," he said. "There were a few potentially matching cars with male drivers. I jotted down their license numbers."

"So that's what you were writing."

He nodded.

"Actually this whole thing was good. I'm glad it happened. First of all we know that Rail was telling the truth when he said it wasn't him that was after you or me. That means he might also actually be telling the truth when he said Susan Smith was still alive. More importantly, though, it gave me a chance to slow down and clear my head. I think I may have come up with a new plan."

"Tell me."

"Sure, we're going to head this way."

"Why?"

"Because that's the way we need to go."

"Why?"

"Because if we don't go this way we won't end up at our destination."

She punched him on the arm.

"You know what your problem is? You never stop being you."

He smiled.

Then he called Sydney and said, "I have some California plates I need you to run. But first, what'd you find out about that Tuesday? What happened that turned Kelly Nine into a contract?"

"Unknown," she said. "Nothing's visible yet."

"Keep digging."

"I will."

"All the way to China," he said.

Dandan lived on the second floor of a narrow house between the financial district and Chinatown, a short walk from the Market trolley. Teffinger circled the area three times before finally finding a parking spot big enough for the 4Runner.

Del Rey wasn't in the best of moods.

"Tell me what the plan is," she said.

Teffinger exhaled.

"I'm technically still not sure I want to go through with it, but here it is in rough form," he said. "Obviously Dandan can't renege on the contract that her broker got for her. She still has the painting, though, at least short-term. What I'm hoping she'll do, if we can get in touch with her, is let me borrow it."

"Borrow it?"

"If I can get it in hand and then prove to Rail I have it—which pretty much means showing it to him—I'll make him give me the information on Susan Smith and on Kelly Nine before I turn the painting over. Once I get the information, screw him."

"You don't give him the painting?"

"No. The painting goes back to Dandan."

"That will be tricky, logistically speaking," Del Rey said. "How are you going to not give him the painting?"

"I'll think of a way to slip it out of the case at the last minute. He'll walk away thinking it's inside. By the time he figures it out, I'll be gone."

Del Rey wasn't impressed.

"I doubt that he's that easily fooled," she said. "And even if you succeed, he'll come back and kill you. Plus he'll figure out that Dandan was working with you and kill her too."

Teffinger cocked his head.

"He's already out to kill her," he said. "The only way she can get out of that is to turn the painting back over to him, which she's not going to do. She'll have to go on the run but that's something she's got to do in any event, at least until Rail is either behind bars or dead."

"You actually want him to come after you," she said. "That way you can kill him and it will be self-defense."

Teffinger shrugged.

"I'm not going to force him to come after me," he said. "It will be his choice. If he chooses to do so he better be prepared."

"This is all a big plan to avenge the death of Kelly Nine."

Teffinger went to deny it.

No words came out.

They were at the front door.

"So what do we hope to find inside?" Del Rey said.

"Something that tells us where Dandan is," Teffinger said. "Rail's calling the truce off at five o'clock. If I'm going to have a painting to show him it's going to have to be quick."

The house had two front doors, one for the lower unit and one for the upper.

They tried the knob for the upper unit.

Surprising, it turned.

The door opened.

A stairway led up.

They took it.

At the top was another door.

It wasn't closed.

It was ajar several inches.

Teffinger put his face to the crack and said, "Anyone home?"

No one responded.

He pushed the door all the way open and walked in.

He wasn't prepared for what he saw.

82

Someone had gotten there first. The kitchen cabinets were open, as were the drawers. Furniture was overturned. Everything cloth was cut open.

"They were looking for the painting," Teffinger said.

Del Rey pointed to a ripped-up chair.

"It wouldn't fit in there."

"It would if you took it out of the frame and rolled it up," he said. "I don't think they found it. I don't see a stopping point. They kept going until they got through the whole place. Hunt around for an address book or anything personal like letters or photographs."

They searched.

Five minutes into it Del Rey said, "I found something."

She was holding a file, rifling through papers.

Teffinger came over.

"What is it?"

What it was, he couldn't believe. There were five or six black-and-white printouts of a woman having sex with a group of men. They weren't being gentle. They were taking her hard. Teffinger looked closer at the woman to be sure he wasn't seeing things.

He wasn't.

The woman was Kelly Nine.

Teffinger put his back to the wall, slumped to the floor and let the papers fall from his fingers.

"That's porn," Del Rey said. "She was doing porn, hardcore porn. Did you know she was into that?"

Teffinger closed his eyes.

"No."

"This is really weird," Del Rey said. "What's just as weird is, Why does Dandan have pictures of it?"

Teffinger groaned.

He didn't know.

He didn't care.

He couldn't breathe.

He focused on the pictures again, hoping to find that the woman was just a trick of the eye and wasn't really Kelly after all.

There were no tricks.

In fact, the opposite; the birthmark on her upper right thigh was visible in two of the shots. In another, the gold tooth in the upper back of her mouth showed.

Her face was Kelly's face.

She was Kelly.

Teffinger felt a hand on his shoulder.

"Nick, are you okay?"

He squeezed her hand and stood up.

"Yeah, fine," he said. "Let's keep looking around."

Del Rey found a digital camera in the top drawer of a bedroom dresser, tried to power it up and said, "The battery's dead."

"Take it," Teffinger said.

They also took phone bills, credit card bills and the framed photos that had someone other than Dandan in the picture.

They took a final look around.

Then they left.

In the 4Runner Teffinger said, "I'm not so sure those photos of Kelly are porn. I think they're rape."

Del Rey looked doubtful.

"She's not fighting."

"How do you fight five or six or seven guys? I think this is what happened to her on that Tuesday night, or on the Wednesday when she missed work. Somehow this is the reason she ended up on the wrong end of a contract."

Del Rey shook her head.

"If it was rape, why would they take pictures? And why in the world would Dandan have them?"

"I don't know but I'm damn sure going to find out."

They pulled into traffic and pointed the front end towards Chinatown.

Del Rey turned on the radio and worked the knobs until she found a Beatles station.

> We've been friends for, oh, so long,
> I let you share what's mine.
> When you mess with the girl I love,
> It's time to draw the line.
> Keep your hands off my baby,
> Ain't a-gonna tell you, but a one more time—
> So keep your hands off my baby

Boy, you get it through your head,
That girl is mine.

"I never heard that one," she said.

"It never went onto one of their albums. We can't sleep at the hotel tonight. That's where our blue-car friend is picking us up from."

"I agree."

"We'll find something cheap and pay cash."

They went to the Green Dragon where Teffinger handed his business card to the woman in the kimono and said, "Please tell Dandan to call me as soon as possible. It's very important. Tell her all I want to do is talk."

"I don't know where she's at."

"Well, tell her if you see her."

Next they went to Dandan's ad agency, b.Box-Media, and had the same conversation with the receptionist.

En route back to the 4Runner Teffinger checked his emails and found one from Sydney on the blue-car plates he asked her to run.

None were of interest.

All the owners turned out to be solid members of the community. None had the earmarks of a killer.

83

Shortly after five o'clock the support staff of Overton & Frey started to thin out. The exodus to the elevators brought a nervous drumming to Jori-Lee's fingers. The end of the workday was here. She'd have to decide whether to stay after hours and snoop around or postpone it for a day or two when she had a better lay of the land.

Leland Everitt's office, that's what she needed to search.

The man was in a conspiracy with Nelson Robertson.

The conspiracy included, at a minimum, getting Jori-Lee away from the man. The question was, how much deeper did it go? Did Everitt know about Robertson's fetish? Did he know that Robertson was being blackmailed by T'amara Alder? Did Everitt play a part in her murder?

Jori-Lee's gut said yes, yes, yes to all of it.

What she needed though was proof.

If she could get that proof, she'd go to the FBI. It was true that she'd broken into Robertson's house, which was a crime of no small proportion. But comparatively speaking, she was a small fish.

She could cut a deal.

Getting into Leland Everitt's office would be problematic. It was at the end of a corridor. There was no good way in or out. It might be ripe with nanny cameras. He might lock his door at the end of the day. His computer might be password protected. His desk and filing cabinets might be locked.

If someone saw her, she had no good excuse for being there.

Wait, that could be fixed.

She could buy him a thank-you card and say she was putting it on his desk.

She could buy it tonight and hit his office tomorrow. Or she could run out now and buy it and then come back.

Her fingers drummed harder.

What to do?

What to do?

Suddenly Zahara Knox walked in and said, "Let's go out and have a drink," she said. "On me."

The drumming in Jori-Lee's fingers stopped.

She grabbed her purse.

"Sounds good."

They ended up at a place called The Vault, a high-energy den of sin crowded shoulder-to-shoulder with pretty people in expensive suits and designer high-heels.

Perfume and sex permeated the air.

"This is where I come to get laid," Zahara said.

Jori-Lee studied her to see if it was a joke.

It wasn't.

"Not tonight though," she added. "Tonight we get drunk and talk."

Over screwdrivers, Jori-Lee spilled it out, the whole mess; Robertson's fetish, the fact he was being blackmailed by T'amara Alder who ended up dead, Leland Everitt's involvement with Robertson to an extent not yet fully known, the fact that Jori-Lee had some concrete evidence in that she secretly kept a flash drive, but she needed a whole lot more, particularly as to Leland Everitt's involvement.

Zahara exhaled.

"Let's go get it," she said.

"Get what?"

"The concrete, darling, the concrete."

"You mean now?"

Zahara nodded.

"We'll use my keycard to get in," she said. "I'm working a couple of cases with Leland. If anyone catches us in his office, I'll have a reason to be there. You'll just be someone tagging along."

Jori-Lee's watch said 7:43.

"Do you think everyone's gone?"

"There's only one way to find out."

Zahara downed what was left of her screwdriver and stood up.

Jori-Lee tapped her fingers and said, "You're serious—"

"Dead serious, darling. Let's do it."

84

Five o'clock silently came and went. Rail didn't call to officially give Teffinger one last chance before the truce forever ended and he went after Dandan. Dandan didn't call. The bird-ripper didn't call. The pale-skinned detective didn't call. No one called. The world uneventfully revolved on its axis as the streetlights kicked on and San Francisco slipped into darkness.

Teffinger toyed with the idea of calling Rail and pretending he had the Van Gogh. The more he played out the realities, though, the less he saw Rail falling for it, and the more he saw one of them or both of them with a bullet in the brain.

Their new hotel room wasn't much.

It was basically a bed, a few cheap things to sit on, a fuzzy TV to stare at and enough basic plumbing to get the job done. If it rained, it would probably keep most of the water off their heads. It was on the second floor of a peeling two level structure. To get to it they walked up outside wooden stairs and down an outside wooden walkway past the other rooms all the way to the end. A smell of urine came from behind the stairs.

Next door a woman broke into a loud orgasm.

Two minutes later a man left.

Teffinger pulled the curtains to the side and

watched him walk away, then turned to Del Rey and said, "The more I think about it, the more you might be right, in that Kelly wasn't being raped and it's nothing more than a porno."

"Does it make a difference at this point?"

He cocked his head.

"If it was a porno then she did it for money," he said. "She wouldn't do something like that for money unless she really needed it in the worst way. So why did she need money so badly?"

"You're speculating, and not very well."

"How so?"

"I can't image anything like that would pay much," she said. "Porn isn't exactly the go-to place for a non-porn woman who needs money. With Kelly's looks, she could land a sugar daddy in a week. That's where I'd go if I was her and needed serious money. But even before that, I'd max out my credit cards first and try to borrow it from friends. Did she ever hit you up for a loan or anything?"

Teffinger grunted.

"No."

"Would she have if her back was against the wall?"

"Possibly."

"You mean probably. Did she mention anything about money problems when she was in Denver?"

"No."

"And her sister never mentioned anything like that to you, after the fact?"

"No."

"Well, given all that, it's pretty clear this isn't a

money issue," Del Rey said. "If it's not rape—and I don't think it is—then she did it for some other reason besides money. Maybe one of the guys in the film had something on her."

"Like what?"

She shook her head in uncertainty.

"It would have to be something big. Maybe she did something she shouldn't have and he knew about it."

"Like what?"

"I don't know," she said. "Maybe she got drunk and ran someone over and he got her license plate number. Or maybe she was anonymously blackmailing someone and someone found out about it and threatened to disclose her name unless she did what he wanted. Maybe any number of things."

Teffinger didn't disagree.

Anything was possible.

Suddenly his phone rang and a man's voice said, "Doug?"

Teffinger didn't recognize the intonation.

It belonged to a stranger.

"Did you say Doug?"

"Yeah, Doug."

"There's no Doug here," Teffinger said. "I think you got the wrong number."

"Oops, sorry."

The connection died.

"Who was it?" Del Rey asked.

Teffinger opened his mouth to say, "Wrong number," but the words that came out were, "I think it was our friend from the blue car trying to track us down."

Del Rey didn't move.

Then she said, "Fine. We'll hide around the corner and kill him when he shows up."

Teffinger winced.

He'd killed two men in the last week.

He was tired of it.

At the same time, he was also tired of being a target.

He was tired of looking over his shoulder.

They pulled the curtains tight, left the lights on and took up a place in the deep shadows at the far corner of the parking lot, behind a rusty van perched on cinderblocks next to a chain-link fence.

Time passed.

The black sky clouded over.

The clouds dropped water.

The wind blew that water into their bones.

An hour passed, then another.

Their bodies stiffened.

Their minds tired.

"I think we're out here for nothing," Teffinger said.

"You think so?"

"Unfortunately, yes. We'll give it five more minutes. Then we're done."

Four minutes passed.

Then something happened.

The dark shape of a man appeared from out of nowhere, silently walking up the stairs at the far end and making its way towards the rear of the hotel, nothing more than a menacing black silhouette hunched against a wicked storm.

Teffinger's blood raced.

He recognized the feeling.

It was the same one he had when Oscar Benderfield lunged at him with a knife.

"Stay here," he whispered.

Then he was on his feet, maneuvering through the shadows to the stairs with the cold steel of his weapon in hand.

He started up, one silent step at a time.

In fifteen seconds someone would be dead.

He could feel it.

85

The law firm was coffin-quiet when Jori-Lee and Zahara entered. Not a voice, not a radio, not a spec of a sound came from anywhere. They did a quick sweep and found the place deserted. Empty trashcans indicated that the cleaning crew had already come and gone.

Zahara grabbed a discovery file from her office, a case she was riding second-chair on, under Leland Everitt. It was their excuse to be in the man's office should they get caught. She tucked the red-rope under her arm and turned to Jori-Lee.

"Are you still with me?"

"Yes."

"Okay. The important thing is to not touch anything unless we have to. And if we do, we need to put it back exactly the way we found it—exactly."

"What if we need to copy something?"

Zahara chewed on it.

"The new copy machines all scan to copy," she said. "If someone got motivated enough they could figure out what got copied, actual images of the paper. I'm sure all that gets stored in a hard drive or something in there. For how long, I don't know. Maybe it even gets backed up occasionally." Her face brightened. "There's an older copy machine in the dead files room."

"Does it work?"

"On and off."

"Ouch."

"Let's worry about finding something, first. There might not even be anything. You got your phone with you?"

Yes, she did.

"Good. Use it if we need to take a picture of anything. Turn the ringer off, though."

Jori-Lee complied.

Then they headed for Leland Everitt's office, not sneaking, walking the walk of hurried associates having to work late and not particularly enjoying it.

As they turned down the corridor that led to their target office, time slowed. Every step took forever. Jori-Lee could see nothing but the closed door at the end of the corridor. It made her palms sweat and her breath jagged.

The screwdrivers were still in her system.

They wobbled her legs.

They fogged her thoughts.

In hindsight, this was crazy.

They were into it, though.

They were too far to turn back.

Zahara didn't hesitate when they got to the office. She put her hand on the knob as if she owned it and twisted. It turned, unlocked. They stepped inside, quietly closed the door behind them and left the lights off. Twilight filtered through the windows, not a lot but enough.

Jori-Lee expected to get worse once inside.

Surprisingly her breath relaxed.

Her brain focused.

"Do you want the computer?" Zahara said.

"No, I'll hit a wrong key."

"Start with the credenza then. I doubt he'd leave anything too incriminating on his desk."

"Okay."

She tried.

It didn't open.

"It's locked."

"He keeps the key in the top desk drawer."

Jori-Lee found it, unlocked all six drawers and

then put it back exactly where she found it.

She opened the top left drawer.

Inside, to the far right, was a black revolver.

Also inside were fifteen or twenty red-rope files.

She pulled the one on the far left out.

It was labeled, "Client X."

Privileged & Confidential was stamped on the front in red ink. Inside were three manila folders.

Attorney Notes.

Investigator's Reports.

Transcripts.

Her chest pounded.

"Point of no return," she said.

Zahara grunted.

"We're long past that, darling. Work fast."

"He's got a gun in here."

"Did you say a gun?"

Yes, she did.

Zahara looked in, then at Jori-Lee.

"What the hell is he doing with a gun?" She pulled it out and checked it closer. "It's a Glock. There should be a serial number on here somewhere—" A beat then, "Here it is. Get a pencil, write this down—"

86

In fifteen seconds someone would be dead. The feeling grew more and more pronounced as Teffinger came up the stairs. The weapon got colder in his grip. The muscles got tighter in his face. The air got heavier in his lungs. His head came up to where he could see down the walkway. The man was at the far end spying in a window.

His face was perpendicular to Teffinger, even pointed away to an extent.

Teffinger raised the weapon and headed that way one silent step at a time.

Then something happened.

A door opened.

A woman's arm came out, grabbed the man by the shirt and pulled him in.

The door closed.

Teffinger exhaled.

It was just a john visiting the whore, just a stupid john making a booty call out in the middle of a cold lonely night.

He shook his head.

You're officially the king of the dumbasses.

Everyone bow to the king.

The pounding in his chest slowed, something in the nature of a speeding car that had a foot suddenly lift off the accelerator. At least fifteen seconds were gone now. No one was dead. No one would be dead. No one would even be close to dead.

He exhaled.

It was all for nothing.

Now what?

The blue-car guy wasn't coming for them. The phone call for Doug was nothing more than that, a phone call for Doug.

Teffinger leaned over the railing and shouted, "Del Rey."

No one answered.

The storm was too loud.

He waved his hands.

"Del Rey."

She didn't see him.

She didn't answer.

He headed down the landing, then down the stairs, then through the endless puddles of the parking lot, no longer a fan of the storm, now only a fan of dry clothes and a soft bed and closed eyes and a mind a peace.

Behind the van, Del Rey wasn't there.

"Del Rey—"

No one answered.

He circled the vehicle.

She wasn't there.

She was gone.

"Del Rey!"

No one answered.

"Del Rey!"

She wouldn't have gone of her own volition, not without telling him, not in a million years. Someone took her, just like Kelly Nine, right out from under his nose. The guy must have been waiting out there in the storm, wedged into a shadow, probably not more than thirty feet away, just waiting and waiting and waiting for the exact right moment.

"Del Rey!"

Teffinger ran toward the street, weapon in hand.

"Del Rey!"

87

The Glock was interesting. More interesting, though, was the Client X file, which Jori-Lee flipped through. "This is strange stuff," she said.

"Should we copy it?"

"Yes."

Zahara grabbed it and said, "I'll do it. I know how to un-jam the machine. You stay here and keep at it."

"What if Leland shows up?"

"He won't."

Then Zahara was gone.

Jori-Lee kept searching.

The other files were nothing of interest.

The other drawers were equally bland.

Suddenly the hallway lights turned on. Zahara wouldn't have done that. Someone else was in the building. Jori-Lee shut the credenza, pushed the locks in, powered off the computer and looked for a place to hide, just in case. In the far back corner was a door. She opened it and found herself in a small private bathroom. She ducked inside and shut the door.

Everything turned black.

She held her breath and listened with every fiber of her being.

Then the worst thing that could have happened

did. Someone came into the office. The heavy breathing didn't belong to Zahara.

It belonged to a man.

A briefcase got set on a desk followed by a squish of air from leather, indicating he just sat down.

Seconds passed.

No discernable sounds came.

Then the computer powered up.

A minute later a printer sprang to life and spit out a page, then another, and then another.

The man walked over to it.

The papers shuffled as if being gathered up.

Feet moved.

The computer shut off.

This was good.

Whatever the man came for, now he had it.

Now he'd leave.

He didn't leave, though. Instead he picked up a phone, dialed and said, "It's me. I have what you want. Ten o'clock at the Big Kahuna. I'll be there."

The voice belonged to Leland Everitt.

The phone went down.

A desk drawer opened, keys rattled, and a credenza door got unlocked. A briefcase snapped open and something got dropped inside. The credenza door closed and the keys went back into the desk.

Footsteps left.

Jori-Lee waited a full minute as she searched for sounds. Then she opened the door a crack, enough to hear clearer. No signs of life came. She poked her head out.

No one was there.

She opened the main door, looked down the hall and saw nothing she shouldn't.

Then she checked the credenza drawer to see if she was right about what she thought happened.

She was.

The Glock was gone.

She snuck down to the dead-files room. Zahara, un-jamming paper, said, "I'm going to shoot this bitch."

Jori-Lee told her what just happened.

Zahara listened without interrupting and then said, "Who's he meeting at ten?"

"I don't know. He never used a name."

Zahara got a distant look, refocused and said, "We'll get the rest of this file copied and get it back in the credenza. Then we're going to the Big Kahuna."

Jori-Lee wasn't so sure.

"I have a feeling we're turning into the cat," she said. "The one curiosity killed."

"Well, here's a little known fact. A lot of those cats never got killed at all. Probably not even a majority, if you had the statistics."

88

The storm cut into Teffinger's face as he sprinted from the back of the parking lot to the street. Fifty yards away, the lights of a vehicle suddenly came to life, quickly followed by movement as they left the curb. Other than the taillights, the vehicle took no shape. It could be a blue car but it could equally be a red pickup or a white SUV.

He hesitated for a heartbeat, deciding.

The vehicle could be innocent.

It could be a mom and a kid.

If it was then Teffinger would apologize afterwards. In the meantime the important thing was to stop it without killing anyone, not until he knew one way or the other.

He aimed for the back tires and pulled the trigger, one, two, three, four, five, six times.

The vehicle fishtailed, crossed the centerline, sped up the road for a long ways and slammed face-first into a telephone pole.

Teffinger ran for it.

As he got closer it took the shape of a sedan.

When he got there the driver's door was wide open.

No one was behind the wheel.

No one was visible in the storm, either running away or on the ground or otherwise. No one was in the back seat.

"Del Rey!"

No one answered.

Teffinger circled the vehicle, searching the ground.

Nothing was there, only black puddles getting further pounded by the weather.

Then he ran.

Ten, twenty, thirty, forty, fifty steps past, then something happened. The silhouette of a figure appeared up ahead, not much more than a dark watery blur coming in and out of focus through the storm, but definitely a human. Teffinger ran faster, raising his knees as high as he could given the massive weight of the water on his pants.

The gap closed.

In ten seconds Teffinger would be able to lunge at it.

It took a clearer shape.

It began to look like a woman.

It was Del Rey.

Teffinger slowed.

Suddenly she shouted, "Teffinger, look out!"

He turned.

A large black shape lunged at him out of the peripheral vision of his left side. A violent kick landed on his forearm. The gun flew out of his grip. He tried to follow it with his eyes but a rock-hard punch hit the side of his head. His feet buckled and his body slammed to the asphalt. Before he could even inhale to get air back into his lungs, weight was on him, a knee pressed him down, then iron fists pounded the back of his head with blow after blow after blow.

They weren't to subdue him.

They were to kill him.

He twisted, then more, and stronger, and somehow got to his feet.

He stood there, wobbly, starved for air, trying to catch his breath, too weak to swing an arm even one more time.

The other man lunged at him.

Teffinger's brain turned to hate.

It made him forget the pain.

It made him not care whether he lived or died.

It made him lunge back with every molecule of strength he had left.

89

The Big Kahuna started life in the 60s as an upscale bar with surfboards on the walls, barmaids in grass skirts and an endless stream of Beach Boys and Jan & Dean spilling out of the speakers. Now it was a faded wave, a dirty lagoon on a not-so-trendy street in a not-so-safe corner of the urban jungle. People still went there, though, and not just the drunks and hookers and the occasional stray, but businessmen and bankers and lawyers and politicians who knew the place from days gone past and wanted to meet off the beaten path.

Leland Everitt's silver BMW was parked on the

street.

Zahara pulled to the curb four or five spaces behind it and killed the engine.

"That's his car," she said. "He's already here."

Jori-Lee's watch said 9:48.

The night was dark.

Streetlights were on but the one in front of the bar was broken.

A neon sign said The Big.

Kahuna was dark.

"So now what?"

"Now we split up and take a stroll," Zahara said. "You take that side of the bar and I'll take this side, plus the back parking lot. Write down the license plate number of every car on the street, especially the nice ones, and especially any that pull in between now and ten. Don't let anyone see you. Keep your face hidden."

"Then what?"

"Then with any luck Leland and the person he's meeting with will come out of the bar at the same time. Maybe I'll recognize him—"

"Or her—"

"Right, or her, but I'm not counting on it. We can see what car the mystery person goes to. We'll already have the number."

"Then what?"

"Then we'll know who Leland met with."

"That's not enough," Jori-Lee said. "We need to get inside and hear what they say."

Zahara shook her head.

"There's no way."

"Is that a gym bag you have in the backseat?"

"Yes, why?"

Jori-Lee hopped into the back and unzipped her dress. "I'm changing out of my work clothes," she said. "What else do you have in here? Sunglasses or a hat or anything like that?"

"Forget it," Zahara said. "He'll know it's you the minute you walk in the door. Just calm down and lay low. I might recognize the person when he shows up. If they came all the way here for a meeting then the last thing they're going to do is talk loud enough for someone around them to overhear what they're saying. If you walk in there, all you're going to do is blow the whole deal."

Jori-Lee kept changing.

"When I get inside I'm going to call you," she said. "Be sure to pick up. Then I'm going to try to get my phone on their table. With any luck you'll be able to hear what they say."

"That's insane."

"True, but insane is all we have."

"How are you going to get your phone on their table?"

Jori-Lee wrinkled her brow.

"Give me a twenty," she said.

"What for?"

"To bribe a waitress."

Zahara hesitated and then pulled out her wallet.

"Here, take a fifty," she said. "For the record,

though, this will never work."

"We'll see."

Zahara cocked her head.

"I'll tell you what, if you're actually going to do this, go in the back door. Don't even go into the bar area itself. See if you can get in contact with a waitress and tell her what to do."

Jori-Lee nodded.

"See, now you're starting to think."

90

A blond Big Kahuna waitress with red lipstick and a short skirt was not only willing to do whatever it took to earn fifty bucks, but actually showed some creativity. She placed Jori-Lee's cell phone behind a menu in the booth next to where Leland Everitt was sitting, then managed to spill coke all over his table. Not having a cloth to clean up the mess, she escorted him over to the adjoining booth while profusely apologizing.

Jori-Lee went back the car and listened with Zahara.

Leland occasionally coughed.

The sound was garbled.

At ten o'clock, headlights came down the street and a vehicle parallel parked across the street. A man got out and went inside The Big.

Jori-Lee recognized the posture.

"I can't believe it," she said. "Do you know who

that is?"

Zahara shook her head.

"That's Preston Wendell."

"The Preston Wendell?"

"Yes."

"As in, the Supreme Court justice?"

"No question," Jori-Lee said. "I've spoken to him in the hall a dozen times."

"Damn."

Right, damn.

"What's he doing meeting with Leland Everitt?"

"Hopefully we'll find out."

Voices came from the cell phone.

The two men were talking.

What they were talking about, though, was unknown. The phone wasn't close enough to pick up the conversation. An occasional word came through but only as an island in an ocean of swill.

"Damn it."

The meeting lasted ten minutes.

The Supreme Court justice left first.

Leland Everitt followed two minutes later.

At Zahara's place with white wine in hand, they went through the mysterious Client X file retrieved from Leland's credenza.

To say it was extraordinary would be an understatement.

Although Leland's client was not identified by name in the papers, it was evident that he was a private investigator with an office somewhere either in

D.C. or the surrounding area.

Someone contacted him anonymously and made him an offer.

The offer was to pay him a million dollars in cash.

He, in turn, was to personally kill, or hire someone to kill, a woman by the name of T'amara Alder.

The investigator took the job.

The cash was paid.

The investigator in turned hired a man named Jean-Luc Baxa to kill T'amara Alder. The deed was done Friday night.

The next day, the investigator hired Leland Everitt to find out who hired him. Who was the anonymous voice on the other end of the phone? The question was critical because the investigator felt that he would be eliminated as someone who knew too much. He wanted to know who to watch out for and who to get some dirt on, if possible, as a shield.

Jori-Lee dropped the file in disgust.

"Nelson Robertson was the voice on the phone. The bastard."

"So now we have the evidence," Zahara said.

"Not really."

"Meaning what?"

Jori-Lee shook her head.

"Meaning this file falls under the attorney-client privilege," she said. "Even if we made it available to the police or the FBI, they couldn't use it in a court of law. Nor could they use it to support a search warrant."

"Yeah, but at least they'd have a lot of facts off the record," Zahara said. "That would get them sniffing around. Once they do that they'll come up with evidence on their own."

Jori-Lee wasn't impressed.

"We'll keep it in our back pocket. I want to break this case open with solid evidence, real evidence, the kind of thing you can slap on a wall."

"You want to be a hero," Zahara said.

Jori-Lee thought about it.

It was partly true but mostly not.

"What I want is to prove that we have a killer sitting on the Supreme Court, and then get his ass off it." A beat then, "I'll bet you anything that Leland Everitt is closing in on Robertson as the mystery voice who hired the investigator. That's why he was so secretly meeting with Preston Wendell tonight. Wendell must know something about Robertson or at least suspect something. He was conveying it to Leland. Wendell's a good guy. He wouldn't want a stained judge on the court any more than I would. Way less, in fact." She took a swallow of wine. "Tomorrow we need to go to work as dumb as dirt. We can't let anyone onto what we know. Not yet."

"Agreed."

"As a footnote we need to figure out who Leland's client is too, this private investigator," she said. "He needs to be off the streets. Well at least now I know who I heard on the other end of the phone when T'amara Alder got murdered—Jean-Luc Baxa. He sounds foreign. I wonder who the hell he is."

Zahara powered up her iPad.

"Let's find out. You want some more wine?"

DAY TEN

July 17
Thursday

91

Whatever sleep came Wednesday night was intermittent and twisty and anything but deep. Teffinger woke at the first rays of dawn Thursday morning in the Intercontinental, not the fleabag, still needing another four hours of rest but knowing he'd never get it, not even four minutes of it, not with his brain on fire the way it was.

He rolled onto his back.

Del Rey was still alive, next to him, sleeping soundly.

The man escaped into the guts of the weather.

The detective who processed the scene last night, a man named Phil Bates out of the Crimes Against Persons unit, wasn't too pleased that Teffinger had been laying wait out in a storm with a gun. "You were going to kill him? That was the plan?"

"No. The plan was to take him alive."

"How?"

"I'm not sure," Teffinger said. "I didn't know if he'd even show up."

Bates wasn't impressed.

"Killing suspects isn't the way we do things out here," he said. "That may pass for okay in Denver but it doesn't here."

Teffinger argued.

It did no good.

"The other thing we don't do here is shoot at cars just because we suspect something."

"That's all I had time to do, assume the worst and shoot. I hit a tire which is what I was aiming for."

"Yeah, well, you also hit the trunk and put a bullet through the back window. There could have been a gaggle of nuns in that car."

"Doubtful."

"Maybe but it was also possible."

The car, it turned out, had been stolen two days ago.

It got towed for printing and processing.

The fibers and blood and minutia of the immediate scene were basically washed away by the storm, which didn't let up all night and if anything got stronger.

Bates' final advice was given with a hard face and tight narrow eyes. "Go back to Denver. If you stay here and end up killing someone, things could end up getting ugly for you."

"Meaning what?"

"You do the math, especially if you injure a bystander."

That was last night.

Now it was morning.

Del Rey was still alive.

The population of the world hadn't gone down by one. That was good enough math for Teffinger.

He took a shower. Halfway through, the curtain pulled back, Del Rey stepped in and said, "That detective last night was an ass."

"He had some valid points," Teffinger said.

"Yeah, well, if you were him, I'd be dead. I'll bet he's never had the balls even once to cock his hand into a fist." She rubbed her stomach against his. "Thanks for being you and not some stupid little pussy."

"Such language."

"Sorry, but it's true."

Toweled off with coffee in hand, Teffinger wasn't quite sure what to do today. Down below the financial district started to get thicker with movement. The air was fog-free. Early morning vessels cut wakes through choppy bay waters.

His phone rang.

It turned out to be the woman from the Green Dragon Oriental Massage, the young one wrapped in the kimono. "I'm not supposed to be talking to you," she said.

"Well I'm glad you are."

"I gave your message to Dandan," she said. "She's not going to call you. You need to help her. She'd going to hate me but I want to give you her new number. Please call her. She's into something and I don't know what it is, but I do know it's serious. She needs someone."

Teffinger grabbed a pencil and pad.

"Give me the number."

She did.

"Please help her even if she won't let you."

"I'll try."

"Thank you."

He dialed Dandan. She hung up as soon as she realized who it was. He dialed again and said, "I just want to talk, just for two minutes. Just talk, nothing else. If you don't like what I have to say, I'll go away and you'll never be bothered by me again."

A beat then, "Talk about what?"

"For starters, keeping you alive," he said. "Rail's after you. My truce with him was over yesterday."

"He's not an issue. He'll never find me."

"You're wrong about that. Do you still have the painting?"

"That's no one's concern but mine."

"I know you sold it," Teffinger said. "I know it's under contract. What I want to know is whether you physically made the exchange yet or whether you still have the painting in your possession."

"I'm not giving it to you so it's a moot point."

"Just tell me."

"The exchange is set for three o'clock today."

"Let me borrow it until two."

He told her why; to show it to Rail, have Rail tell him where Susan Smith was, and who killed Kelly

Nine, then switch it out from under his nose.

"That's insane. No one's that stupid."

"I can make it work," Teffinger said. "Trust me. You'll get the painting back in time for the exchange. I'll even go to the exchange with you, to make sure everything goes the way it should."

"It's already going the way it should," she said. "Half the money's already been paid."

Teffinger exhaled.

"Susan Smith is going to die if you don't cooperate."

"She's probably already dead. But even if she isn't, and even if your plan works and you trick Rail into telling you where she is, he's going to kill her as soon as he finds out you suckered him."

"I'll get to her first."

"You don't know that," Dandan said. "An associate of his could be holding her captive somewhere, which makes sense; otherwise she would have popped up somewhere. All Rail has to do is make a phone call. We both know that the only way Rail won't kill her is if you give him the real painting. Either that or you kill him as soon as he gives you the information. Is that what you're going to do? Kill him on the spot?"

"No."

"So what's your plan then? Give him the real painting?"

"No."

"Well, then you don't have a plan, not one that will work, anyway. I'm sorry about all this, I really am, but

I think we're done talking. I'm smashing this phone as soon as I hang up so don't try calling again."

The line went dead.

Teffinger called Sydney.

"Two minutes ago I just made a phone call to a cell number," he said. "I need the physical location of where that phone was, as in an address if possible. Here's the problem, I don't have time to go the warrant route. Do you have any markers you can call in?"

Silence.

"Maybe—"

Del Rey studied him with a sober face after he hung up and then said, "You're going to get Dandan killed."

He opened his mouth to argue.

No good words came out.

He shoved his wallet in his back pocket, grabbed the car keys and headed for the door. "I'll be back in an hour. Stay here where it's safe."

She grabbed her purse, fell into step and said, "Where we going?" When he looked at her and she said, "I don't listen very well, do I?"

"Now that you mention it, no."

92

They headed to Dandan's apartment and found it unlocked as before, but now even more of a mess. "Someone's been here," Teffinger said.

"Rail?"

Teffinger shrugged.

"I'm guessing he made the first mess and someone new made this one, probably the guys after Rail, or more to the point, after the painting. Right now though I don't give a rat's ass about anything but the movie."

The movie.

Teffinger's theory was simple.

The papers showing Kelly Nine in a porno weren't printouts from a camera shot, like he first thought. They were still prints taken off a movie. That movie was somewhere in Dandan's apartment. If they could find it they might be able to get a better handle on who was in it, where it was taken and how Kelly ended up in it.

In the corner was a flat screen TV on a small table.

Under that table on the carpet were one or two hundred DVDs.

Basic Instinct.

The Wedding Singer.

Body Double.

Perfect Strangers.

The Hangover.

The Lincoln Lawyer.

They opened them, one at a time, throwing the boxes and the discs to the other side of the room. Five minutes into it, Teffinger found something interesting.

In Failure to Launch was an unlabeled disc.

"Bingo, maybe," he said.

He fired it up.

Kelly Nine filled the screen, frame after frame after frame, in unforgiving clarity, not enjoying what she was doing but going with it, almost as if she was drunk or in a trance or resigned to the fate because of something that happened beforehand.

He ejected the disc and said, "This has something to do why she was targeted for murder."

"I agree."

"She wasn't enjoying herself."

"No, not hardly."

Teffinger stuck the disc back in Failure to Launch, slipped the case into his rear pants pocket and then he let his eyes sweep around. Maybe there was something here they missed the first time, something that would tell them where Dandan was.

He grabbed a Diet Coke from the fridge and took a long swallow as his eyes roamed.

Suddenly the door pushed open.

A man walked in.

It was Rail.

He had a gun in his hand

Attached to that gun was a silencer.

He pointed that silencer at Teffinger's chest.

"Stay calm," the man said.

Teffinger swallowed what was left in the can, crumpled it in his hand and let it drop to the floor.

"It looks like we meet again," he said.

93

Jean-Luc Baxa—the man who killed T'amara Alder—was an Internet ghost. His name was nowhere, his footprint was nowhere, his shadow was nowhere, his keystroke was nowhere. He was invisible, which wasn't surprising given the nature of his work. A man in his profession wouldn't get sloppy enough to let someone hunt him from the privacy of a living room.

Jean and Luc were popular French names.

Baxa was an established French surname.

So, the man was French, assuming the name wasn't an alias.

Physically, Jori-Lee couldn't differentiate a French national from an American one. If Baxa came for her, she wouldn't suspect him based on looks. Language was another matter. If he spoke, there would be an accent, however faint or buried. That's what she had to watch for.

Thursday morning, if Leland Everitt knew anything about the events of last night, he gave no clue; not when he came to Jori-Lee's office to be sure everything was going to her satisfaction on her second day of work, and not when she bumped into him in the hall an hour later.

Shortly before lunch, Jori-Lee walked into Zahara's

office and closed the door.

"I think I figured out who Leland's mysterious private investigator Client X is," she said. "I think he's a guy named Oscar Benderfield."

"Why?"

"Because—get this—Benderfield got killed last week."

"How do you know?"

"I went down the list of investigators in D.C. and Googled them this morning, just trying to get a feeling as to whether one of them seemed shady enough to hire a hitman. I came across an article in the Post about Oscar Benderfield's death. It didn't say how he got killed but I called his office. A woman by the name of Danielle answered—his Secretary, I assume—and told me that Benderfield got killed by a Denver detective who came to town to question him about a case. Apparently there was a fight and Benderfield lost. The local police weren't pressing charges against the detective."

"What was the detective's name?"

"Nick Teffinger."

Zahara chewed on it.

"If Benderfield's the client, why would Leland still be working the case last night if his client was dead?"

"Good question," Jori-Lee said. "My guess is that he hasn't heard about it, either that or he's figured out that Robertson is dirty and is on a mission to bring him down."

Zahara exhaled.

"Either way, I guess it's not important," she said.

"What we need to do is get into Benderfield's office and see if we can find some evidence that ties him to Robertson, plus the guy he hired, the Jean-Luc guy; especially Jean-Luc, since he might be after you."

"Jean-Luc."

"Right," Zahara said. "We'll do that tonight."

"Do what, exactly? Break into his office?"

"Yes."

Jori-Lee swallowed.

Then she said, "Okay."

94

Teffinger's brain sparked with the force of a renegade lighting storm. There was no move he had that would be faster than Rail's squeeze on the trigger. He was helpless against the man and, worst, so was Del Rey.

"I don't have the painting and I don't know where Dandan is," he said. "Whatever you're hoping to get out of me, you're not going to get it."

Rail wasn't impressed.

He nodded towards the couch and said, "Sit down."

Teffinger hesitated and then complied.

Del Rey joined him.

Rail leaned against the wall, out of distance of any possible lunge, and kept the barrel pointed at Teffinger. "Dandan's broker in Rome, Savina Bandini, was murdered last night. Did you know that?"

Teffinger's forehead tightened.

He could still hear the woman's voice in his ear.

The voice disappeared as he realized Rail wasn't bluffing. The fact was too easy to verify.

"By who?"

Rail retreated in thought and then said, "Let me ask you a question. Have you ever heard of a man named Yoan Foca?"

Yoan Foca.

Yoan Foca.

"No."

"That's good for you," he said, "because just hearing his name takes you halfway to death. He lives in Havana, Cuba, and has never once in his life left the country, at least to my knowledge. His minions, though, are all over the world. There's no place they can't go. There's no one they can't kill."

Teffinger hardened his face.

"Why do I care?"

"You care because Yoan Foca is my client," Rail said. "He's the one who originally owned the Van Gogh. He's the one I was in the process of selling it for when Dandan took it. He's the one out there in the shadows hell-bent to get it back. He's the one who killed Savina Bandini last night. He's the one who's a heartbeat away from getting his fists around the throat of Dandan, whether she knows it or not." A beat then, "He's the one who will hunt you to the ends of the earth once he knows you refused to help me." He nodded towards Del Rey, focused back on Teffinger and said, "And your pretty little girlfriend here? She's nothing more than a scream in the night. Then, poof, she's gone. She's gone so far and so deep that it's questionable whether she ever even existed."

"Is that one of his men in town?"

"Meaning what?"

"The one who's after me or her," he said. "The one who rips the wings off birds—"

"Him? No, he's not one of Foca's," he said. "Foca doesn't hire people that sloppy. You're going to have a talk with your little Dandan friend. You're going to let her know just how deep in she is. You're going to explain to her that the only way to come out of this alive—and un-tortured for that matter—is to turn over the painting while she still has a chance. Like I said, Savina Bandini's dead. She was killed before the new buyer sent her any money."

"She told me the opposite."

"If she did she was lying," Rail said. "Even if she wasn't, Dandan would will never see a cent of it, not at this point. The woman has no upside in keeping the painting. It's not going to bring her riches. It will only bring her death, worse than death, actually. This is your chance to save her from a horrible, horrible thing. I'll call you in two hours. Have some good news for me."

He shoved the weapon in his waistband and headed for the door.

"Hey, Rail. Where's Susan Smith?"

The man stopped and said over his shoulder, "I'll tell you in two hours when you have that good news for me."

Then he was gone.

Teffinger didn't get up. Instead he pulled out his cell phone and dialed Leigh Sandt in Quantico. "It's me, Nick. Look, I know I'm being a huge pain in the ass but I need whatever you can get me on a Havana, Cuba guy named Yoan Foca."

"Yoan Foca—"

"Right. Yoan Foca."

"Why?"

"He has henchmen out here in San Francisco that are a heartbeat away from killing someone. I'd like to figure out who those henchmen are."

He hung up and said to Del Rey, "I'm not a huge fan of Rail's style but I have to agree with him that Dandan is playing at an end-game that's about to take her down."

"So what do we do?"

"We find her and knock some sense into her."

95

An hour passed and nothing good happened. Dandan hadn't shown up at the Green Dragon, the kimono girl had no new information and Teffinger had no idea where to look next. Then Sydney called and said, "Get a pencil, here's the address of where that cell phone connected."

Teffinger's blood raced as he wrote it down.

"It didn't come easy," Sydney said. "I officially owe two blowjobs. Plus—"

"Syd, I got to cut you short, I'm sorry, I'll explain later. Good work. No, not good work, great work. I'll call you later today."

He hung up.

The address was in Chinatown, two blocks from the Green Dragon, and belonged to a small shop that sold pastries and tea and coffee. Dandan wasn't there. The customers were few. Teffinger smiled at the woman behind the counter and said, "I'm looking for Dandan. Do you know her?"

"No Dandan."

"Does that mean she's not here or you don't know her?"

"Know no Dandan."

Teffinger's shoulders went limp.

"Okay, thanks."

Outside a stiff wind blew.

Teffinger called the woman's cell phone again. Like every time before, he got nothing. She had destroyed the phone just like she said she would.

"Now what?" Del Rey said.

Teffinger surveyed the street.

There was buzz, cold buzz, cold buzz that wouldn't help him.

Then he looked up.

Above the shop were two stories, both living quarters judging by the window coverings and the balconies.

"She's staying in one of those," he said. "That's where she was when my call connected."

"How do you know?"

"Because it's time for something in my life to work out the way it's supposed to."

The entrance was a plain wooden door to the right of the shop labeled Private, invisible unless you were looking for it. They quietly climbed narrow wooden stairs to the second level and listened at the door. No sounds came from inside. They continued up and listened at the top door. From inside came the sounds of kids speaking in Chinese and the occasional muttering of a woman who wasn't Dandan.

They went back to the second floor.

No sounds came from behind the door.

Teffinger tried the knob.

It was locked.

He knocked.

No one answered.

"Come on," Teffinger said.

They headed down onto the street and then found an alley that led to the back of the building. As suspected, a fire escape ran up the side, a beautiful, beautiful fire escape. Teffinger scouted up and down the alley. A few eyes were around but none were paying attention.

They headed up to the second floor landing.

A window was open.

It had no screen.

A fan was blowing.

Teffinger poked his head in just in time to see the

backside of a woman darting out the front door.

It was Dandan.

"Dandan! Hold on!"

She didn't even slow enough to slam the door behind her.

Her footsteps pounded down the stairs.

Teffinger wedged through the window, twisting and struggling a lot more than he expected. Then he was across the room and down the stairs.

At street level he looked to the right.

She wasn't in sight.

He looked to the left.

She wasn't that way either.

He checked both directions again, got nothing, and then raced to the right with a fifty-fifty chance.

96

Teffinger's sprint to the right turned out to be a bad, bad, very bad choice. Dandan didn't appear ahead of him, not in fifty steps, not in half a block and not in a full block, at which point he gave up. Del Rey wasn't at street level when he got back to the apartment. He found her inside with the door closed.

In front of her, on a small kitchen table, was an aluminum case.

It was open.

The Van Gogh was inside.

"This was under the bed," she said. "Is this it?"

He nodded.

"Yeah, that's it."

"It's okay," she said. "But to be honest, I don't know if I'd hang it on a wall."

"You're in luck then because you'll never have to."

She smiled and closed it up.

"Let's go."

He considered it and then surprised himself by sitting down.

"We'll wait for Dandan to come back," he said.

"What for? We don't need her anymore—"

That was true.

"It's her life on the line," he said. "She deserves a say in what happens."

Del Rey tilted her head.

"I thought we already concluded that the painting would kill her if she tried to hang onto it. I thought getting it away from her was her only chance at living."

He nodded.

"It is."

"So what's the issue?"

"The issue is it's her life," he said. "She deserves a say in it."

"Yeah, but if she says anything other than get rid of the damn thing, she'll be dead. There is no other right answer, none, not now, not tomorrow, not next year. If she gave any other answer, all that would mean is that she's not thinking clearly enough to save herself. She's too drunk with the money, which will never come. Plus, don't forget about Susan Smith."

"I haven't."

"Personally I think Rail's lying through his lips when he says she's still alive, but you never know. The only way to find out for sure is to give him the painting."

Half a pot of coffee was on the counter.

Teffinger found a cup, splashed a little milk in and topped it off from the pot.

It was hot.

It was good.

"We'll wait for Dandan," he said.

Del Rey shook her head.

"I can't believe you're doing this."

He took a careful slurp.

"They might kill her even if we turn the painting over," he said.

"Well, that's a risk she took when she stole it," Del Rey said. "We didn't get her into this mess. She got herself into it. So, yeah, they might kill her on general principles even if we turn it over. But they'll definitely kill her if we don't."

Teffinger nodded.

That was true.

"I want her to turn it over voluntarily," he said. "I think that will bode better for her. Rail was going to give her a million for it. Maybe we'll go back to that arrangement. Then at least she'll have some money to help her disappear."

His phone rang.

It was Leigh, the profiler.

Teffinger took a sip of coffee and said, "What do you got?"

"Did I just hear coffee?"

"Yeah, sorry."

"You're drinking coffee?"

"Yes."

"While you're driving somewhere?"

"No, I'm sitting at a table."

"You're sitting at a table drinking coffee?"

"Yes."

"How come I'm busting my butt on your case— repeat, your case, not mine—while you're sitting at a table drinking coffee?"

"Because you're a better person than me."

"This is wrong, Teffinger, this is wrong on so many levels that I don't even know where to begin."

He took another sip, a noisy one.

"Ah, good. Don't worry," he said. "I'm going to do some work tomorrow, or the day after for sure. Now, tell me what you got. This is about my little Havana friend, Yoan Foca, right?"

It was.

It was indeed.

What she had to say about the man wasn't pretty.

He was a mean, powerful bastard.

He was a mean, powerful bastard who rode the riches of drugs, weapons, human trafficking, extortion, computer crimes, political rigging, and all the filthy little things in between.

He was the uncontrolled and uncontrollable King Kong of Cuba, rich beyond numbers, although that wasn't his defining mark. No, that honor went to his power. Inside the country he had a network of lawyers, judges and politicians slithering up to his feet with puckered lips whenever they were summoned. Outside Cuba he was networked into the deepest depths of filth and violence.

The smart thing was to never become his enemy.

He could reach you no matter where you were in the world.

His arms were long and stretched across oceans.

His primary areas of operation were Mexico, the Middle East, the Bahamas and Europe. All of it was orchestrated from his compound outside of Havana, which he never, ever left.

Because of his size and the ripple effect into the United States of what he did in Mexico, the CIA kept him in its peripheral vision. To date, though, as far as they knew, he'd been smart enough to stay outside the borders. There was no current operation in progress to take him down in whole or part.

The compound sat on a hundred barbwire-encased acres, meticulously monitored with weapons, dogs and cameras. Inside were three mansions, each more opulent than the other, each with ready access to a labyrinth of tunnels and secret escapes.

He liked women, young women, young women of all races and designs, and maintained a well-stocked supply.

Teffinger hung up, grabbed the Van Gogh and said, "Let's go."

"I thought we were waiting for Dandan."

He hesitated, then scribbled a note, "Call me," followed by his cell phone number, and set it on the counter.

"There's only one right answer," he said. "We need to get the painting back to this Yoan Boca guy. Otherwise Dandan is dead a hundred times over."

"I thought you were going to give her a say—"

"I was but now I'm at the point where it doesn't matter what she says," he said. "She works at an ad agency. This other world that she's strayed into is just words and blurred images to her. I don't think she appreciates just how real it is."

Del Rey headed for the door.

"Okay, your call," she said. "But I don't like putting the target around your neck instead of hers. Call me selfish but that's the way I feel."

"Our neck," he said. "Not my neck."

"Yeah, thanks for that, by the way."

"It's only temporary. Hopefully this will all be wrapped up by the end of the day."

Del Rey shifted her feet.

"Do you think it's smart to leave your number? What if Boca's men show up and find it?"

"That's fine. That will give me a chance to tell them Dandan doesn't have the painting any more."

97

Ten minutes, that's how short a time it took for Dandan to call Teffinger after he left. "Damn you to hell," she said. "I told you about that painting in trust. I trusted you, you son-of-a-bitch."

"Savina Bandini got murdered last night," he said.

"Bullshit."

"It's true," Teffinger said. "Rail told me and then I verified it on the web. You're next."

Silence.

"Who killed her?"

"Who do you think? When you stole the painting, you didn't steal it from Rail, you stole it from his client, who's a Cuban guy named Yoan Foca."

"I never heard of him."

"Good because you don't want to."

"Is he the one who killed Savina?"

"Yes, his men, technically, but yes."

The woman exhaled.

"I don't have time for this stuff. I have to deliver that painting at three o'clock."

"That's not going to happen."

"It's already been bought," she said. "Do you know who bought it?"

"No," Teffinger said. "I've actually been wondering about that."

"Mun Yin. He operates out of Hong Kong," she

said. "Everything nasty that happens in that part of the world, he's got his hands in. I don't know who your little Cuban friend is, but there's one thing I know. I'm not going to screw around with Mun Yin."

Teffinger exhaled.

"Has he actually paid for the painting?"

"He's paid ten million of it," she said. "That was wired to a Cayman account Savina has."

"How about you? Did she send any to you yet?"

"No."

"So you don't have any money in hand to give back to the guy—Mun Yin?"

"No, plus you don't understand, that's not the way this works," she said. "He bought the painting. He's already paid half. He's entitled to the painting." A beat then, "After I deliver it I can tell him what happened to Savina. I'll have him pay the balance directly to me."

"He'll blow you off."

"I don't think so."

"So you're still looking for money, even after all this—"

"I'm looking to complete a deal that's already half done," she said. "He's not going to be too happy with this Cuban guy who killed Savina. That guy better watch out. I want the painting back and I want it back now. If you don't give it to me then I'm going to show up at three o'clock and tell them who took it. Then you better watch out."

Teffinger cocked his head.

"Call me back in an hour," he said.

Then he hung up.

In the 4Runner heading east on Market with the Van Gogh in the back, he called Leigh Sandt to see if she could get him a read on Mun Yin. Twenty minutes later she got back to him with pretty much what he expected.

Mun Yin was an even deadlier dog than Yoan Foca.

It was almost noon.

He looked at Del Rey and said, "Are you hungry?"

"Starved."

"Keep your eyes out for a drive-thru. I don't want to leave the painting alone."

She put a hand on his shoulder.

"You can't save Dandan," she said.

"So what would you do if you were me?"

"I'd just give her back the painting and let her decide which is the lesser of the two evils. She seems to think it's the Cuban guy. I tend to agree with her. If she carries through with the Mun Yin sale, maybe he'll actually pay the balance directly to her. That way at least she'd have a good chunk of cash to help her disappear. Plus, maybe Mun Yin will kill the Cuban guy for killing Savina and trying to hijack the deal. If that happens then Dandan will have the problem solved at both ends."

He spotted a McDonalds and swung in.

"I can already taste the fries," he said.

Fifteen minutes later, back on the road with a cheeseburger in his left hand and fries wedged in the console, Teffinger got the call from Dandan, exactly one hour from when they last spoke.

"You can have the painting back," he said.

"I can?"

"Yes. Go up to Twin Peaks and pull into the viewing area," he said. "I'll be in a white 4Runner. Don't look at me and don't park next to me. Get out of your car, take a look at the view for a few minutes, then get back in your car and pull away. Call me while you're driving. I'll follow you. When I'm sure no one's on your tail, I'll let you know to pull over and you can have the painting."

"Fine. When?"

"I'll be up there in half an hour. Tell me something first. We found a porno DVD at your apartment."

"With Kelly Nine—"

"Right. Where'd you get it?"

"Someone came across it on the Internet," she said. "He knew Kelly and thought it was her but he wasn't sure. He downloaded part of it onto a DVD and sent it to me to get my opinion, which was that it was definitely her."

"You never told me about it," Teffinger said.

"She was dead," Dandan said. "I didn't see a need to tarnish her reputation."

"It has something to do with why she got marked for murder."

"Then you know more than me."

Teffinger exhaled.

"Who's going to help you deliver the painting this afternoon?"

"No one."

"Think about whether you want me to come along."

He hung up.

Del Rey wasn't impressed.

"You're a homicide detective, not a stolen arts dealer."

"True, but I'm also all she has."

"Nick, listen to yourself. She's a criminal at this point. Homicide detectives aren't supposed to spend their days helping criminals commit their crimes. We came here to catch Rail, remember? Why? Because he killed that investigator back in Denver."

"And he took Susan Smith."

"Right. So why aren't we focused on Rail?"

He shoved a fry in his mouth.

"Remember when we were at your house and it was storming out with all the lightning and you danced for me all sexy and everything?"

"Yes."

"That was nice," he said.

98

At the top of Twin Peaks, Dandan pulled the Targa into one of the few empty parking spaces unclaimed by tourists, which happened to be four down from Teffinger's 4Runner. There she got out, slipped on sunglasses and walked to the guardrail to take in the panoramic view of the relentless congestion that stretched in all directions until it got slapped to a stop by water.

Teffinger kept his concentration on the vehicles that arrived after her.

They were few in number.

None looked suspicious.

Dandan was dressed down, in Jeans, a black T and tennis shoes. Up top she wore a black baseball cap turned backwards. A breeze blew her hair, sometimes far enough that she had to brush it out of her face.

After a few minutes she got back in the Targa, fired it up and pulled out.

Teffinger waited ten seconds and then followed.

A car was between them, a black BMW with tinted windows.

"Where'd that come from?"

"I don't know."

The road down twisted through grassy slopes that provided unobstructed views in all directions.

Teffinger's phone rang and Dandan's voice came

through.

"There's a bimmer behind me."

"I know. Who's inside?"

"Two men."

"Okay, I'll tell you what, when you get down the hill to Portola put on your right turn signal. We'll see if they do the same. Then, instead of turning right, head straight across the road into Glen Canyon. Hopefully they won't follow and we'll just prove to ourselves that we're overly paranoid."

"Okay."

"Stay on the phone. Don't disconnect."

"I am."

Teffinger dropped back.

The BMW stayed behind Dandan as she cut into a twisty canyon road with a steep incline to her left. As the bottom on the hill she did as instructed.

It had no effect.

Her voice was stressed when she said, "They're still on my ass."

"I know. I'm closing the gap."

"What should I do?"

"Don't panic. Cut over to Market."

"Then what?"

"Get into the financial district," he said. "Pull into the first big hotel you come to. There'll be security cameras. They won't try anything there."

Suddenly something came out of the BMW's passenger window, possibly an arm and a head.

A bright flash of orange fired.

Instantly the windshield of the 4Runner shattered with an explosion so deafening and so horrible that Teffinger's entire body jerked.

Del Rey screamed, "Nick!"

Orange flashed again.

A tire exploded.

The vehicle jerked to the right.

Teffinger fought for control.

Then the vehicle flipped into a death roll.

The violence of the motion prevented any sense of orientation. Up was down and down was up. Sounds tore through the air, horrific sounds of popping glass and twisting metal and things being ripped to their death. A seatbelt snagged Teffinger's chest and pelvis time and again as airbags exploded around his head and body.

Then almost as quickly as it began, all motion stopped.

The crash was over.

The vehicle was on its side.

Teffinger wasn't dead.

How badly he was hurt, he had no idea, but he wasn't dead.

"Del Rey!"

"Teffinger—"

She was alive.

A pungent odor of gas or oil invaded the air.

"Come on!"

His door wouldn't open but the glass was busted. He climbed out, ignoring the damage to his body as best he could, then pulled Del Rey through behind him.

No one was around.

He checked his body.

Everything worked.

Blood came from wounds but none of them were profuse.

Del Rey was in equal shape.

Teffinger felt her body.

Nothing seemed broken.

She could stand okay.

She could walk okay.

She could bend to the right and to the left.

There were no obvious injuries to her skull.

Up the road quite some distance was the Targa, immobile and strangely angled, most likely wrecked. A black BMW was in the same vicinity, not strangely angled, not most-likely wrecked. Two men were carrying something between the two, something that was probably Dandan.

The Van Gogh was still in the back area of the 4Runner.

Teffinger pulled it out through the broken glass and handed it to Del Rey. "Take it. Head down the hill into the trees. Just keep going until you come out the other side."

"Okay."

"Grab the first cab you see," he said. "Take it into Sausalito, get a hotel and stash the painting the best place you can find, behind the curtains or something.

Then leave."

"To where?"

"A coffee shop; I don't care. Just get away from the painting. I'll call you."

She took a step towards the trees then turned and said, "I need my purse."

It was scattered inside the vehicle.

Her wallet, however, was intact.

He got it for her, plus her cell phone and said, "If anyone finds you with the painting, don't argue with them. Just give it to them."

"What are you going to do?"

"I'm going to head up the road."

99

Jori-Lee's end of the law firm turned into an orchestration of controlled chaos Thursday afternoon, caused by the Tangent case, which she wasn't involved in. From what she gleaned, the case had churned into a perfect storm of trial motions, proposed jury instructions, identification of witnesses and draft exhibit books that all needed to be filed and served by the end of the day.

Jori-Lee kept her door open.

She left it open because the buzz felt good; it felt like money, it felt like danger, it felt like the preparation of war.

More importantly, she left it open because people

needed to know they could walk in and grab her if they needed to.

She was available.

She was on their team.

She wasn't afraid.

Time passed.

Then Jon Ryan walked in and said, "Can I jerk you out of whatever you're doing?"

"Sure."

He pushed a stapled set of papers across the desk and said, "This is a brief we're filing in support of a proposed jury instruction on liability. Give it a read and see if you spot any typos or anything that needs to be changed, improved, modified, stricken or whatever. Don't be shy. Be brutal. Make sure if the girl enters the scene wearing a red dress she doesn't leave wearing a blue one. Okay?"

She nodded.

"Okay. How fast?"

"It's due today but we're going to file it electronically, which means midnight. So you have some time."

"Good."

"Give your changes directly to Dottie. She'll do a redline/strikeout so I'll be able to see what you've done. Again, be brutal. I want this thing to be suitable for framing. I want it hanging in the Smithsonian."

"I'll see what I can do."

"You'll do fine."

Five minutes later, Sanders called.

The sound of his voice briefly took Jori-Lee to a

moment in time with the man's golden body before her and the sand under her feet and the sun in her eyes and a dance in her heart.

"I'm still shadowing your apartment," he said. "All's quiet."

"Good."

"There was a Supreme Court case about a year-and-a-half ago called Texas vs. Certileo," he said. "Do you remember it?"

"No."

"Well, it was a criminal case. The defendant, Cisco Certileo, was a young Hispanic boy, thirteen years old at the time. His father was long gone. He lived with his mother and her screwed-up boyfriend, a man named Hector. Hector wasn't a very nice person. He beat the mother and, as it turned out, visited Cisco's bedroom whenever his drunken cock felt like it, which was a lot. The mother knew. She did nothing to stop it. Eventually the kid snapped and murdered them both in their sleep with a butcher knife. He was tried as an adult, assigned to an incompetent public defender, found guilt and sentenced to death."

"I vaguely remember reading something about that."

"It was in all the headlines," Sanders said. "Anyway, the case eventually made its way all the way up to the Supreme Court, the issue being whether it was cruel and unusual punishment to give a death penalty to a kid who was only thirteen years old at the time of the crime, particularly given all the stressors in the kid's life that led to the event, coupled with the questionable competence of the kid's attorney. The Supreme Court reversed the death penalty sentence in a 5 to 4 decision. Robertson was one of the judges in the majority who voted for reversal."

"Okay, but I don't get what this has to do with anything."

Sanders exhaled.

"Robertson threw his vote," he said.

"How do you know?"

"I found it on the flash drive," he said. "He's been throwing cases for almost two years. What he has is the decision he would have written together with the decision he actually submitted."

"How can that be? He didn't get blackmailed until a week or two ago."

"I don't know but I do know one thing," Sanders said. "He's thrown eight votes so far. In five of the cases, his throw really didn't matter. The decision ended up 6 to 3 instead of 5 to 4. In three cases the whole decision flipped. The one that concerns me the most is the one I just told you about. If and when we ever expose him, his vote in the Certileo case will be vacated. That will leave the decision as four to four. A tie means that the lower Court's opinion stands. It doesn't get reversed."

Jori-Lee processed it.

"That means the death penalty will stand," she said.

"Right," Sanders said. "That wouldn't be good. I would have done the thing as that kid in those circumstances."

Jori-Lee exhaled.

"We're so deep in uncharted territory that it's not even funny," she said. "Maybe his vote won't be vacated."

"It's fraud by a judge," Sanders said. "Something has to happen."

"Well then, alternatively, maybe there will be new legal arguments, to the effect that it would be cruel and unusual to have a final decision holding no death penalty and then modifying that decision with the effect of reinstating the death penalty. The reversal itself would be cruel and unusual."

"I wouldn't want my future hanging on that, would you?"

She considered it.

The pushback wasn't kind.

"Maybe the case will be re-submitted fresh."

"That leaves the original eight judges, meaning the death penalty won't be reversed. Even if the Court was to hold the case in abeyance until a new judge is installed, who knows how the new judge would vote. In the meantime, the poor kid has to have everything hanging over his head again, not to mention that new precedent might be set. The way it is now, states basically have a red light when it comes to executing kids. That's fine with me."

"So you're saying we don't expose him—"

"I'm not saying that per se," Sanders said. "All I'm saying is that if we do, a lot more than just his life will end up changed."

Jori-Lee's eyes fell to the brief.

"I can't get my brain around this right now," she said. "I have to work late and then me and Zahara have a little mission to complete."

"A mission?"

"I'll tell you about it after it's done," she said. "I'll be home late but I'll make it up to you. Wait up for me."

"Okay."

"Promise?"

"Yes, promise."

"Hey, you still there?"

Yes, he was.

"Maybe Robertson just flip-flops," she said. "Maybe instead of throwing cases, he honestly wasn't sure which way to go. To help resolve it in his mind, he wrote the opinion both ways and then figured out which version fit better."

Sanders wasn't convinced.

"I've never known a lawyer's brain to work that way, to the point of actually writing it out in detail both ways. But I can't for sure say that it would be impossible."

"We'll talk tonight. I want to see the flash drive."

"I put it back where we keep it."

"See you tonight."

100

The two men dumped Dandan into the trunk of the BMW and then squealed away long before Teffinger got his feet to the scene or his eyes to their faces. One of the Porsche's rear tires was shredded, presumably from a well-placed slug. A long fishtail etched in the asphalt led to where the vehicle slammed into a boulder.

The slam wasn't hard.

The front end was crumpled but not destroyed.

The hood was jacked up enough that you could see inside.

There was some blood on the interior but not a lot.

Teffinger looked up the road.

No vehicles were approaching from either direction.

The men must have been operating under the assumption that the Van Gogh was in the Porsche with Dandan. Finding their assumption wrong, they then took her for interrogation.

She wouldn't hold up well.

She'd tell them that Teffinger had the painting.

Then they'd come for him.

There was only one play left at this point, namely to swap the painting for Dandan; make an even exchange. It was doable but only if Teffinger kept the painting under his control. It wouldn't be in his interest to let the cops know he had it. They'd take it; not just because it was stolen property, but because it would shine a worldwide spotlight on their pretty little hero faces. Keeping the painting meant he needed to get out of here, now. They'd trace the 4Runner to him at some point but that would be later. He'd handle it—including the fact that he left the scene of an accident—when the time came.

A vehicle swept around a far bend into sight, still a distance away but already slowing as it approached the 4Runner.

Teffinger disappeared into the trees.

He was a ghost.

He was already gone.

Five minutes later in the thick of the silence he did something he didn't anticipate, namely he called Rail. The man's phone still worked, which was a surprise.

"Have you come to your senses?" Rail said.

"You told me before about Yoan Foca when you didn't have to."

"That's true."

"I owe you something in return," Teffinger said.

"Such as what?"

"Such as the ability to have the painting in your hands and place it in Foca's hands. That would get you out from underneath him, don't you think?"

"It would." Fingers tapped and then Rail said, "What's your angle in all of this?"

"Foca's men took Dandan," Teffinger said. "They didn't get the painting, though. I have the painting."

"You have the painting?"

"That's right. I have the painting and I want to exchange it for her. I want you to help me."

Silence.

Then Rail said, "That sounds reasonable. Does this mean we're back on truce?"

"Yes. We'll meet tonight. I'll call you with time and place. In the meantime, call Foca and tell him an exchange will be in the works. There's no need for his men to interrogate Dandan as to where the painting is because I have it. Dandan needs to be well and unharmed for this to work. If she's tortured or killed, all bets are off. I'll rip the painting to shreds with my own bare hands."

"Tonight," Rail said. "No tricks."

"Me? I'm not smart enough to know any tricks. In fact, I'm hoping that you'll thrown some of your old ones my way."

It took some logistics but he eventually made his way to Del Rey's place in the universe, which turned out to be coffee shop down the street from Hotel Sausalito, a two-story structure with nice awnings seamlessly embedded in the middle of a happy seaside strip.

"We're in 212, facing the street," she said.

"Is it safe?"

"Yes for what it is," she said, "but I had to use a credit card."

He told her about his plan to exchange the painting for Dandan and his most recent twist on that plan, which was to enlist Rail's assistance.

She didn't approve of the Rail part.

"He's just another way things can go wrong. Why don't you just bring in the FBI?"

"Can't," he said. "They'd take the painting, they're duty-bound to. Once they have it in their possession they're not at liberty to do anything with it other than keep it safe and return it to the original owner, meaning the museum."

"But they're trained in hostage situations, you're not."

Teffinger grunted.

"Without the painting, Dandan's dead. I wish it was otherwise but it isn't."

She ran a finger across his hand and said, "So how do we do this without getting everyone killed?"

"I don't know. That's what Rail's for. He's also going to have to cough up Susan Smith."

"You think he'll do it?"

Teffinger hardened his face.

"I'm not going to give him a choice."

101

Thursday night, a drizzle dripped down on D.C., eerily steady, not letting up, not getting worse, not doing much of anything other than getting things wet. The wipers of Zahara's car swept back and forth on intermittent, bringing the nightscape slowly in and out of a soft watery focus. Oscar Benderfield's office was dark and deserted both times they drove by.

Zahara looked over and said, "Do you still want to do this?"

This referred to breaking in to see if they could find any evidence to conclusively verify that Benderfield was in fact the mysterious Client X from Leland Everitt's credenza. More importantly, *this* was breaking in to find something to show a connection between Benderfield and Robertson, who was undoubtedly the one who anonymously hired Benderfield to kill T'amara Alder.

Did Jori-Lee still want to do this?

"Sure. Why not?"

"No reason. I was just wondering if you were having second thoughts."

"Why would I?"

Zahara frowned.

"I know we've been talking about how the FBI would view you as a small fish if we got a case on Robertson and turned him in. The more I think about it, though, this would turn out to be the news story of the century. The spotlights would be intense. A lot of people would be taking the position that someone—i.e., you—shouldn't be allowed to break into the house of a Supreme Court justice and then walk free, or simply get a slap on the wrist, just because they got lucky and found something incriminating while they were there." She paused and said, "The more I think about it, the more I see the FBI taking a more serious view of what you did. Even if they didn't want to come down hard on you, they'd almost have to, not to mention that there are probably more than enough zealots in that organization who would argue that what you did was a breach of national security, the same as if you'd broken into the white house."

"So what are you saying? That I shouldn't go to the FBI?"

"What I'm saying is that I'd really think it over."

Jori-Lee wasn't impressed.

"If Robertson's throwing his vote and/or hiring people to kill people who are blackmailing him, there's only one course of action to take," she said. "If that means that I get caught in the collateral damage, then so be it."

"Okay."

"I don't know why we're having this conversation."

"Because I cringe at the thought of you in prison."

Jori-Lee patted Zahara's arm.

"That's why we need a solid case," she said. "I don't want to leave Robertson with a way to wiggle out. And I don't want to give the FBI something that they might shove in a drawer when the politics start going off."

"Okay, then let's do it."

"I'll go into Benderfield's on my own," she said. "That will keep you clean."

"Staying clean isn't my main concern," Zahara

said.

"Okay, then let's go."

102

Thursday night after dark Teffinger pushed into the guts of the Dusty Beat, the same corner dive off Haight where he met Rail before. The man was in the same back booth, not much more than a shadow in the dark. As Teffinger approached, the man's ponytail, solid chest and python arms took shape. He wore a blue cotton shirt rolled at the cuffs. His face, as before, belonged on the cover of a magazine.

A draft sat on the table, waiting for Teffinger.

He slid in and took a swallow.

It was cold.

It was good.

"Before we begin, I want to know what you did with Susan Smith," Teffinger said.

Rail smiled.

"Right to the point, huh?"

"Seems that way."

Rail shrugged.

"Sure, why not?" he said. "But just to be sure, we're still off the record—"

"We are."

Rail's face got serious. "I gave her to Yoan Foca,"

he said. "It was sort of a peace offering for losing the Van Gogh. It was to keep his mind off killing me while I tried to get it back."

"She's in Cuba?"

Rail nodded.

"He has her." He tapped his fingers on the table. "Rest assured she's not that important to him. She's one of twenty or thirty. She's chump change. What's important to him isn't her. What's important to him is the Van Gogh."

Teffinger took a long swallow.

"So you're saying we could get her back?"

"I don't see why not," he said. "We could do a double deal, the Van Gogh in exchange for her and for Dandan. Of course, the logistics would get more complicated, with Dandan here in the city and Susan Smith all the way over in Cuba."

Teffinger exhaled.

"Tell me about Yoan Foca," he said. "What kind of man is he?"

"Actually, he's a lot like you and me."

Teffinger almost said, I didn't know you and me were alike. Instead he said, "In what way?"

"Violent if you give him a reason," Rail said. "Not so violent if you don't."

Teffinger leaned in.

"I'm not violent."

"You killed two men last week."

Teffinger almost argued but didn't see the upside. "You're right about the logistics. We need both women in the same place. We need to get them both at the exact same time."

Rail nodded.

"Agreed."

"That means either Dandan goes to Cuba or Susan Smith comes here," Teffinger said. "I don't see an upside to trying to do this thing in Cuba."

"Agreed again."

"Okay, that means he needs to bring Susan Smith here." He cupped his hands, giving it one last thought. "Call him and tell him that's the deal. And tell him I'm only going to deal with him personally, not his lackeys. I want to look him right into the eyes and be sure we have an understanding. I want to be absolutely sure he has no plans to send someone around a year down the road to kill someone, including me."

Rail frowned.

"He doesn't go outside Cuba."

Teffinger stood up and swallowed what was left of the beer. He set the glass on the table and said, "He does now."

Then he left.

He was halfway to the door when Rail called his name from behind. He turned and the man waved him back. He sat back down, impatient.

"Do you know why I always get here before you?" Rail said.

Teffinger wasn't in the mood.

"No, tell me."

"So I can keep my eyes on the door," he said.

"Well, that's nice."

Rail shrugged.

"Sometimes it saves your life," he said. "Two or three minutes ago a man walked down the street. He's someone I met in Tangiers a long time ago. He's in the same business as me."

"He's a hitman?"

"Among other things," he said. "His name is Jean-Luc Baxa. He's a crazy little bastard. By that, what I mean is, that he's crazy enough to rip wings off birds."

"Are you saying he's the one after me?"

Rail nodded and leaned forward.

"I'm going to give you one more Ace to put up your sleeve," he said. "But first I want to be absolutely sure that I'm included in this exchange with Foca. If you have any plans to cut me out, I want you to be honest and tell me now."

"No, you're in," Teffinger said. "You've already earned your keep."

Rail nodded.

"You remember I told you before about how I fell in love with Kelly Nine," he said. "I didn't do the contract and of course someone else got hired to do the job. That person was Jean-Luc Baxa."

"He killed Kelly Nine?"

"Yes." He exhaled. "There, I've given you everything."

Teffinger processed it.

"What was he wearing?"

"A red hoodie and a black baseball cap," he said. "It was too dark in here for him to see me. I can help you take him down if you want."

"Why would you do that?"

"Because if he kills you then I don't have a painting to give to Foca."

Teffinger's chest pounded.

"We'll wait and see if he makes another pass."

103

The beat in Jori-Lee's chest of possibly finding a smoking gun in Benderfield's office got dimmer and dimmer the more they searched without finding anything. Half an hour into it, that beat was almost completely gone when her phone rang and Sanders' voice came through. He sounded like he just crawled out of a burning house.

"Did you hear what happened?"

No, she didn't.

Hear what?

"Robertson's dead. It's all over the news, every channel—"

"What happened?"

"He was out on the street and got robbed," Sanders said. "He resisted and ended up shot. A couple of witnesses got whisked off by the FBI."

"Why would he resist?"

"I don't know but get home," he said. "We need to figure out how we're going to handle this."

"I'm bringing Zahara with me."

"Whatever, I don't care. Just get back here."

Sanders was a wired mess when Jori-Lee and Zahara got there, pacing in front of the TV with a beer in hand and two empties on the table. The news depicted an eerie scene of a body on the sidewalk, covered with a blanket under a forlorn drizzly night, awash in an endless sea of red and blue flashing lights.

"I've been thinking what we should do," Sanders said.

Jori-Lee pulled her soaked blouse off, headed for the bedroom and said over her shoulder, "Tell us."

"Nothing," Sanders said. "We should do nothing."

She came back in, slipping a T-shirt over her head, and tossed a similar one to Zahara, who made the switch.

"Do nothing?"

"Robertson's gone," he said. "There's nothing he can do bad to the world at this point and there's nothing left for us to expose."

Zahara wasn't convinced.

"There are eight cases where he threw his vote," she said. "And he hired Oscar Benderfield to kill that girl who was blackmailing him."

"T'amara Alder."

"Right, her."

Sanders shook his head.

"We don't have proof," he said. "The best thing we have is the flash drive and that's not something we can cough up without getting Jori-Lee in a position where she'll probably end up in prison. It was already questionable, going to the FBI, even when we had a trump card—namely, a Supreme Court justice to bring down. But now he's already down. The trump card is gone. It's history. If Jori-Lee voluntarily admits she broke into Robertson's house, she'll end up in jail just as certain as the day is long. Hell, there will probably end up being an inquiry as to whether she was somehow involved in his death."

Jori-Lee frowned.

"I did more than just break into his house," she said. "I also broke into T'amara Alder's place. You can also add Oscar Benderfield's office, thanks to tonight."

"That makes my point all the more right. As far as the eight votes that got swung, the ultimate outcome only changed in three of them, the rest were all six to three. Personally, I don't have any heartburn the way they turned out, especially that case down in Texas involving the kid."

They debated it.

Robertson was dead.

He wasn't in a position to hurt anyone anymore.

Oscar Benderfield was dead.

He wasn't in a position to hurt anyone anymore.

The hitman that Benderfield hired to kill T'amara—Jean-Luc Baxa—was still alive. He needed to be brought down, but they could do that with a well-placed anonymous call to the police.

So in the end, Sanders was right.

They would just let the dog lie where it fell and hope that it didn't spring back to life and bite them in the face.

"It's settled then," Jori-Lee said. "We'll go to work tomorrow like nothing happened. We'll never tell anyone what we know."

Zahara nodded.

"Agreed," she said.

"Agreed," Sanders said. "We take it to our graves."

He went to where the flash drive was hidden, waved it in his hand and said, "This ties Jori-Lee to Robertson's home computer. I say we get rid of it. Any objections?"

Jori-Lee's brain was fuzzy.

She couldn't run the implications either way.

"Whatever you think is best."

Zahara shrugged.

"Fine by me."

Sanders fired up the stove and held the drive in the flames with a spoon until the thing melted. Then he put it under cold water and snapped it in two.

He tossed the pieces to Zahara.

"Throw these out your window while you're driving home Two separate places, at a minimum several blocks apart."

"Will do."

104

Teffinger was a tiger in a cage, just waiting for the door to open. His prey, Jean-Luc Baxa, was somewhere out there in the night, somewhere outside the Dusty Beat, pounding the pavement of Haight Street. Rail kept his eye on the window waiting for the man to make a pass.

In the interim he called Yoan Foca in Cuba, where it was the middle of the night.

The man didn't appreciate being woken up.

He didn't appreciate the demand that he personally come to San Francisco.

He swore and hung up.

Ten minutes later he called back.

"We'll do what you said," he said.

"You're personally coming?"

"Yes. This better go perfectly. Do you understand?"

The line died.

Rail lit a cigarette, blew smoke and looked into Teffinger's eyes. "Foca's afraid that Mun Yin's going to find a way to get his hands on the painting. He wants to close the deal before that happens. That's why he doesn't have an interest in you trying to get the painting all the way to Cuba. That's why he's coming here. He wouldn't be doing that if you hadn't gotten me in the loop. I might have lost his painting but he still trusts me." He took a long drag and tapped ashes. "That's what years and years of building a reputation gets you."

Teffinger understood.

"So, tomorrow night, then?"

Rail nodded.

"He's bringing Susan Smith?"

"Yes."

"What's the best way to do the exchange with no one getting killed?"

Rail blew smoke.

"Personally if it was me, I'd do it at sea, maybe out in the Bay," Rail said. "We'll get each one of you a nice stable rubber dinghy, fourteen feet or so, with an outboard on the back. You can each have night vision goggles. He can verify that you're alone. You can do the same, plus verify he has the two women. You pull together and you open the painting so he can see it's the real thing. Then, at the same time, you get into his dinghy while he gets into yours. You shove apart and go your separate ways."

Teffinger worked through the details.

It was as good as anything he could come up with.

"I've done a dozen deals like that," Rail said. "I never had a problem."

Rail did a double take at the window, said "Bingo," and mashed the half-smoked butt into the ashtray. Teffinger followed Rail's eyes behind him just in time to see a red hoodie and a black baseball cap disappear from the window.

He got up and swallowed what was left of his beer.

"I'll handle this by myself."

"The hell you will."

Rail fell into step.

Teffinger didn't care.

The tiger was out of the cage.

This was the man who stole Kelly Nine out of Teffinger's bed.

It was the man who tried to steal Del Rey from the fleabag.

It was the man the world didn't need.

105

The red hoodie was already twenty steps up Haight Street by the time Teffinger pushed out of the Dusty Beat. He followed, walking briskly through the city chill, closing the gap while Rail tried to keep up.

Lightning was in his blood.

He knew the feeling.

He knew it only too well.

It was there last week in that one-second freefall just before he unleashed a deadly blow at Jack Cold-er's face. It was also there back at Oscar Benderfield's house, when the man suddenly sprang at him with a knife. It was there a year ago when he first came face to face with the fact that someone had stolen Kelly Nine right out of his bed.

He quickened the pace.

Then he broke into a trot, a quiet, quiet trot.

Ten steps, that's how far the gap was now.

Suddenly the man turned.

Teffinger recognized the face.

It was definitely the man who tried to steal Del Rey and, by implication, the man from the blue car who shot a bullet through the 4Runner.

Teffinger charged.

The man squared off, which wasn't what Teffinger expected. Then he jerked to the left as Teffinger's momentum kept him going in a straight line. At the same time, he swung at Teffinger's head with a powerful right fist that landed with the impact of a hammer.

Colors exploded inside Teffinger's head.

He was on the ground, flat.

Cold concrete sponged up into his clothes and sent an icy chill through his skin and into his bones. He tried to muscle to his feet and managed to get up on one knee. There he balanced precariously for a heartbeat before toppling to the side.

He tried to get up again.

His muscles didn't respond.

A terrible fight was taking place above him.

Teffinger couldn't get up.

He couldn't stop the pain in his head.

Then the fighting stopped.

Suddenly iron fingers grabbed his hair and yanked his head off the concrete. A bloody face leaned in. It belonged to Jean-Luc Baxa.

"Lucky for you that you're not the mark," he said. "Tell Rail I didn't kill him and that makes us even. The score is settled."

Then he was gone.

DAY ELEVEN

July 18
Friday

106

Teffinger got out of bed before dawn Friday morning without waking Del Rey, downed two Tylenols and slipped outside for a jog. The air was cold but felt like medicine in his lungs. One major thing was clear from last night, namely that he wasn't the target. The clarity of that came not only from Jean-Luc Baxa's words but also from the fact that the man didn't kill Teffinger when it would have taken only two iotas of effort.

That meant that Del Rey was the target.

Teffinger repeatedly questioned her as to why.

She repeatedly didn't know.

"You tell me," she said. "Kelly Nine was the target too. What do me and her have in common, other than you?"

As near as Teffinger could figure, Baxa had somehow got onto him last night, possibly by tracing Rail. The man's plan was to follow Teffinger to Del Rey. Luckily, Teffinger figured that out on Haight Street before he left the scene. He figured it out good enough to flag down a cab, crisscross all over town, jump into a second cab, cross the bridge and then walk through shadows the last mile to the Hotel Sausalito.

The effort proved worth it.

Nothing happened last night.

No one came for Del Rey.

No one came for the Van Gogh, either.

They were ghosts but it wouldn't last long.

Luckily, it didn't need to.

The exchange was set for tonight, man to man with Yoan Foca; the Van Gogh for Dandan and Susan Smith. Things could go wrong a hundred different ways and the number increased every time Teffinger thought about it.

Rail would be busy today securing the dinghies, night goggles, and the rest of it.

His words from last night still resonated.

"It's not the logistics that makes or breaks an exchange," he said, "it's the groundwork that takes place long before the exchange ever comes into being. Each party needs to be sure the other party can't gain anything significant from a double cross. That's a lot harder in a case where you're exchanging a painting for money. Both items are valuable to both sides. Neither side would mind walking away with everything. But in this case, on Foca's side, all he really wants is the Van Gogh. He has no real use for either Dandan or Susan Smith. If things hadn't turned out well, he would have made it his mission in life to kill Dandan, but after he gets the painting in hand, his passion for her death will quickly pass. He certainly won't make a move before he has the painting safely tucked away. On your end of things, all you want is the women. You really don't have a use for the painting. So the exchange should go smoothly. The only thing that could go wrong at this point is if you don't show up with the painting."

"We'll see."

"Trust me."

Teffinger studied him.

They were still on Haight Street.

Rail was bloodied from his encounter with Jean-Luc Baxa, bloodied but alive.

"Did I ever say thanks for the help?"

"It wasn't much help, in hindsight," Rail said.

Teffinger grew serious and then smiled.

"Yeah, that's true. Never mind, then."

"I'm never minding."

"Good."

"This is what I look like when I'm never minding. How do I look?"

"Not very good."

"I could say the same. Right now between the two of us, I don't think we could get a girl unless there was money involved."

"A lot of money."

"And if she was blind, that would help."

Teffinger narrowed his eyes.

"Foca has some guts coming here."

Rail nodded.

"He'll have men with him, you can count on that. They'll be off-screen but they'll be there. They'll have rifles. They'll have scopes. But they'll only come into play if you try some kind of slick move, which you're not, so don't worry about them."

Teffinger spotted a coke can and kicked it.

"Is he really going to let you off the hook once he gets the painting?"

Rail grunted.

"I'm not going to stick around to find out. I'll be going deep as soon as this is over. I'll send you a postcard."

"Make it from Iowa."

"Why?"

"I'm going to be jealous if it's from Fiji."

Rail slapped Teffinger on the back.

"We're not so different, you and me."

That was last night.

Now it was morning.

The jog went for three miles.

When Teffinger got back to the hotel, something happened that he didn't expect.

Del Rey was gone.

The Van Gogh was gone too.

107

Friday morning at the firm, Jori-Lee kept her face buried in papers, hoping that Robertson hadn't left the security footage of her break-in lying around where the FBI would stumble on it. If they showed up to interview her, she didn't know how to handle it.

She didn't want to lie.

She didn't want to tell the truth, either.

Maybe she'd just hire a lawyer and take the fifth.

Bits and pieces of what happened to Robertson trickled in throughout the morning.

Yesterday over the lunch hour, he'd withdrawn $5,000 in cash from his checking account.

The murder happened in a gritty part of town given to hookers and pimps and trannys and people of the night.

Robertson had just stepped out of a sleaze-infested place called the Blackmore Hotel and was walking down the street with his head down. He was incognito, dressed in jeans, tennis shoes, a baseball cap and sunglasses.

A man approached from the opposite direction.

At the last second he stepped in front of Robertson. At first it looked like they were talking, as if the man was possibly asking for directions or for a cigarette or a handout. Then a scuffle ensued. A gun fired, twice. Robertson fell to the sidewalk. The shooter rifled through Robertson's pockets, pulled something out and ran.

The only witness was a prostitute, across the street and down half a block. Through the distance and drizzle, she never got a look at the shooter, not even close. The rumor was that she was on serious drugs at the time.

Robertson's wallet was found on the sidewalk fifty steps down from where he got shot.

It was empty.

His car was located on a side street, three blocks down.

Jori-Lee's cell phone rang and Sanders' voice came through. "How are things going?"

"So far so good. Are you hearing all this stuff that's coming out on Robertson?"

"Yes. I want to meet you for lunch. Can you break away?"

"Sure, if you want."

"I want."

108

Del Rey was gone and so was the Van Gogh. Teffinger scooped up his phone as fast as his motor skills would let him and called Del Rey's cell number. She answered on the third ring.

"Where are you?"

"Across the hall in 216."

He went over to find her safe, with the Van Gogh.

She was crying.

He took her in his arms and pulled her close.

"There were people out front," she said. "They were talking in some kind of an Asian language. I thought they were Mun Yin. I thought they'd somehow tracked the painting to here. I grabbed it to run out the back of the hotel. The people across the hall were just leaving. I asked them if they had any clean towels. They said they did and left the door open for me. I came in and shut the door and this is where I've been for the last ten minutes."

Suddenly talking came down the hall.

Teffinger peeked out the keyhole.

A muscular Asian man was standing in front of his room across the hall, putting his ear to the door, listening with intensity. The man examined the keycard device as if memorizing it and then disappeared quietly down the hall.

Teffinger's eyes tightened.

"We got to get out of here."

"You go," she said. "I'm done."

"What do you mean, you're done?"

Her eyes got even more watery.

"Nick, I love you," she said.

"I love you too."

"No you don't," she said. "You love who you think I am. I'm not that person though."

Teffinger wasn't in the mood.

"Pull yourself together," he said. "I'll take all the drama you can give me tomorrow but right now isn't the time."

"This isn't drama," she said. "This is serious."

She meant it.

It was in her eyes.

He held her shoulders.

"What's going on?"

She stepped back.

"I've been blackmailing a Supreme Court judge by the name of Nelson Robertson," she said. "I've been doing it for two years. I've been getting him to swing his vote. He's done it eight times."

Teffinger smiled, waiting for the punch line.

It didn't come.

"This is a joke, right?"

The woman lowered her head.

Teffinger said, "Blackmailing him for what?"

"He was kinky," she said. "I found out about it and set him up. My friend T'amara Alder helped me; she's the one you and me had a threesome with, the one I call Trouble. We videotaped him having his sick little sessions, both with me and with T'amara. I didn't want money. I just wanted his vote. We came to an arrangement. Everything was working just fine but then T'amara saw his picture somewhere and realized who he was. She called me up and said, *Remember that creep we were videotaping? He's on the freaking Supreme Court of the United States. This is going to be worth a fortune.*"

"So she wanted to blackmail him for money,"

Teffinger said.

"Right," Del Rey said. "I told her I already had a deal going with the man and for her to just stay out of it. She said, no way. The dollar signs were already in her eyes. I did everything I could to talk her out of it but it did no good. She tried to shake him down even though I disapproved. This happened just a few weeks ago. That put Robertson over the edge. He decided to take both me and her out."

"That's why you're a target."

She nodded.

"From what I can figure out—and a lot of it's guesswork, I'll admit—Robertson somehow got that hitwoman Portia Montrachet on my ass. The Susan Smith she came to murder in Denver was me."

Teffinger shook his head.

"That can't be," he said. "She was killed outside the apartment of the other Susan Smith, the model. She was the target, not you."

Del Rey exhaled.

"What I'm about to tell you, you have to promise it's off the record."

He shrugged.

"We'll see."

Del Rey paced.

"I knew Portia was after me because you were feeding me information on her," she said. "I didn't know what to do. I told a friend about it. He decided he was going to step in and help me. He thought that if Portia ended up dead, Robertson would back off.

He killed her. It didn't happen at the alley outside Susan Smith's apartment. He did it somewhere else and then dumped the body there. That way it would keep the attention off me and, correspondingly, off him."

Teffinger grunted.

"The boxer," he said. "Danny Rainer."

She shook her head.

"No, he's not the one," she said. "If you start digging you'll find that I actually did some legal work for him a couple of years ago. We have some history together and it looks incriminating. It wasn't him though, I can promise you that."

"Then who was it?"

"I can't tell you," she said. "You'll never figure it out, otherwise I wouldn't even mention it. The bottom line is that Robertson didn't take the hint. All he did was hire someone else to kill me."

"Jean-Luc Baxa."

She nodded.

"He killed T'amara first and then came after me. Teffinger, I'm going to tell you something and it's the honest to God truth," she said. "I've been hanging around you for protection but that's not the only reason. It's not even the main reason. The main reason is because I've fallen back in love with you. It happened the second you walked into my law office and I looked back into your eyes after so long. That's why I'm done. Baxa's after me, and you've almost been killed twice because of it. I'm not going to put you at risk any longer, not one second more. I can't be selfish anymore. I've done a lot of bad things in my life but if you end up dead that'll be something I can't live with."

He smiled.

"Me either."

The corner of her mouth turned up ever so slightly.

Teffinger squeezed her.

He squeezed her long. He squeezed her tight.

He squeezed her until the sobbing stopped.

Then he held her by the shoulders, looked into her eyes and said, "We're going to work this out. We're going to survive this. Right now though we need to get out of here."

"You don't hate me?"

"No," he said. "Nice try, but no. You're stuck with me so just get used to it."

109

Sanders said very little at lunch, which was strange given that it was his idea. Jori-Lee knew something was wrong but couldn't imagine what. Finally she said, "Are you breaking up with me?"

"No."

"Something's wrong."

He nodded.

"I think Leland Everitt killed Robertson," he said.

Jori-Lee understood the words but they were so strange she couldn't process them beyond their four corners.

"That's crazy."

"I think Leland Everitt's dirtier than dirt and that Zahara Knox has been acting as his spy all along," he said.

"His spy?"

He nodded.

"Think about it," he said. "Here he is, taking you into the firm at Robertson's request. Obviously you're still a potential threat to Robertson, even though supposedly you and him had reached a truce. Leland is going to want to monitor you. He's going to want to be absolutely sure you're no longer a threat to Robertson. So what he does is set up Zahara as a spy."

Jori-Lee shook her head.

"No, that's nuts," she said. "She's been on my side since moment one."

"That's my point," Sanders said. "There she is in your very first meeting with her, warning you—a perfect stranger—to stay away from the firm. That immediately creates a bond. From there she capitalizes on it. It's called keeping your friends close and your enemies closer."

Jori-Lee shook her head.

"You're being paranoid."

"Am I? It was her idea to break into Robertson's office, right? And what did you find in there. You found a mysterious Client X file, which I believe was planted there for you to find. It made it seem like Leland was representing Oscar Benderfield, trying to find out for Benderfield who hired him to in turn hire someone to take out T'amara Alder."

"Right—"

"That exonerated Leland and at the same time gave him a reason to have been talking to Benderfield, as a client, in case anyone ever asked. In reality, I think the whole file was a hoax. I think Leland actually hired Benderfield to take care of the person who was blackmailing Robertson. He did it at Robertson's request."

The smile fell off Jori-Lee's face.

She didn't expect Sanders to make a case.

He was, though.

"What about the gun in the credenza?" she said. "Why would they let me see it if the whole thing was a hoax?"

"My opinion? I think that was just a slipup. Maybe Zahara wasn't supposed to break in with you until the following night. Maybe she jumped the clock." A beat then, "If my guess is right, that's the gun that was used to kill Robertson."

Jori-Lee frowned.

"If Leland was going to all these lengths to help Robertson, then why would he kill him?"

Sanders took a sip of water.

He smacked his lips.

"I don't know," he said. "That's the one thing that doesn't add up. It's the one thing we need to figure out. I know this seems sudden but I've been building this theory up in my mind over the last few days. It was already in my mind last night. When you and Zahara came back home and I made the argument that we should never tell anyone anything we knew, that was all for Zahara's benefit, knowing she'd relay it to Leland. It was the only way I could think of to keep you safe short-term. The disc that I burned on the stove, by the way, wasn't the real one. I still have the real one."

"You do?"

He nodded.

"Go back to work as if you didn't hear a word of this. Watch your back though. Leland Everitt killed Robertson. He'll kill you just as fast if he has even an inkling that you're onto him. He's in too deep at this point to do anything other than murder his way out." He put his hand on hers. "I love you so don't go and get yourself killed."

"Likewise."

"Likewise on the love part or on the don't-get-killed part?"

She smiled.

"Both."

110

Friday night after dark Teffinger carefully set the Van Gogh in the belly of the dinghy, throttled up the 5hp Johnson and let it warm up.

"This will go smoothly," Rail said. "Trust me. You'll be back in half an hour. Everything will be fine."

"We'll see."

The night was full dark, moonless to a fault.

An eerie thin fog played over the salty water, allowing fairly good visibility for a hundred yards and then messing with it. The brighter lights of San Francisco managed to punch through.

The weaker lights had no chance.

The exchange was to take place directly under the Golden Gate Bridge, midway between the two towers. Teffinger was to motor out from the city side. Yoan Foca would come from the Sausalito end. They'd meet, they'd exchange, they'd motor away in separate directions and everyone would live happily ever after.

Teffinger swallowed.

He didn't like water.

He especially didn't like cold water.

Cold water had tried its best to kill him on more than one occasion.

A breeze blew, stronger than Teffinger preferred.

Small waves washed in from the Pacific, not more than one to two feet, not to the point of whitecaps but more than enough to make the dinghy nervous.

"Do me a favor," Teffinger said. "If he kills me, I want you to kill him back."

Rail chuckled.

"He's not going to kill anyone."

"Yeah, but if he does, I want you to, too."

"He won't but if he does, I will."

"Do you promise?"

"I promise. Time to go." Rail pushed the dinghy

off shore and said, "I'll be waiting for you. Good luck."

Teffinger kept the motor in reverse until he got clear of the rocks, then swung the vessel around bow-first and headed for the massive orange structure, which was three or four hundred yards up the shore.

The waves slapped at the boat.

The noise was louder than Teffinger expected.

It made his eyes narrow and his palms sweat.

He got directly under the bridge and followed it.

He passed the first tower.

He kept going.

He had a vision of Yoan Foca pulling a gun at the last minute and shooting everyone dead—Teffinger, Dandan and Susan Smith, all of them, dead. He had a vision of their bodies falling into the merciless cold water and sinking deeper and deeper into the horrific darkness.

He should have brought his gun.

Should he turn back?

Suddenly a small vessel punched out of the fog up ahead.

Teffinger flashed his light.

The other vessel did the same.

Then they slowly approached one another.

DAY SEVENTEEN

July 24
Thursday

111

Del Rey kept her eyes on the back entry of One First, waiting for Justice Preston Wendell to emerge. Her chest was tight. What she was about to do was serious. Every word mattered. The day was hot. She stayed in the shade of an elm.

Lots of people emerged at the end of the day.

Wendell wasn't one of them.

He was a hard worker.

He packed a snack.

That let him work until 7:30 or even 8:00.

Tonight he came out at 7:42.

He had a spring in his step.

He'd had a productive day.

Del Rey closed the gap and said, "I'm a friend of Judge Nelson Robertson. I was hoping I could talk to you for a minute."

The man paused.

"How do you know Judge Robertson?"

"I was the one blackmailing him," she said. "You

know he was being blackmailed to throw his vote, don't you?"

The man took a step back.

"What'd you say your name was?"

"My real name's Susan Smith," she said. "I go by Del Rey, though. I'm a lawyer from Denver."

"And you say you were blackmailing Judge Robertson?"

She nodded.

"He swung eight votes for me," she said. "All that changed though when you killed him."

The man looked at her with shock.

"I killed him?"

Del Rey ran a finger down his arm.

"How'd it feel when you did it, just out of curiosity?"

"You're about one step away from me calling the police," he said.

"I've been working out the pieces ever since he got murdered last week," she said. "I've put a theory together. Do you want to hear it?"

"No."

"Good because here it is," she said. "Everything was fine until a friend of mine named T'amara Alder jumped in and wanted to blackmail him for money. That's when he went to his good friend, you."

"Me—"

She linked her arm through his.

"Walk with me," she said.

He obliged.

"You knew some of his votes were off the charts

so you weren't all that surprised when he told you why, namely that he was being blackmailed. Being the good friend that you are, you told him you'd try to think of a way to get him out of his little jam. After all, the court would change if he left, and not in a way you wanted. Then you came up with a plan."

"Which was what?"

"You went to Leland Everitt and talked to him, knowing full well the attorney-client privilege covered your conversation," she said. "You impressed upon him that the solution needed to take place at the source, meaning that the two blackmailers—me and T'amara—needed to be eliminated. Leland, being the man of bad genes and greed that he is, told you about a little a friend he had, a friend named Oscar Benderfield, who could arrange to get things done. You told him to proceed. You wired money to the firm to cover the so-called expenses."

Wendell wiped his brow.

"Hot out, isn't it?" Del Rey said. "Anyway, Robertson found out that T'amara Alder got murdered. It was in the papers. He confronted you about it. You admitted that it might have happened but it was all for the better. It was for his benefit. The world was better off. The system was back to pure." She exhaled. "The problem was, he might be a pervert but he wasn't a killer. With every day that passed, you got more and more concerned that he would break down and go to the police. So you followed him one night when he made one of his dirty little journeys out there to pervert-land, and you put two bullets in his gut and made it look like a robbery."

"You're crazy."

"Relax," Del Rey said. "I have no plans to mention any of this to the police. My game is much bigger than that."

Wendell looked at her with a sudden recognition of what she was after.

"You want my votes," he said.

Del Rey nodded.

"You're my new Robertson," she said. "Don't panic though. It's actually not a bad deal. You'll only hear from me now and then, when there's a particular case that interests me. I really should be mad, given that you tried to have me killed. The guy who got hired by Benderfield to do that job, by the way, ended up dead."

"You killed him?"

She nodded.

"It felt good," she said. "How'd it feel when you killed Robertson?"

The man grunted.

"It felt like he didn't appreciate everything that I'd done for him."

"Meaning the whole thing that I just outlined—"

"Right."

"We're going to get along just fine," she said. "In many ways you and I are exactly the same. We know how to get things done. Just for grins, where'd you get the gun that you used?"

He smiled.

"Leland Everitt gave it to me."

"It worked well."

"Yes it did."

"What kind was it?"

"It was a Glock."

She patted his arm.

"Small world," she said. "That's the same exact weapon I used on the man who came for me. His name was Jean-Luc Baxa, by the way. Did you know that?"

"No. I never knew his name."

"You only knew that he'd been hired—"

"Right."

"Well, that was his name, Jean-Luc Baxa. I'll say one thing for Benderfield, he sure had a lot of friends in low places. I wonder how he and Leland Everitt ever got tangled up together in the first place."

Wendell shrugged.

"It probably started small."

"Most things do. So, do we have a deal?"

"It doesn't look like I have a choice."

Del Rey studied him.

"Let me ask you something," she said. "If you could go back in time to that night when you pumped two slugs into Robertson's guts, would you do it differently?"

"You mean kill him differently?"

"No, I mean not kill him at all."

He didn't hesitate.

"Not killing him wasn't an option at that point," he

said. "He put me in a corner; not just me, but Leland. He brought it on himself as far as I'm concerned. How about you? Would you not kill that man—"

"—Jean-Luc Baxa—"

"—Right, Baxa---would you not kill him if you had the chance to do it over?"

She shook her head.

"No," she said. "I'd kill him again. I'd kill him a hundred times over. It was self-defense, that's how I look at it. It was him or me."

"Then you know exactly how I feel."

"I think I do. I'll be in touch."

"I'll wait for your call."

She broke off.

Five steps later she turned and said, "Hey, judge. There's just one more thing."

"Which is what?"

"Have you ever heard of someone named Jori-Lee Kent? She was a law clerk for Robertson."

His face got somber.

"What about her?"

"Well, it seems that she got onto some things, which I'm sure you already know about. What you might not know is that she eventually ended up talking to a detective in Denver by the name of Nick Teffinger, who happens to be the man who killed Benderfield. She was pretty impressed with that and felt she could trust him. Anyway, unfortunately for some people--people like you for example--Teffinger's a pretty smart guy. Between what I was able to tell him, and what Jori-Lee was able to tell him, he started putting things together, and now, here we are. Do you see those four men coming this way? They're with the FBI so I wouldn't resist them too much if I were you." She tore her blouse open. "Did I mention I was wearing a wire?"

The man broke into a run.

He didn't get far.

He went down hard.

Bodies were on him.

A knee went to the back of his head.

His arms got pulled roughly behind his back.

Handcuffs went on.

He got jerked to his feet.

He looked around wildly, spotted Del Rey and said, "You bitch!"

She pulled the wire off her chest and threw it at him.

"See you in hell."

Then she left.

ONE MONTH

LATER

112

Tuesday night after dark, a mean thunderstorm rolled out of the mountains and unleashed a demonic fury on Denver. Teffinger watched it from the garage, through the windshield of the '67 to be precise, with a Bud Light in his gut and another in his hand. Del Rey sat in the passenger seat sipping an iced wine.

She wore a white tank top and white shorts.

Her legs were tan and strong.

Teffinger's phone rang.

It was someone he never expected to hear from again.

It was Rail.

"I want you to do me a favor," the man said. "I want you to meet me in Miami tomorrow."

"What for?"

"For something important."

"Like what?"

"I can't give you any details."

Teffinger exhaled.

"That's a pretty big commitment," he said. "I'm in the middle of five hundred things."

"Make it five hundred and one," Rail said. "You trusted me once before and things worked out. Trust me a second time."

Teffinger didn't have the time.

He didn't have the cash.

He didn't have the curiosity.

"Come on," Rail said. "You owe me."

That was true to a point.

Last month under the Golden Gate Bridge, everything worked out exactly as Rail had orchestrated it. Dandan and Susan Smith were both delivered unharmed. Dandan since went underground on the run from Mun Yin, but that was her problem at this point. Susan Smith was back in Denver, already readjusted to her life.

"Okay," Teffinger said.

"Take the first flight you can get," Rail said. "Call me when land and I'll tell you where to go."

"This better be good."

"It will be."

Lightning arced across the sky, immediately followed by a slap of thunder so loud and absolute that it rolled all the way to Kansas.

"I'm going to Miami tomorrow," he said.

"What for?"

"I don't know. Rail wants me there."

She wrinkled her face.

"This doesn't smell right."

"Rail's okay—"

"He's a well-polished killer," she said. "Don't get fooled by his pretty little smile. It's entirely possible he's offered you up to someone."

113

The Next Day

Miami was hot and humid when Teffinger touched down Wednesday morning. Rail picked him up at the airport, drove to a marina and said, "Can you drive a boat?"

"To a point."

They rented a 32-foot Baja go-fast and headed southeast into open water with Rail at the throttle.

"Where we going?"

"I'll tell you when we get there."

They went for a long way, seventy or eight or ninety miles, until Cuba was in their sights.

"We're still in international waters," Rail said. "Don't be concerned."

"I'm not, but why are we here?"

A sail was on the horizon, a mile or so off, tacking in their direction.

Rail killed the engines.

The vessel bobbed.

The waves were gentle.

The sun was magic.

The water was aqua.

"I told you about that night when I sat out in your backyard and watched you and Kelly Nine make love," he said. "I decided to not protect her any more and left. I walked away, got in my car and drove off."

"I remember."

"What I didn't tell you is what happened next," he said.

"Why, why happened next?"

"I came back."

Rail paused and let the words float.

"To my house?"

Rail nodded.

"I tried to leave but I couldn't," he said. "My hate was too much. It was in control. I broke in and walked into your room. You were sound asleep, curled up and facing the wall. The storm was beating down. I put my hand over Kelly's mouth. She woke up. She saw me. She knew how bad things were. She knew I'd kill you if she woke you up. She got up without waking you and she left with me."

Teffinger hardened his face.

"You're the one?"

Rail nodded.

"I got there before Baxa," he said. "He never touched Kelly. He might have showed up that night, I don't know one way or the other, but she was already gone if he did."

"You had her."

"Right, I had her," he said. "We fought. I almost killed her but didn't. Instead I took her to Yoan Foca. It was the perfect solution because Kelly would end up with a terrible life for betraying me and Foca would be most grateful. I'd get more work from him in the future."

Teffinger cocked his fist.

"You little bastard."

Rail held his hand up in defense.

"Hold on," he said. "It gets worse. Foca kept Kelly as part of his stable for a while but quickly got tired of her. He likes his women more animated and cooperative and enthusiastic than she was. So he sent her out to one of his porn operations."

"He forced her into porn?"

"Yes."

Teffinger punched Rail as hard as his fist would go.

The man fell back.

Teffinger pulled him to his feet, picked him up and threw him over the side.

The man disappeared under the surface, then gasped for air and treaded water.

Teffinger headed for the controls and said, "Have a nice swim back."

"Wait," Rail said. "There's one more thing."

Teffinger almost cranked over the key. Instead he said, "Tell me."

"What I did was wrong," he said. "It was born from my hate of her, but that hate faded. When we arranged the deal with Foca to exchange Dandan and Susan Smith for the painting, I asked him to throw Kelly Nine in as well. He wouldn't do it, plus he said the logistics were bad. She was all the way on the other side of the island. Plus, it was already going to be risky flying Susan Smith all the way to San Francisco."

"He never even mentioned her to me," Teffinger said.

"No reason he would," Rail said. "Anyway, I later cut a deal with him. Mun Yin was out to kill Foca, first because Foca killed Savina Bandini in Rome, which ended up getting ten million of Yin's money stuck in a Cayman account that he can't get out, and second because Foca jacked up the whole painting exchange. My deal with Foca was simple. I would kill Mun Yin for him. After I did that, he would return Kelly Nine to me and throw a small amount of money my way—five million. I killed Mun Yin three days ago. It took me a whole month. Do you see that sailboat heading our way? Kelly Nine is on it. That's Foca's part of the bargain."

Teffinger processed it.

Then he pulled Rail out of the water.

As the sailboat approached Rail said, "Kelly is supposed to be blindfolded. I don't want her to know I'm here. I don't want her to see me. I don't want to feel her hate. I'm afraid it will kill me."

Teffinger nodded.

He understood.

The boat came closer and closer.

A rough, brown-skinned man threw a rope.

Rail grabbed it and tied the boats together.

A timid woman was led out of the sailboat's cabin.

She was blindfolded.

Rail hopped aboard the sailboat, held the woman's hand and carefully helped her into the go-fast.

He stayed on the sailboat, untied the ropes and pushed the boats apart.

He said nothing.

Then he took one last look and disappeared into the cabin.

Teffinger removed the woman's blindfold.

When she saw who was in front of her, a measure of life returned to her eyes. She hesitated for a second, almost as if she wasn't sure if this was some kind of a cruel trick. Then she put her arms around Teffinger and pulled him tight with every ounce of strength in her body.

Her body trembled.

"It's all over," Teffinger said. "You're going home."

ABOUT THE AUTHOR

Formerly a longstanding trial attorney before taking the big leap and devoting his fulltime attention to writing, RJ Jagger (that's a penname, by the way) is the author of over twenty hard-edged mystery and suspense thrillers. In addition to his own books, Jagger also ghostwrites for a well-known, bestselling author. He is a member of the International Thriller Writers as well as the Mystery Writers of America.

RJJAGGER.com